DARK SIDE:
The Haunting

J. M. Barlog

CHICAGO, ILLINOIS

DARK SIDE: The Haunting
Published by BAK Books

ISBN 0-9654716-1-6

BAK Books are published by BAK Books, a division of BAK Entertainment, Inc. Its trademark, consisting of the words "BAK Books" is Registered in U.S. Patent and Trademark Office.

BAK Books
333 N Michigan Ave Suite 932
Chicago, Illinois 60601
www.bakbooks.com

Printed in the United States of America
OPM 0 9 8 7 6 5 4 3 2 1

Other novels by J. M. Barlog

Windows To The Soul

Necessary Measures

Red Hearts

*To my daughter Janice.
Her smile is the sunshine in my day*

1

Echoes. Jenny Garrett's first inkling of life came as echoes. Indeterminate sounds really, buoying to the surface of a tumultuous crashing sea. But from amidst this chaos emerged a faint tinny beep—a homing beacon guiding her through a twisting and turning tunnel of darkness. Steady and reliable it came, like the faithful ticking of a clock; the sound grew in intensity but maintained a near constant frequency.

From somewhere beyond, a warbled voice wormed its way into her brain. A voice she knew. Her own voice trapped inside her head. Jenny listened, straining to capture words barely decipherable. She could sense her chest rising, feel her lungs expand then collapse in that gentle life-sustaining rhythm.

...beep...beep...beep...

Moments passed. Jenny never thought to keep track of them, never realized how precious they could be. She commanded her eyelids. They refused her, sending a wave of dread spilling into her mind the way wretched flood waters overwhelm everything in their path. For her, darkness held steadfast.

Then, like night yielding begrudgingly to the brightness and comforts of dawn, shrouded layers of gray and white poured in through rushing waters.

The darkness—and now the dread—were gone. Sight exhilarated her with a sense of being.

Jenny listened to the thump of her heart, pumping strongly and regularly, and in synchronization with that artificial beep funneling into her brain.

Seconds passed, measured now by heartbeats. Jenny listened, then sought to explore the far reaches of the flat colorless canvas stretched endlessly before her. Their tiny tails of crystalline blue, she peered through a shower of motes hurling this way and that like miniature comets. When they abated, water-stained acoustic panels, faded by a half century's time, came into focus, and for the first time, Jenny realized she existed still in the world of the living.

She felt no pain, only a deep, penetrating chill that coursed her entire body. But could she still feel her body? Or was her mind tricking her? What remained out there in the abyss beyond her eyes and ears? What dread would she face when she commanded her limbs to move?

Beep...beep...beep...

That artificial sound, so rock stable, so comforting in its regularity, became her measure of time, and as such, her measure of life. How had she come to be in this desolate place? She tasked her brain to dole out answers, to make sense of what collected in her consciousness.

No answers came.

Overcoming a leaden inertia seizing her limbs, Jenny risked movement. She had to take stock of herself, had to know what remained of her. There must be more. Hell's fires shot up her spine, punishing her attempt and tearing into every corner of her head to force an immediate cessation.

...beep...beep...beep...

The rhythmic hollow chime marched steadily into her ears like soldiers.

With ever-clearing vision, Jenny could discern only what presented itself before her eyes. Twisting her head slightly left, she sought the outskirts of her uncharted world.

Please, God, let there be more to me, she heard a desperate inner voice cry. Let me exist as a whole person. Was this all that remained? She would refuse a life of only sight and sound. She had to know if there were more.

Jenny commanded her arms. They responded, though not without reproof. It felt like someone was pumping her with a thousand volts of electricity. But in excruciating pain, her answer came. Joyful tears rolled out the corners of her eyes. Her body was out there, though just beyond reach.

Exalting briefly in an exhilaration that comes from wholeness, Jenny tilted her head further. The throes of pain seized her neck. It felt like iron clamps held her in check. She issued a scream, but no strident cry fell into her ears. Only that steady beep.

Beep...beep...beep...

On the edge of her world, entangled plastic tubes descended from three clear bags dangling on a bedside pole. Jenny now knew this place, yet still had no understanding of how she came to be here.

Poised to endure whatever the consequences of her decision, Jenny sought the furthest reaches of this place. Through a dim light filling the room, and across a chasm of uncertainty, Jenny discerned the outline of a feminine form, whose hair reached her shoulders and cloaked behind a black veil of obscurity. For a time, the form stood stone still; no sounds other than the beep marched into her head.

Beep...beep...beep...

Jenny's mind sharpened; her eyes focused with improved clarity. While Jenny stared, the voiceless form advanced, falling for the first time under the scrutiny of a sallow light that radiated out from somewhere behind her head. Matted hair became the color of honey stained red. The flesh took on the pallor of parchment. Cracked lips, bluish in color, remained thin meaningless lines across the face. Where eyes once were, black orbs, devoid of life, existed.

The face!

Jenny fought to breathe, urged a scream.

Beep—beep—beep—beep—beep.

The sounds lurched into frenzied staccato. Terror seized Jenny's pounding heart as a wavering alarm sundered the rhythm of life.

The face and the body poised before Jenny were those of herself.

Then Jenny Garrett saw no more.

2

A drowsy autumn sun washed into the hospital room through water-stained glass. Jenny perched herself anxiously at the edge of her bed, staring at her legs and feet as they dangled. More than six arduous weeks had passed—forty-five days to be exact, and now Jenny was going home under the power of her own legs. Something five weeks ago she wondered if she would ever experience.

A thick fuchsia robe trapped her warmth against her sinewy form, staving off the almost constant chill from windows rift with cracks that allowed the outside air into the room. Jenny hesitated, glancing once more at the hand mirror set beside her on the bed. It taunted her, daring her to pick it up, to use it. She resisted, knowing full well she must at some time face what demons existed on the other side of that glass. She had refused up until this moment to confront what could no longer be held off. Her sweaty hand clutched the mirror's cool metal stem.

The voice inside her head dared her. What do you look like now? You must know, it chided.

After a moment's indecision, Jenny mustered her courage, lifted the glass from the bed, and brought it between her face and her legs. She stared at it with loathing and disgust. Hideous.

Jenny slammed the mirror to the floor, shattering the glass into a thousand sprawling pieces across green speckled tiles that had gone out of fashion a generation ago.

The bandages that had long hid her face and protected her from this moment had been weeks removed. Now what remained, exposed to the world, was a thin scar that hooked from the base of Jenny's nose to the right corner of her mouth. *Hideous.* Never, ever would she smile again. Never could she allow anyone to see her this way.

The crash brought her nurse rushing in with panic writ across her face.

"S-s-sorry, I d-d-dropped it."

Relief washed over the nurse.

"That's okay, Jenny. Just stay on the bed. I'll get maintenance to clean it up," the nurse said, with hands on her robust hips.

Jenny despised what had become of her face and her still-butchered hair. She dreaded the time it would take for her hair to return to its former feminine length and luster. After wiping teary azure eyes, Jenny used her finger to inspect another small scar bisecting her right eyebrow. She recoiled briefly when the tip of her index finger made its first contact.

"Rumor has it you're looking to leave us today," a throaty Dr. Vance Morrison said from the door as he checked Jenny's chart. He looked fiftyish, yet he maintained the youthful stature of someone half his age. Today he appeared unshaven and drained from a shift that seemed unending. His entrance into Jenny's room preceded that of an elderly black maintenance man and a nurse assigned to assist him.

"A small accident?" Morrison asked, noticing the glass. He had hoped Jenny would have accepted her present state better. All his encouraging words, in the end, had done little to ease Jenny's moment of truth.

The black custodian picked his way carefully into the room ahead of the doctor, and within a minute, had the glass swept into a neat pile and whisked into a dustpan. Morrison's nurse took up her position just inside the room, yet safely beyond the range of the shattered glass.

"D-dr. M-m-morrison, can I go home?"

"What's the matter, Jenny, you don't like our hospitality? Warren informs me his cooking is considered a scandal to food." Morrison hid a faint smile, then replaced it with an all-business expression.

"Before I let you go, I want one more good look at you. This really is one hell of a piece of work. If you'll pardon my French."

Morrison's intense hazel eyes slipped down below the top rim of his glasses and did little to soften a clinically distant face. He saw anatomy and physiology and little else beyond. His proffered smile could easily be mistaken for admiration of his work rather than an interest in his patient's well-being.

How could he even look at her with such pleasantness? Jenny thought as Morrison examined his handiwork.

But Morrison saw not disgust and disfigurement; rather he saw a miracle. A miracle from God that had plucked a worthy soul from Death's clutches and returned it to the world of the living. Nothing on earth could be more precious than life.

Not at all what Jenny had seen when she gazed into that mirror.

With his fingers, he studied a thin, almost invisible scar along Jenny's hairline, pleased at the results of the hours of work it took to perform the delicate task.

"You're healing just fine. In time, these can be permanently removed," he offered, smoothing with a gentle finger over her brow. His eyes caught hers.

Jenny looked askance.

"W-w-when?"

"Soon, Jenny. I know how you feel. But first let's make sure everything else is in good working order."

Jenny brought her eyes to meet Morrison's, feeling tears filling the corners.

"A little nip and tuck and that scar will be barely noticeable."

Morrison pocketed his pride, knowing Jenny needed more time to accept her new life. The accident had irrevocably altered her. Now she had to come to terms with that. But she would have help.

With a surgeon's gentle caring, Morrison assisted Jenny back into a prone position.

Jenny's Pavlovian response was to avert her eyes when Morrison opened her robe to examine the measures he had taken to staunch the internal bleeding and ultimately save her life. A crescent moon incision frowned across the entire breadth of Jenny's abdomen. A stabbing reminder for the rest of her life of what she had endured.

Jenny refused to acknowledge it; she wished that somehow it could be erased from her like a mistake on a chalkboard. How could Warren ever become passionate seeing her this way?

The handiwork displeased Morrison equally, but desperate times called for desperate measures. And though successful, desperate measures tend to leave an unpleasant aftermath.

Jenny would probably never know how close she came to death that night in the operating theatre. Nor would she hear of the measures the doctor and his team took to snatch her from death.

"I'm afraid bikinis are out," Morrison offered with a wry glint of medical humor.

You have the perfect bikini body, Warren's words flooded into her mind at that moment. He had spoken them to her the first time they made love on the sofa in her uptown apartment. He had stared at her with such desire that now she feared he would never be able to see her in that way again.

But now...she could never expose such a monstrosity.

"Jenny, I hope you believe in miracles," Morrison said, after closing her robe and cupping her hands into his. "Because that's what you've been granted. Only a miracle could have pulled you through after that crash. I'd like to take the credit, but I can't. You make sure that husband of yours realizes how lucky you both are."

Morrison wrapped Jenny's cold hand in his, skillfully maneuvering her to a sitting position without the aid of the attending nurse, who still stood quietly near the door.

"H-he already d-does. Dr. M-m...M-M-Morrison...h-h-how..."

Frustration locked Jenny's jaw. Her temples pulsed. The harder she tried, the more the words clogged her throat. Tears left her eyes.

"It's okay, Jenny," Morrison was quick to interject. "Just try to relax. Your speech should normalize in time. Don't force it. Give your body time to heal; time to make itself right again."

"H-h-how come I c-c-can't remember?"

"The accident?"

Jenny nodded.

"That's not unusual in head trauma cases. I expect you'll experience gaps in your memory for awhile. These, too, should correct themselves over time."

"H-how long i-is a w-w-while?"

"Few months. Maybe more, maybe less. If all goes well, they'll get filled in. I've spoken with Warren about this. He knows what to expect and how to help you through it. He'll fill in those gaps for you."

For the first time since Morrison entered the room, Jenny offered a faint glimmer of a smile.

"Look at it from the bright side—it's not amnesia. It's just a short gap in your life. Portions of your memory are lost for now. But don't worry, it only gets better."

"And...i-i-if all doesn't g-g-go w-well?"

"Jenny Garrett, you are alive! You're walking out of this hospital and you've got a husband who loves you like crazy. Count your blessings, and take the rest one day at a time."

Jenny tightened her robe, smiling, though her eyes remained uncertain.

"Any pain sitting?"

"No. Last n-night I got t-terri-b-ble pains..."

"I'm going to keep you on the Demerol for at least another week. You've come a long way in six seeks, but you're not fully recovered. You understand that?" Morrison's face turned into a paternal frown while he spoke.

Jenny nodded.

"You take it real easy at home," Morrison said, leveling an emphatic finger.

Despite all his training and efforts, Morrison realized there were some things only love and nurturing could fix. And that's what Jenny needed most right now. Doctors repair the body, but only loved ones can repair the spirit. The hospital and staff had done all it could to put Jenny back together again. Now Warren needed to provide a husband's love to help Jenny the rest of the way.

And for Jenny, the road ahead would be rocky and difficult. Warren became the best person to help her overcome the obstacles still facing her. Maybe he was the only person who could restore her spirit to what it once was.

"W-will...I b-be..."

Jenny tensed up.

Morrison patted her hand.

"H-h-have ch-ch...b-ba-by?"

"It's far too early to tell. You're young and strong. Only time...and God can answer that."

Jenny quelled a sudden rush of guilt rising out of her question. Why should those words trigger such an unusual reaction? Something in that exchange had knotted her insides, and at the same time, eluded understanding.

"Just remember, strict convalescence for the next four weeks. No working, no straining to do anything. You just lay around and do nothing. I'll see you again in two weeks. Then we'll see if you can start getting out and about. If anything comes up before, you call me right away."

"Jenny, it's time," Warren said from the door, his smile the brightest part of his face. Yellow tea roses overflowed in his arms—Jenny's favorite. His cinnamon-colored, thatchy hair was long overdue for a trim and wind-blown it looked like he did no more than hastily rake his fingers through it upon rising. His clothes, despite attempts to remedy it, looked like they had been plucked from a clothes hamper, smoothed by hand and then climbed into. But Warren had made it through this ordeal and now Jenny was coming home.

"Right on time, Warren. I think Jenny's all ready to go."

3

Home. There's no place like home. Home was a meticulously renovated three-story Victorian set at the rear of a cul-de-sac in the small town of New Brighton. Home was close enough to commute to New York City, yet far enough away to be classified as exurbia. Thirty-seven miles of rolling rich countryside acted as a levee, holding back the crime and grime from the city. Home had been Jenny's refuge of security and comfort since marrying Warren. Now Jenny wondered what home would become for her. A prison? A fortress, impenetrable by the outside world?

Warren cradled Jenny in his arms while climbing the stairs with the grace of a man whose physical condition was in dire need of repair. He situated her comfortably onto their bed, struggling to keep from dropping her prematurely onto the mattress. Scents of jasper and wild flowers wafted through the bedroom.

Jenny was home. And nothing else mattered at this moment.

After propping a trio of marshmallow pillows behind her, Warren kissed her softly. The scar made her lips feel different, but Warren buried his observation. He held his kiss until his lungs forced him to release her.

WELCOME HOME JENNY - I LOVE YOU - WARREN, was emblazoned on a banner which hung on the wall opposite the bed. The very wall that had previously had her dressing table mirror before it. The banner only accentuated the mirror's absence more. But in reading the banner, Jenny's mind flashed reflections of the face she had witnessed in the hospital—as if the mirror had still been in place. The images sent waves of revulsion through her before dissipating into smoke. Warren's well-meaning intentions had accomplished more to harm than to charm.

"You're home now," he forced out, his breathing burdened by an unbreakable weakness for smoking. "I love you more than life itself," he whispered, clutching her hands in his with such fierceness that the blood stopped flowing through her fingers.

Jenny thought she detected a tear in Warren's green eyes. This moment, though anticipated for weeks, seemed less than Jenny had hoped it would be.

Running her fingers through his collar-length hair reminded Jenny of the wonderful length hers had once been. Before...

"I-I...l-lov..."

Frustration flamed in Jenny's eyes.

"It's okay, Jenny. I love you."

Warren had festooned strings of white carnations over the door frames and situated vases of fresh flowers on every surface in the room. With all the color, one would have thought they had entered a florist shop.

"T-this i-is..."

"I'm glad you like it. I wanted it to be special for you."

"Where's M-mr. C-Chips?"

"Outside. I wanted this moment just for us. I'll bring him in after you're settled."

Jenny smoothed her hand across their comforter, thick with down and fashioned with lavish splashes of orchids. Stitched painstakingly by her grandmother's own hands, used by her mother before her death and given to Jenny and Warren on the occasion of their marriage from her father, who himself had since passed away. This was their bed. The place where they made love. Yet, though she thought it, she was unable to feel the passion two lovers shared here. Those wonderful memories they made together during the nights and mornings and afternoons of their marriage seemed now distant and vague. Something seemed profoundly absent from this moment— something had been stolen from her.

She had contemplated this moment every waking minute for the last three weeks. Home—there's no place like home. Home is where you are safe. But now as she experienced it, it seemed empty; she had expected so much more.

"I love you, Jenny."

"I-I love you, t-too, W-Warren."

"That was great, Sweetheart. You're improving already."

The words rumbled out like jagged rocks. Rocks that Jenny had to spit to get out. Now she was glad they were gone.

"I-I w-wan..."

"It's okay. Morrison said to expect this. We'll work through it together."

Jenny nodded, squeezed his hand, then let every muscle in her body go limp. She held no doubts that Warren really loved her. No doubt that she could find in her mind. But then again, there were now places where she was unable to look. Dark corners that held dark secrets. Something felt wrong; something still hovering beyond her understanding.

"Everyone misses you. Later, after you rest, I'll read you the cards. Everyone sends their love and prayers."

Warren opened the window a crack to allow a fresh stream of air to swirl into the room. Did he intentionally keep his back toward her now? Did he not want to look at her?

"I'm to keep you in bed. Just like on our honeymoon."

Warren's mischievous wink brought a forced smile from Jenny. A smile that sent an obviously empty message. Jenny recalled only fleeting visions of that time and the pleasures they had shared.

Warren buried his disappointment by feigning interest in the arrangement of the flowers beside her bed. His eyes studied the vase for a long moment.

"There that's better, don't you think?"

"Sure.

"Do these need more water?"

Jenny offered no answer. Instead, she slowly scanned her surroundings, searching for articles that might trigger her memory. She sought the reassurance of a photograph, a color, or an even a household object that might open—just a crack—the door that had closed on her memory. She remembered so much: the wedding pictures on the bureau, the bric-a-brac she brought back from their Cayman Islands honeymoon five years ago. Yet she drew only blanks when she sought to recapture those days leading up to that moment.

"I-I c-can't see...a-anyone yet. You understand?"

"Don't worry, I asked Bridget and Kate to give you time. They understand what you're dealing with."

"They k-k-know about..."

"No. Only that you need time."

Warren was quick to take her hand into his to reassure her of his loyalty. He would never say anything that might make her recovery more difficult.

Jenny's relief shone upon her face, though her free hand rose instinctively to cover her scar.

"I thought, only when you're ready, maybe we could have a little homecoming get-together for your closest friends."

Warren detected immediate anxiety rising up into Jenny's eyes. He had erred. This was something he should have waited to talk to her about. Only Jenny would know when she was ready to face her friends.

"S-s-sure. When I'm ready. I a-appreciate them allowing me the time. I don't think I could h-h-have faced anyone but you during this."

"I've also removed the telephone, so you won't be disturbed by my incoming calls, and I've set up a roll-away bed in the den for myself."

Jenny's face flashed first surprise, then disappointment, and finally hurt. What did he mean? Was she now so hideous that he could no longer be close to her?

Warren responded quickly and decisively, kneeling beside the bed, taking her hands into his and kissing her gently on her lips.

"It's best if you had a few days alone in the bed. Morrison cautioned me not to rush into anything physical. We'll have plenty of time to make up for it when you're better. That's all."

But was that all? Jenny thought. What would Warren do when he saw her? Jenny's weak smile disappeared when she kissed him. During that intimate moment, something shuddered through her mind. Warren had been without her for more than six weeks. The man who believed getting out of bed was the second thing you did upon awakening. Sex to Warren was a daily vitamin. He must be a saint to have endured through this.

But the very thought of making love sent an ocean of panic through her. That scar across her stomach repulsed her. How would Warren react? What would be in his eyes when he saw her naked? What would be in his mind when he touched her? What if...she could no longer excite him?

Mr. Chips, the Garrett's perpetually perky Scottish terrier, bounded up the stairs, leaping onto the mattress to greet Jenny. Warren's quick arm shot out just in time to intercept the mutt before he could reach her. All Mr. Chips could comprehend was that Jenny was home, and he was excited to see her.

Warren clutched the dog tightly, bringing him just close enough to allow him to sniff and lick Jenny's outstretched hand while his nub of a tail wagged gleefully back and forth.

This was the way Chips remembered it. Jenny, Warren and him.

"I'm glad to see you, too, Mr. Chips," Jenny said.

Her voice and gentle stroking calmed the dog, and after a minute of begging on his haunches, Mr. Chips circled himself into a ball and settled down beside the bed. Everything had returned to way it used to be. Almost.

4

Jenny barely grasped her first four days at home. Pain brought Demerol and Demerol brought sleep or, at best, a state of semi-wakefulness. The days seemed nothing more than a smear of time that jumbled her surroundings. She slept between her meals and found the least exertion completely exhausting. Only the Demerol enabled her to slumber pain-free through the night, though occasionally an electrifying jolt would sneak through to steal her from sleep.

After finishing all her breakfast on the fifth day— Warren insisting she consume everything he prepared—Jenny browsed the current issue of Advertising Age then dozed until early afternoon. She awakened mid-afternoon to a steaming bowl of chicken soup and crackers, following which she drifted off into a long nap.

While Jenny slept, Warren spent the afternoon hours locked away in his cherry wood-paneled den, where an assortment of medieval accouterment adorned the walls. From chest plates, to gauntlets, to swords, Warren surrounded himself with pieces of a time when men's nerves were tested by steel instead of silicon.

His computer was the primary occupant of his desk, a paradox to the centuries-old decor. It updated columns of green and blue numbers spread across the screen. The market today seemed unusually restless. Warren had predicted it, allowed himself a momentary indulgence in the accolade, then focused his concentration on the rows of numbers changing on the screen. One might have thought he was playing a casino game the way the numbers kept flipping. But this was no game. His diligence and patience were beginning to pay off. Warren was ready to make a move. With a predatory eye, he tracked oats, corn and pork bellies, following each price fluctuation, waiting for that exact right moment to sell.

In commodities, as in many other businesses, timing is everything. It took steel nerves and a cast-iron gut to win. He felt akin to the medieval knights, and realized how they must have felt moments before the battle. In today's hotly-contested arena, however, multitudes play, a few succeed, but most die a brutal death. Trading commodities was not for wimps or the faint of heart.

Warren knew his time was running out; he had to begin Jenny's dinner shortly. If pork bellies closed on the uptick, he'd have another chance at a profit tomorrow. If not, a false move now could wipe out the entire week's gains. Six-figure gains that could evaporate the way alcohol evaporated on a hot skillet.

The pressure was boiling over now. Warren was hanging on by a thread. A tenuous thread that could snap at any second.

"Come on," he muttered, his eyes bouncing between the numbers in the columns on the computer screen and the clock ticking off seconds in the upper left corner.

****

The nimble fingers of a gentle breeze luffed the window curtains and brushed across Jenny's face while she slept. She felt them pulling at her, drawing her out of her slumber. They lasted only a moment and seemed like the fabric of a dream.

Moments later they returned. This time though, they were more like the low rumble of distant thunder crawling across a crowded sky. In a matter of seconds, the rumble dissipated.

Jenny refused to be taunted and settled back into a shallow sleep, her body leaden against the mattress, her eyelids refusing to pull up.

Again it came. A vibration of objects moving against each other.

Jenny lifted one eye, then the other. The light stung and her mouth turned cottony. What had taken her out of her sleep? A fear began to swell inside, though she found no reason for it to root.

The noise came, this time as a short burst.

Jenny turned toward the source.

A vase of wilted flowers toppled off the bureau, crashing to the floor. Then another and another.

Jenny screamed—grabbing at her side. The sudden spasm sent a wall of fire into her head.

Warren half stumbled into the bedroom, stopping with bare feet inches from glass shards splayed across the hardwood floor.

"I'll kill that friggin' dog!" he scowled. Then he turned to Jenny. "Are you okay?"

"Just some sharp pains. What happened?"

Mr. Chips bounded up the staircase, a guttural growl rumbling from deep in his throat. He arrived just in time to confront a scolding and be towed back down the stairs by his collar. He would spend the remainder of the day outside without water and food. Warren secreted a special hatred for the dog. One that he had been free to unleash while Jenny was in the hospital. One that he kept buried otherwise, because Jenny loved the stupid animal so.

Without displaying any signs of his anger or frustration, Warren returned with the vacuum, an armful of hoses, and shoes to protect his feet. He silently and meticulously removed every bit of glass. When he finished, he stared at the water rings left by the vases on the bureau. Rings clearly at least three inches from the edge of the bureau. Warren had made certain to place them far enough on the interior to prevent such an accident.

"Warren, Chips came from downstairs. He couldn't have been responsible."

"What? Sure he was. How else could those vases have fallen? Chips ran into the bureau and knocked them over. He's going to...oh no!"

Warren dropped the vacuum with a crash. He dashed to his den, muttering something about pork bellies. Jenny endured a long, continuous string of gutter-mouth vulgarities that reached her bedroom when Warren pulled up the latest price update on the screen. He had missed an opportunity to take a hefty profit. Six figures down the crapper.

"Damn that friggin' dog!" he wailed from down the hall, as if cleaning up his language now could somehow erase what he had said earlier.

Jenny found herself staring at the bureau for a long time after Warren's departure. Mr. Chips had not been in the room when she opened her eyes, nor did she see him run out after the vases crashed to the floor.

After a dinner of pasta with olive oil, Warren recounted for Jenny those blank days leading up to the accident. He described their hours together and gave Jenny insight into where she would have been during those times they were apart. However, he stopped short of recounting that fateful Friday night. Those missing days, and exactly how many Jenny had no way of being certain, were at the center of her questions, the heart of her curiosity. Why couldn't she remember? In her mind, the accident never existed. She was doing something, although she wasn't exactly sure what it was, then she came to in the hospital after the accident and a brief coma.

Warren never mentioned the accident, nor did Jenny venture to ask. Each time Warren said anything that would lead to that night, he would change abruptly and begin something new. Listening to his descriptions, it seemed more like Warren was relating to Jenny the events of someone else's life—since she could remember none of what Warren told her.

A secret part of her relished that such a horrible experience had been erased from her memory. Another, darker part, haunted her for answers, refusing to rest until the truth came to the surface.

By the end of the sixth day, Jenny's stutter had diminished to only occasional slips. Warren's insistence that she parrot everything she said, finding that her second iteration was always perfect, had paid off. A small but significant triumph Jenny lofted high like Olympic gold. As Morrison had predicted, she was getting better, improving with every hour. Yet her memory refused to reappear.

She resolved that she would overcome any impediment the accident had forced upon her. But as she lay alone in bed that night, listening to the wind draw the branches against her window, she had no inkling of the terror poised to invade her life.

With only faint moonlight seeping around the edges of her curtains, exhaustion drew her into a dreamless sleep. But soon afterward something plucked her out of her rest. An icy chill cut to her core.

In that shallow light, she turned very carefully to observe a silhouette in the overstuffed chair beside her door. So fatigued was she though, that she said nothing, only smiled briefly and found her way back to sleep.

With the morning's light came Warren and a loaded breakfast tray. A spicy western omelette was today's main fare, with wheat toast and English breakfast tea on the side. While Jenny devoured her food, Warren watched her from the chair, cleaning his wire-rimmed glasses and smoking a cigarette.

"You look tired this morning," he commented. "You sleeping okay in here?"

"I woke up last night. But you know that."

"How could I know that?" Warren asked, genuinely puzzled.

"You could have joined me in bed."

Warren said nothing, but noticed her stutter had completely vanished.

"Do you realize that was perfect?"

"It's o-okay. When I woke up, I saw you sitting in the chair."

"Jenny, I wasn't in here last night. I worked in the den until about midnight, then I went to bed. Did I disturb you?"

"No. I thought...I-I saw you, you were sitting in the chair just the way you are now. You were staring at me."

Warren said nothing, seemingly anxious to get started on his daily routine. He had to make up for yesterday's lack of profitability. He pressed out his cigarette, placed the ash tray on Jenny's night stand and left to get on-line with the markets.

Jenny finished her meal in solitude.

With her breakfast tray at the end of her bed awaiting Warren's return, Jenny browsed through the Wall Street Journal with no particular interest in mind. Nothing interested her, though she knew that before the accident she had made the Journal part of her daily ritual. Something kept playing on the back of her mind. Something that refused to make its presence known.

After about a hour, Warren returned to collect up the breakfast tray, kissing her gently first on the forehead and then on her lips before exiting. Downstairs, Warren cleaned up the kitchen, the occasional clamor of pan banging the counter drifting up to her. Warren, for the most part, was clumsy and anything but

perfect; however, he was trying. And his culinary
skills seemed to be better than Jenny had expected.

After putting Mr. Chips out in the yard, Warren
set to his daily work in the den. Jenny paused when
she heard him tapping away at his computer keyboard. He stopped when the telephone rang, then
started up again after a few minutes. Since there
came no grumbling or outbursts of profanity, Jenny
surmised that Warren's day must be progressing on a
positive note.

After an hour of light reading, Jenny tired and
switched on the television to the Cable News Network. Warren returned at noon with Jenny's lunch
only to find her sound asleep. His attempt to leave
her undisturbed seemed to awaken her. She lifted
drowsy lids to stare at him.

"I'll check back in an hour."

"Uh-huh."

Jenny drifted into a deep sleep aided by the surrounding quiet and a breeze floating in from outside.

"...pressure...slipping...I can't," came a gruff,
demanding voice. The words were like explosions
inside her head.

"We're doing...it's below sixty," a female voice shot
back.

"Can't sus...tain the..." another urgent voice cut
in, sounding like a scratched record.

"Damnit...pump...up...bag..."

Jenny's heart pounded out of control. She felt
herself reaching out to grab onto something beyond
her reach.

As quickly as they arose, the strident voices evaporated. But they left Jenny sweating, frightened and
confused. Awake now, she sought to recapture what
she had heard, but gave up moments later and turned
to the refuge of 'Judge Judy.'

This night's dinner was heavenly. Steamed hali-
but in a delicate lemon butter sauce and crisp—not
flimsy—oriental vegetables. Warren had hid well his

culinary talents over the past five years. He had feigned complete ignorance of the workings of the kitchen. Jenny expected canned soups, those newfangled boxed meals, or prefab microwave dishes that looked and tasted like the cardboard they came packaged in. Instead, she was being treated to gourmet food meal after meal.

"So where d-did you learn to cook like this? A-and more importantly, how c-c-come you never told me about this?"

"That must mean you like it. And if I had told you, you'd have enslaved me in your kitchen. I'd rather be your bedroom slave. Jenny, baby, you get the full treatment until you're back on your feet."

"How'd your day go?" Jenny asked, indicating the den with a slight nod of her head.

"Don't ask."

Jenny grimaced in sympathy.

Later that evening, as an ocher sun set outside their window, Warren read Hugo's *Hunchback of Notre Dame* to Jenny. He had a wonderful bass voice suited for storytelling, and though he hated to tell stories, he did enjoy reading the classics to Jenny. They locked hands the entire time, releasing them only when Warren needed to turn the page. Before leaving, Warren made sure he emptied his ashtray from the night stand and banished it to the bureau.

"I need to meet with a client this evening. Two hours tops. Do you mind?"

"Not at all. I've got everything I need right h-here by the bed. I'll watch an o-old movie on cable."

"Promise me you'll stay in bed."

"Promise."

Warren leaned down, kissed Jenny first on her lips, then on her cheek, and finally on the forehead. His hand clung to hers until distance forced him to release it.

"I love you, princess," he whispered, just before letting go. He turned away quickly to hide wet eyes.

"I-I love you, too," Jenny said, concealing an edge of confusion that seemed to creep more frequently into her voice. Those words seemed so difficult to say, and not because of her stutter. She almost felt guilty in uttering them.

Jenny heard the door close. The empty house became soundless. Mr. Chips lay dutifully beside her bed, forcing his eyes closed, snoring gently, but ever-vigilant.

Twice the telephone rang in the den. Jenny fought down the urge to answer it. She would have enjoyed talking to anyone, but knew better. After the fourth ring, the answering machine took over. Both times Jenny heard faint voices leave behind a message.

Warren returned two hours later just as he had said he would. He informed Jenny that Bridget was one of the two calls. She'd said she'd call again tomorrow afternoon. Jenny seemed excited. Maybe she was ready to return to her old life? As he tucked Jenny under her blanket, Warren decided to re-install the telephone in the bedroom. Jenny's stutter was almost gone, and she certainly seemed ready to talk to her close friends.

Besides, they would certainly understand her little rough spots after all she'd been through. Sooner or later, Jenny had to face the real world again. Warren hoped it would be sooner, even though it was something Jenny feared.

Jenny settled into her pillows and listened in the darkness while down the hall Warren talked on the phone. Tears rolled down her cheeks, but not from any pain in her body. Something was missing inside her. She felt it when Warren was close to her. She could hide it from him, but never from herself. He was her husband; she loved him. So what was wrong with her? Why did she have to tell herself she loved him? Why? And why did their contact feel so foreign and strange? This was not the way she remembered love to be.

At eleven, Warren came in to kiss Jenny good night. Jenny opened sleep-laden eyes, stroked his cheek, then held his hand tightly. When their lips parted, she motioned him onto the bed.

"I love you so much, Jenny," Warren whispered, lowering himself gingerly beside her, burying his face into the soft warmth of her neck. His kisses worked passionately up to her waiting lips.

"I love you too, Warren."

His gentle kisses showed the utmost concern for her injuries. He never pressed against her, though she could feel his excitement building against her thigh.

"I was terrified that I was going to lose you. I don't want to face my life without you, Jenny."

"I'm not going to die now, Warren. That's behind us. I'm going to be here with you."

Warren's kisses grew more urgent. His need had become more insistent.

Jenny felt the fired passion in his breath and the six weeks of abstention bottled up in his manhood. He needed to release all that had built up inside him. He needed her. She sought deep inside herself for her own passion, but came up empty.

"You can touch me, honey. But I can't make l-l-ove yet."

"It's okay, Jenny. I want to wait until we can both enjoy our lovemaking."

"I d-don't know how long that will be," Jenny whispered, fighting back her tears.

"I'll wait until the last sunset if I have to."

Warren drew himself from their marriage bed, hastily wiping away tears. He snatched up Mr. Chips, switched off the light at the wall and eased Jenny's door closed.

"Sleep well," he whispered; then he was gone.

In the quiet solitude, Jenny fretted over the melange of emotions churning helter-skelter inside of

her. Why was there no spark when Warren kissed her?
Passion's fire had all but faded inside her. She felt
fraudulent, as if she wore a facade to spare Warren.
Finally, she drifted off to sleep.

In the lightless still, Jenny awoke, gasping for
breath. Immediately, she turned toward the corner.
Her door was ajar, but no light entered from the hall.

He was sitting there.

"Come hold me," Jenny whispered, then shifted
carefully onto her side.

She waited. No sounds arose. No sweet caress
from her husband contacted her skin.

Then an icy hand brushed her cheek.

Jenny turned.

Her own face, luminous against the night, hovered inches away. The eyes were black and sightless.

Jenny screamed.

The apparition vanished.

Seconds later, a confused and stumbling Warren
tumbled into the room, slapping on the lights.

"Jenny, what is it?"

"Warren, there was..."

"It's okay, Jenny. I'm here. It's okay."

Jenny trembled in Warren's tender arms. Holding
her closer did little to quiet the trembling.

"Jenny, what happened?"

"She was in here."

"She?"

"Warren, I-I saw her. I saw m-m-myself. There was
a woman in here, she looks e-exactly like me."

"Jenny, there's no one in here. There's no one in
this house but you and me. There's nothing to be
afraid of."

"Warren, last night, were you sitting in that chair
watching me?"

Jenny's voice overflowed with consternation; her
eyes were penetrating and serious.

"No. I told you, I went straight to bed. I promise
you, Jenny, I was not in here last night."

"Then she was here. She was watching me from that chair."

"Jenny, what do mean she? You saw a woman in here?"

"I saw me...I m-m-mean...she touched me. I felt her touch me."

"Honey, sweetheart, it was just a bad dream. It wasn't real."

Jenny struggled to sit up in bed, struggled to make sense of what she had seen and what she was saying. She locked her hands in Warren's. Her trembling worsened.

"I never told you...b-b-because I wasn't sure that I really saw it. But in the hospital when I first came around, I thought there was someone standing across the room staring at me."

"Jen, you were really drugged up. It could have been a nurse..."

"N-n-no, listen to me. I know what I saw. There was this woman standing in the shadow staring at me. When she moved forward, I saw the face. Warren, it was me!"

"Jenny, baby, your brain is just healing right now. You can't always trust what you see or hear."

"I saw her more than once in the hospital. Now she's h-here...a-at home."

"Jenny, try not to think about it. It's just a dream. You don't have to be frightened."

"Warren, it's not a dream. I felt her touch me. Don't you understand?"

Warren stared into Jenny's terror-stricken eyes. With pupils fully dilated, Jenny stared back. She grasped his arm desperately. He felt terror in her touch.

"Warren, stay with me, hold me."

5

Warren's morning began as a disaster and was about to get worse. Mr. Chips heaved up his breakfast all over the kitchen floor, right after wolfing down a full bowl of canned dog food. The stench drove a retching Warren to the bathroom. But dutifully he returned, pulled a mop from the closet, and though weighted down with lethargy from a near sleepless night, set about the task of cleaning up the animal's vile mess.

Jenny's bizarre story had kept him tossing until dawn. It had to have been a dream—Jenny's claim that she saw a ghost of herself. The very notion stretched beyond all reaches of rational thought. And Jenny had always been rational. How could the accident have changed that?

But Jenny's insistence regarding what she saw left an indelible mark on Warren's mind. Not only did she claim to have seen it in her bedroom, but also that it had touched her. The only real, sane answer was that Jenny's head injuries were more severe than the doctors originally thought.

A punishing headache scraped at Warren's already frayed nerves. Things were deteriorating all around him. The market had been open for more than an hour, and he still had yet to get the opening numbers for the day. But Warren sucked in a deep, calming breath, composed himself, put Mr. Chips out into the yard, and then finished scrubbing the floor.

"If I'd known you were going to do that, I'd have only given you half as much, you stupid shit," Warren scowled while a whimpering Mr. Chips looked on morosely through the glass.

Thanks to Chips, the Belgian waffles became carbon chips and had to be dumped down the disposal. Even before he could start breakfast anew, he had to dash for the ringing telephone in the foyer, beating the answering machine by no more than a second.

"Thanks for returning my call so promptly," Warren said. His eyes immediately went toward the upstairs bedroom door.

"Sounded urgent," Dr. Sy Rosenstein said. "If not a little cryptic."

"Sorry, but I figured it best to speak with you directly. I hope your secretary understood."

"She understands. But what is this all about, Warren?"

"I'd like you to see Jenny. She's having...problems."

"What kind of problems? Medical?"

"Not medical. Can you fit her in, say in the next day or so?"

Shifting papers filled the silence on the line.

Warren was cashing in a chit and couldn't discern whether it came begrudgingly or not. Rosenstein had left Warren with an open invitation to call on him any time he needed, as a result of a solid 26% annual return portfolio Warren had set up for the doctor a few years ago. At the time, Warren never dreamed he'd have reason to use that invitation. Now he hoped a psychiatrist could help Jenny.

"I'll shuffle. We'll get her in. Tomorrow at five good for you?"

"Great, Sy. I really appreciate this."

By eleven, Warren departed the now immaculate kitchen. Jenny had enjoyed her Belgian waffle breakfast, never realizing what had preceded it, and Warren settled down in front of his computer to get some work done. Almost nothing was following his plan. He had already lost out on two important trades today and was now scurrying like a starving rat to make up the deficit. Corn was down, live hogs up. Warren watched lumber go limit up before noon and now further regretted his month-old decision to unload his lumber contracts. That was another load of money he'd never see. He mentally tallied up the lost revenue opportunities and realized he was quickly running out of options.

Everything had been much easier when Jenny was in the hospital. Now, he got only half as much done as he needed, and his business was suffering more than he dreamed it would.

Nerves of steel, he told himself as the light played off the sword, Excalibur, he kept on the wall near his computer.

It wouldn't take much more to go belly up at this rate.

A persistent doorbell brought a growling Warren up from his scrolling computer screen. More damn distractions. He bantered around the notion of just letting it ring until the caller eventually gave up and went away.

"Just go away, you shit," he groaned to himself.

No such luck.

"This better be friggin' important," he grumbled all the way down the stairs and to the front door.

"Just a minute," Warren yelled when Mr. Chips issued a low, angry growl at the shuffling that seeped beneath the door.

Interruptions were the one thing Warren had no patience for.

With Chips safely locked away, Warren returned to the door. Mr. Chips had become strangely protective since Jenny's return and exhibited aggressive behavior at the most inappropriate times. Warren chalked it up to the dog's advancing age. Though he learned—much to his dismay—that these little shits could live to be fifteen years old. Another three years of the little bastard.

"Can I help you?" Warren offered in less than a neighborly tone, staring at the backs of a neatly dressed man and woman.

"Hello, Mr. Garrett, I'm Detective Rick Walker, and this is Detective Vicki Chandler. I was hoping we might have a few words with Jenny?" Rick flashed his shield and ID without waiting to be asked, though Warren ignored them. At that same time, Rick observed Warren's face. Was there surprise? No, more like irritation.

People tend to react spontaneously when suddenly face to face with the law: A constricting jaw muscle, a furtive glance, something the trained eye catches that can be very revealing. Warren's stone face and lack of gestures seemed impossible to read at the moment.

Rick's linebacker shoulders and towering frame consumed the doorway on his entrance. His gray-flecked hair gave him a seasoned authoritative appearance. His eyes never left Warren. Warren's eyes never left his. Vicki remained motionless waiting for Rick to enter.

"She may be sleeping. If you want..."

"You don't have to wake her. Her recovery is much more important than what we have. We'd be more than glad to come..."

"No. Come in. I'll see if she's awake. Is this about the accident? I told the police everything I knew about the accident at the hospital and during their follow-up."

"It's just routine, Mr. Garrett. We just need a few more details about that night, that's all."

Warren's smile was slight. He stared at Rick's steel-gray eyes a moment longer than appropriate. Was he sizing up Rick?

Warren showed them to the sitting room while he climbed the stairs.

Rick scanned the room with a careful eye and poker face, cataloging the lavish and meticulously maintained furnishings. A floor-to-ceiling mahogany book case covered the entire far wall. It held both the classics and numerous objects d' art. Rick tallied the numbers in his head. Tens of thousands in furnishings in this room alone.

Vicki whistled and shook her head as she ran her fingers along a peach-colored Victorian sofa. The Persian rug alone under her feet had to cost thirty to forty grand.

"We're not talking K-mart stuff here," she murmured, careful to keep her comment from rising to Warren's ears.

Standing deep in the heart of Yuppieland, Rick flipped through the pages of his notebook to review the questions he had prepared on the drive over. On a blank page, he scribbled a large dollar sign, then a question mark to indicate he needed to look deeper into the Garrett's source of money.

"She's awake, Detective Walker, you can come up."

"It's Rick. Call me Rick."

Rick and Vicki entered the bedroom to find Jenny sitting up in bed in her fuchsia robe. Her smile was slight and uncertain, and her hand went immediately to cover the scar on her face when she spoke.

Rick could see the hasty measures Jenny had taken to primp her hair. There was no mistaking the confusion in her eyes, and the discomfort Jenny felt at facing visitors.

Both Rick and Vicki avoided the scar on Jenny's lip, instead maintained what they thought to be friendly eye contact. However, Rick's fixed gaze only served to make Jenny more self-conscious and nervous.

"The detectives said it's just routine," Warren offered, taking Jenny's hand.

"How are you feeling today, Mrs. Garrett?" Rick started.

"I'm g-g-getting b-b-b-better."

Jenny's jaw tightened at her sudden regression. Her heart hammered inside her chest. Why were they here? What was happening? She could feel the sweat in her hand as Warren held it.

"That's good to hear. I'm sorry to intrude during your convalescence. Do you feel up to speaking with us? We'll only take a few minutes."

"S-s-sure."

Warren slid the chair beside the bed, offered to bring in another from the den, and when Rick refused, took his place across the bed from the detectives, retaking Jenny's trembling hand.

Why would detectives come here? Jenny thought, waiting for Rick to speak.

"Mr. Garrett, we need to speak with Mrs. Garrett alone. Could you wait outside? It'll only be a few minutes."

Jenny searched Warren's eyes. Why must he leave? What possibly could be going on? She bounced her eyes off Rick to Vicki. She found no compassion in those eyes either. Something felt terribly wrong.

Warren let concern stream off his face. There was an edge of hesitation in Warren's response, as if he initially thought he should refuse. But he nonetheless departed, closing the door quietly in his wake.

"Mrs. Garrett..."

"Jenny, please, call me J-Jenny. I-I hate being called M-m-mrs. Garrett. Makes me seem like I'm my h-husband's p-p-possession or something."

"Jenny, we just need to ask you a few questions regarding your accident on the night of September fifteenth."

"Okay. B-but I must tell you, I-I c-can't remember much."

"Do you remember driving your the car that night?"

"N-no."

"Not at all? Do you remember where you were just prior to the accident?"

"No."

Rick sought to conceal the surprise in his voice. Although he maintained his poker face, his voice, however, was a different matter. He glanced down at Vicki, who had taken the chair in hopes that it might make Jenny feel more at ease with them. It appeared, though, as if the gesture offered little in the way of easing the tension of the moment.

"Jenny, it's very important that you remember what happened that night," Vicki said.

Jenny detected their concern; her eyes moved from Rick to Vicki back to Rick. A sudden burning erupted in her stomach surging into the back of her throat. A electrified pain clawed its way up the back of her neck.

"I d-d-don't remember."

"Do you remember leaving the restaurant?"

"I c-can't remember that night at all."

Jenny's voice cracked. She clung to the edge, on the verge of tears.

Rick switched tactics fast, burying the growing anger that was now trying to buoy to the surface. He stowed his interrogator's voice and pulled out a seldom-used paternal tone. Jenny was having trouble dealing with his questions.

"You have no recollection of having dinner at Diamante's that night?"

"N-no, none."

Rick scribbled a line in his notebook.

"Jenny, your husband said you and he shared a bottle of champagne at the restaurant. Do you remember that? Was that all you had to drink?"

"I'm sorry. But I-I can't remember. Oh, my God! Did I kill someone?"

For a moment neither spoke.

Jenny's hands trembled out of control.

Vicki reached out to calm them.

"You sideswiped a car before going over the guard rail. A woman and her nine-year-old daughter were injured in the accident. I'm afraid the daughter's still in a coma," Vicki said.

"Oh m-my God."

"Mrs. Garrett, it's our job to reassemble the pertinent information about the accident. We need to get a clear picture of exactly what happened that night. We were hoping you could help us," Rick said.

"You're saying I...injured someone."

"I'm afraid so."

Jenny pulled her hands from Vicki's and began working her sheet nervously through her fingers. For a moment, she sought the dark recesses of her memory, hoping to force something into her conscious mind. Something that might help explain what these detectives were talking about. Nothing surfaced.

Rick noted Jenny's nervous habit. Could that have contributed to the accident that night?

Tears found their way into the corners of Jenny's eyes. Why were they questioning her? More importantly, a part of her deep inside needed the truth about that night. Did she cause the accident?

"W-was I...at fault?"

"Jenny, that's exactly what we need to determine. At this point, we have very little information about your accident. I was hoping you might be able to fill in some of the gaps."

"I'm sorry, Detective, I can't remember. I'm sorry if I hurt someone. I can't even remember what happened before the accident."

"Jenny, can you remember anything that occurred that Friday, the day of the accident? Where were you in the morning or the afternoon?" Vicki asked plaintively, though she was cleverly probing for the least little scrap of useful information.

The detectives had come here to determine if Jenny could be held criminally responsible for the accident, and if so, what charges should then be filed against her. How much did Jenny drink before leaving the restaurant? If the little girl died, they may have to charge her with involuntary manslaughter. That is, if Jenny were driving while intoxicated that night.

Jenny paused.

Rick could see her mind churning behind those seemingly-innocent blue eyes. It would appear she was trying in earnest, but failing.

"No. I'm sorry. I just can't remember."

Jenny's voice grew frantic.

"Jenny, can you tell us what you are able to remember clearly?"

Leaden moments dragged on; Jenny ransacked her jumbled memory. Bits and pieces of her life lay scattered about. Her pounding heart echoing in her ear only worsened matters. She had to put the pieces back together. But where to begin?

"I was h-having lunch with K-kate," she said. There was triumph in her voice. "We were...I'm n-not sure where we were. There's a black waiter...we had...I can't remember."

"Who is Kate, Jenny?"

"Kate M-Matheson, m-m-my partner. We own a small uptown advertising agency. Matheson and Garrett."

"How long have you been in business?"

Jenny thought. Why didn't that come automatically to mind?

"Our fourth year." She felt relief in knowing that. "We're still s-s-struggling, but we're getting better."

"When might this lunch have taken place?"

"I don't know." Jenny closed her eyes. "We were happy, excited...Kate had to leave...everything after that is blank. It's like I didn't exist."

Vicki looked up at Rick. Was that lunch on the day of the accident? Had they been drinking at that lunch?

Rick scanned some scribbles in his notebook. He stopped suddenly, looking at Jenny, then he returned to his notes.

"Is there any c-c-criminal..."

"Right now, Mrs. Garrett, we're investigating. I understand your husband has been handling the details with the insurance company, so we'll be able to get some of the information we need from him. We would like to come back as our investigation continues...to interview you again."

"I understand. I really wish I c-c-could help you. But I can't remember. I-I didn't d-d-do anything wro..."

Vicki stood up, her eyes concerned, her face like stone. Rick slipped his notebook into his coat pocket, signaling the end of the interview. Afterward, he removed a card from his wallet and slid under the ashtray on the table beside Jenny's bed.

"Here's my number. If you remember anything about the accident, or the days leading up to it, please contact me immediately. It's very important that I hear your side of what happened that night."

Jenny took in the card. The words beneath Rick's name sent a wave of nausea into her throat: SPECIAL INVESTIGATIONS. Jenny felt no relief at their departure. Guilt swarmed over her like angry bees. What had she done?

****

Warren sat waiting with cigarette in hand at the bottom of the stairs when Rick and Vicki came down. He tapped his cigarette nervously along the edge of the ash tray he held in his other hand. The action seemed more an unconscious tick rather than a sign of unrest.

"Could we ask you a couple questions, Mr. Garrett?"

"Sure. But I gave everything I know about the accident to the police at the hospital that night. A couple of days later someone from the county sheriff's department called me for a follow-up. I haven't learned any more since then."

Rick's face remained expressionless, his tone level and unrevealing.

Warren led them from the foyer into the sitting room, where he settled into his overstuffed leather chair with its own standing ash tray beside it. He indicated that Rick and Vicki should sit on the sofa. It implied that no one occupied that particular chair but him.

"This shouldn't take long."

Rick and Vicki took opposite ends of the damask Victorian straight-backed sofa, finding it impossible to sit comfortably upon. A sure way to keep the interview short was to force the detectives to sit on that sofa, which appeared to be an expensive antique, but felt like sitting on a rock.

Did Warren intentionally choose a position distant from the officers?

Rick surmised that the room's lavish accouterments, along with the cloth-bound original edition books on the shelves, were meant definitely for show rather than use. Warren seemed the type who needed to display the accumulations of his accomplishments. Only if others could drool over it, did it mean anything to him.

Vicki remained silent during their brief interview. Her task now was to carefully monitor Warren's mannerisms to see if she could detect anything out of the ordinary that might aid them in analyzing the little they already knew.

"That night, Mr. Garrett, you said Jenny had not been drinking, correct?"

"Yes...no. Wait. I said we split a bottle of champagne. That was, I guess, two glasses each."

"Did you have a long wait for a table at Diamante's?"

"I don't know. I arrived late. Jenny was already at the table when I got there."

"Did you have a reservation?"

Warren looked down his nose at the detective.

"We're regulars."

"Did Jenny consume any alcohol while she waited for you?"

"I don't know. I wasn't there. Why? What are you suggesting?"

"Were there any empty cocktail glasses at the table when you arrived?"

"This is ridiculous."

Warren pressed out his cigarette, fumbled in his pocket for his pack, but abandoned it when it refused to come out without effort.

"Just answer the question, Mr Garrett."

"No. I don't remember. Jenny's not a drinker anyway."

Warren looked back at his crushed out cigarette in the standing ashtray. His eyes came back to settle on Rick's in a stare that, though it was meant to intimidate, did little to affect Walker.

"We spoke to a Ruben Alejandro. He was your waiter that night. He informed us about the champagne, but he said he also remembered bringing drinks to the table during dinner."

"That was me. I had a Scotch, neat, and a refill."

"Mrs. Garrett had no cocktails with dinner?"

"No, she nursed the champagne. I told you Jenny's not a big drinker. Wine mainly, or occasionally a whiskey sour when it's socially required."

"She's an advertising agency executive, correct?"

"Yeah, so."

"Do you normally have champagne with dinner?"

"Sometimes."

"Was it a special occasion? An anniversary or a celebration of some kind?"

"No."

Rick paused intentionally, the silence meant to afford Warren a chance to add to or alter his statement. A sign that there might be something more Warren wanted to get on the record. He didn't.

"How would you describe Jenny's state of mind during dinner? Did she seem preoccupied or upset?"

"No. We talked about work and the house."

"Did you argue or disagree at any time during dinner?"

"No. And I can't see..."

Warren shifted uncomfortably at the insinuation. He reached for his cigarette pack, worked it out of his pocket this time and brought one to his lips.

"I trade commodities for a living, and I'm losing money every minute we spend going over and over what's already been put on record."

"I know that, Mr. Garrett, I'm almost finished here."

While he spoke, Rick jotted Warren's obvious agitation to these questions into his notebook. The very act of writing would grind away at Warren's brain. There was something behind this investigation. Rick could feel it in the way both Jenny and Warren responded to his inquiries.

"Your waiter said he thought he saw you lean over the table to kiss Jenny."

"There was no special reason."

"You weren't attempting to make up for anything then?"

"No."

Rick remained silent for a long minute, offering Warren a chance to continue, if he was so inclined.

Warren, however, sat dutifully silent, tapping his cigarette along the edge of the ash tray. He stopped suddenly, anticipating Rick's next question.

Rick, instead, scribbled in his notebook, keeping his eyes focused intently on his scribbling. He was writing nothing in particular, but Warren would never know that. Clicking the top of his pen, Rick seemed to stare through Warren for a moment, then rose suddenly.

Warren pressed the cigarette out in the ash tray, despite being only half consumed, and hesitated before getting up.

"No other questions then?"

"None for now. Thank you for all your help."

"So what's the verdict?"

"We're still investigating. I left my card with your wife. Please contact me if you think of anything that might be helpful to our investigation."

"Helpful? What is this all about? Jenny's accident was just that—an accident. Your questions are way out of bounds..."

"We just need to confirm that we have all the facts. That's all."

"Was Jenny able to help you?"

"Afraid not."

Rick and Vicki remained silent during their descent down the stairs and the short walk back to their car. They had hoped to gain more information. Jenny's selective amnesia could be legitimate, or it could be feigned to allow time to prepare her story.

Rick scratched at the graying strands standing up on his neck. They did that each time he took a case with the word *ringer* written all over it. In his nine-year career attached to the State's Attorney's office, Rick had three other ringers, cases where he knew the party reeked with guilt, yet he failed to unearth the necessary evidence to prove it. His gut told him to stay with his feelings.

But, if Jenny legitimately had no memory of that night—which was not that uncommon in cases involving head trauma—that would gravely complicate matters. He would have to find another way to uncover what really happened those thirty to sixty seconds before impact.

The woman driving the other car involved in the crash believed she saw headlights coming up behind Jenny's as she came around the bend in the road. Still, no one had come forward with testimony as to what really occurred that night. That elusive other car might reveal insights into Jenny's driving just before impact. Driving under the influence, Jenny could have crossed the center line. If he could locate the other driver who had been on the road that same moment, Rick could get corroboration. But he had nothing to go on. No license number, no vehicle make, not even the color.

Rick needed some indication of erratic driving, since due to the nature of the crash, the officers at the scene were unable to get blood alcohol samples right after the accident occurred. A mix-up at the hospital during those first critical hours had deprived the authorities of the much needed evidence of DUI.

"That pretty much got us nowhere," Vicki said, once they were ensconced inside the car.

"Well, for right now, let's let them think about us."

6

Dr. Sy Rosenstein maintained an austere tenth-floor office on the west side of the city. The unadorned cubicle was one of a thousand in the West Lake Insurance building. The mahogany door displayed simply his name and the suite number.

Jenny's mind was a jumble as Warren assisted her into the anteroom, which offered a secretary's desk and chair, a worn brown leather sofa and a side table with a lamp, whose shade had faded over the years, and an ashtray. The magazines arranged neatly on the table were at least three months out of date and dog-eared from use. Jenny could only wonder how long she would have to wait to see this man.

She was anything but crazy. What possibly could a psychiatrist do to help her?

Warren grabbed a magazine, flipped through it in record time and returned it to its place on the table.

A prunish sixty-year-old secretary, wearing clothes as faded by time and use as the lamp shade, addressed Jenny by name, maintained warm eye contact, and offered not the slightest hint of a smile, making it equally obvious she was intentionally avoiding Jenny's scar.

Jenny found her hand moving instinctively to cover her mouth. She forced herself to bring her hand back down to her lap, and battled the urge to walk out. Finally, logic won out with Jenny realizing that talking to someone like Rosenstein could only help her now. If he would believe what she was about to tell him.

Sy kept them waiting less than ten minutes. When he opened his inner office door, Jenny hid her surprise. He stood no more than a heel taller than five feet, his sparse hair stretched to minimize his typical male-pattern baldness, and his black plastic glasses rimmed narrow hazel eyes. Bushy gray and chestnut brows grew over the glasses and afforded Jenny an inkling of what his hair must have looked like decades ago. He certainly was the image one might expect to find on the cover of 'Psychiatry Today' magazine.

He greeted Jenny first with a smile that seemed a permanent fixture to his face and meant to ease the anxiety inherent in a first visit. Jenny wondered if he knew why Warren had brought her here, or if this would be one of those exploratory sessions.

Warren was quick to assist Jenny into Sy's office with a steadying hand tightly around her waist. Once inside, he helped her into the chair directly across from the doctor's and drew the side chair to be right beside her. Jenny's eyes never left Rosenstein's; Warren's eyes never left hers.

Save for the half-dozen framed degrees on the wall behind his desk, the walls remained barren and faded from the sun's influence over the years. A man of frugality seemed to be an understatement in Sy's case. He refused to afford himself even the slightest luxuries that one would have thought he would be entitled to by his profession. Sy obviously sought the inner satisfactions of the work he performed over material gain. And his gentle manner certainly supported his profession.

"How are you feeling today, Jenny?" Rosenstein asked, as if they had known each other for years, when in fact this was the first time either had laid eyes on each other. Rosenstein's voice was as light and as gentle as his smile. Though, in fact, it seemed to ease Jenny little under the circumstances.

Warren remained silent, reached for a cigarette pack in his pocket but stopped when Rosenstein's eyes indicated a THANK YOU FOR NOT SMOKING sign on the edge of the desk. Warren thanked Rosenstein for seeing them on such short notice while he unobtrusively returned his cigarettes back to his pocket.

"You look wonderful for someone having come through what you've experienced?"

"I-I'm g-getting b-better."

"Would you care for coffee, or perhaps some tea?"

Both Warren and Jenny declined, Jenny breaking Sy's eye contact and looking at her balled hands in her lap when she detected Sy's eyes moving to the scar on her face. She forbade herself from covering it with her hand.

Jenny knew she was expected to start. Would he believe what she needed to tell him? For a long moment, Jenny considered abandoning her whole story, reaching for Warren's assistance and leaving this place. But the hardest part so far had been in just getting here.

"Warren has filled me in about your accident, and I've taken the liberty of reviewing your medical history," Sy said, keeping his eyes on Jenny.

"Jenny's been having..." Warren started.

"Perhaps, Jenny, you'd like to tell me?"

Sy's words brought Jenny's eyes off her hands and back to his. His smile seemed to indicate his willingness to, at least, listen. Sy leaned slightly forward in his chair, which turned him more toward Jenny and seemed to indicate he wished for her to begin.

"Where s-should I-I start?"

"Anywhere you feel comfortable."

"As I told you over the telephone..." Warren injected.

"Warren, perhaps you might wait in the reception area. There's an ashtray out there and you are free to smoke."

"I'm sorry, I'll be quiet."

"After m-my a-accident," Jenny already needed to take a breath, "I was recovering in the hospital when I thought I saw a ghost. It wasn't a ghost. This i-is..."

"It's okay, Jenny."

"It w-was me. I saw a ghost of myself standing in my room staring at me."

"You said you thought? When was this?"

"I don't know exactly when. The first time I saw it was when I awoke...after the accident. I'm not even certain I saw it or just thought I saw it. But it appeared again outside my door about a week before I was discharged."

"Did it remain?"

"No...yes. Only for a few moments. I'm certain I saw it the second time. She—it was looking at me—but it didn't have eyes."

"How was it looking at you?"

Sy remained calmly dispassionate during Jenny's telling of her story. His eyes emanated trust, his voice though, never conveyed the same feeling.

"With black holes. I mean I could tell it was looking at me."

"Why do you say it was a ghost of yourself, Jenny?"

"It was me. I'm sure of it. The hair, the face—it was me."

Rosenstein remained expressionless behind his desk, always listening, but never once did he pick up his gold-plated pen sitting on a yellow lined pad an inch from his hand.

Warren shifted in his chair. His untimely move-ment stole the doctor's attention from Jenny as if there had been something to read in Warren's sudden gesture. Was that his way of demonstrating silent disbelief in what she had said?

"Jenny, can you tell me what you remember about your accident?"

"Nothing. I can't remember anything of the days leading up to the accident, either."

"Please go on."

"At first, I thought maybe it was just my mind playing tricks on me. The ghost I mean. I-I, but when I came home the ghost appeared in my bedroom."

"How did she appear?"

"Sitting in a chair near the door watching me."

"And this was during the day?"

"No, the middle of the night. A stabbing pain awakened me, and she was sitting there...staring at me."

"Your hospital records indicate you're still taking Demerol for pain. Had you taken pain medication prior to this episode?"

"Earlier in the evening."

"The prescribed dosage?"

Jenny nodded, growing uncomfortable and shifting in the chair herself. Warren, too, seemed to display a sudden restlessness.

"Was this..."

"It a-appeared again the next night. I t-thought it was Warren. I said, 'Why don't you come lay beside me in bed.' I thought it was Warren."

Jenny's hands trembled, her voice weakened. Her constricting chest made breathing difficult. It seemed to Rosenstein that Jenny was reliving the episode in her mind as she spoke.

Sy scribbled for the first time on his pad. His eyes, though, never left Jenny's. He saw something in her eyes; something that conveyed an undeniable terror rising up inside her as she related her story. The horror she felt in the presence of her ghostly self was returning to her now.

"It touched me. It touched me, and when I opened my eyes she, it, was before my face."

Jenny was teetering....

"What did it look like?"

Jenny hesitated.

Sy could see fear swirling behind her eyes. A fear that bonded truth to her words.

"If this is too diffi..."

"No. It was my face. Without eyes. My hair was long, like it was before the accident. But her face—my face—was mangled, ripped open."

Jenny reached out suddenly, snared Warren's forearm and gripped it so tightly that her nails dug into his skin.

"Jenny, what did you feel when it touched you?"

At first Jenny said nothing, looking instead toward Warren, who slid his hand over hers. The contact allowed Jenny to loosen her grip and release him.

"I was eight when my mother died. Breast cancer, though I didn't know that at the time. My Aunt Theresa said I had to touch my mother's cheek as a way of saying good-bye one last time. I didn't want to, but I did as she told me. I never forgot what it felt like...to touch a dead person. It was cold and like clay. That's what it felt like. I felt a cold, dead hand stroke my cheek."

"Jenny, why do you think your aunt insisted you touch your mother?"

"I don't know." Jenny's voice began to crack and quiver.

Sy recorded another few lines, then rose from behind his desk. He rubbed the bridge of his nose under his glasses before he spoke.

"Warren, I wonder if Jenny and I might have a few minutes alone together."

"Sure," Warren said.

But Sy detected an uneasy edge in Warren's manner. He agreed but found discomfort in leaving Jenny alone to talk to him.

Jenny's eyes caught Warren's as he departed.

"Jenny, I've read through all your medical records from the hospital. I'm sure you understand that you suffered a very severe head trauma in the accident, and it is very possible that certain brain tissue was damaged as a result."

"M-m-morrison s-said the s-stutter..."

"Yes, your stutter is one result. A brain injury, unlike other injuries, takes a very long time to heal after such an accident. During this healing process, you may find that things will happen in your life that you are unable to understand. I think maybe these manifestations of yourself are merely the result of that healing process."

"You think what I-I'm seeing...is from the injury?"

"It's not so important what I think. But looking over your records, and knowing the types and dosages of drugs administered to you in the hospital, it is possible that these visions are simply hallucinations caused by the drugs."

"But what about what I saw in my house? I'm only taking pain killers now. Could they affect me like the drugs in the hospital."

"Very possibly. But I'm afraid our time is up for now."

"But I also hear strange voices inside my head."

The words stopped Sy.

"What kinds of voices?"

"I don't know...voices. Voices I've never heard before."

"What are they saying?"

"Just words. Parts of words. I can't understand them. But they're there. I know they're there."

Rosenstein said nothing. But as a result of Jenny's latest comments, he added a few more words to his pad.

"What do you really think, Dr. Rosenstein?"

"I think we should get together again next week. Do you have any trouble traveling?"

"A little."

"Jenny, are you afraid of what you saw?"

Even coming from a trained clinician, the question seemed stilted and clumsy.

"I don't think so. I never got a sense that the thing wanted to harm me."

"Good, because I don't believe there is anything to be frightened of. I'll set you up for an hour next week."

Sy secreted a pleasure derived in the contact of assisting Jenny out of her chair. He opened the office door, but remained in his office while Warren hastened over to take Jenny's arm.

"Warren, could we have a moment together?"

After Warren helped Jenny to the anteroom sofa, he returned to Rosenstein's office, where they stood just behind the closed door.

"Jenny may have sustained more damage than the physicians originally thought. The problem we have is that there is no way of knowing for certain if brain damage has occurred," Sy said.

"How do I deal with this? Morrison told me what to do for the stutter and the memory lapse. Tell me what I'm supposed to do about this."

"I don't have answers for you right now. These episodes are most likely hallucinatory in nature. They might be brought on by drugs or by a change in the brain's chemical makeup. Very likely Jenny is just receiving jumbled electrical signals from her brain."

"Sy, when I held her the other night...after she screamed...she was trembling out of control. I don't know what's going on, but it's scaring the hell out of Jenny."

"I'm afraid I'm without an explanation that addresses this. But remember, Jenny's mind is undergoing tremendous change that is likely to last for months. Her vision could be a residual effect of the drugs. It could be her mind healing, trying to fit pieces back together again. It could be piecemeal memories of the accident. Sometimes those pieces don't fit right—maybe Jenny's witnessing just such a mismatch."

"What do I do?"

"Just stay with her and see she convalesces. The best thing for Jenny now is time for her body to heal. I've asked Jenny to come back next week. We'll see what happens then. Sometimes just vocalizing these things can make them go away."

7

It was too late to even try to cook something for dinner and Warren seemed to lack the enthusiasm anyway. So, he brought in Chinese, and afterward handed Jenny tissues while she cried during the colorized version of Casablanca, though he never could figure out what had brought on the tears. Then he tucked her in for the night at ten o'clock. Jenny began nodding off around nine, but forced herself to remain awake to see the end of the film despite having seen it in its original black and white splendor years earlier.

It had been an exhausting day for both, though when Warren reviewed the day's events, he realized he had accomplished little. His trades had soured early in the day and he had to drop off before he wanted to in order to get Jenny to Rosenstein's office.

That night, Jenny fell off to sleep without the aid of pain medication, and Warren hoped she would sleep through the night without waking. In truth, he was hoping the previous night's episode would not be repeated.

In his makeshift bed in the den, he lay awake long past midnight, staring at the ceiling through the darkness. Sleep taunted him from beyond his reach. Would she see it again? Would she scream again?

Warren wrestled with his blanket, while outside gnarly bare branches scraped across his window. He seemed unusually alert to the night sounds and to the changes in light as clouds crossed before the gibbous moon outside his window.

He flipped his mind from Jenny to his business. Everything was going wrong at once. His dealings were suffering dearly at a time when his attention needed to be at its sharpest. His primary bank had called twice in the past week. He was overextended—way overextended—and sinking fast.

"Them shits," he muttered out loud.

Jenny had no inkling of the precarious threads he had been clinging to for the last six months. And now he must keep it from her until she grew strong enough to deal with it. Only Jenny's agency income had prevented them from losing the house.

Two secondary banks held notes over Warren's head, and they, too, were getting nervous about his loans. They would require reassurance, Warren thought, before being convinced that Warren could pull himself out of this slump. He took stock in himself while he sought the outline of the window. He had recovered from difficult stretches three times in the past four years, and he had survived the cyclical downturns in the market that were inevitable. He knew with time and tenacity he would do it again.

But did he have the time?

Caring for Jenny was proving more of a burden than he had thought. The trades had to start going his way soon, or else he'd need a large infusion of cash. Before falling off to sleep, he ruminated over the ways he might get his hands on cash in the six figure range.

****

Jenny awoke with a start as bright sunshine streaming through her window. Mr. Chips pawed at her bed, beckoning to be put outside for his morning constitutional.

"Go see Warren. He'll let you out."

"Let's go, Chips," Warren growled from the doorway, while he scratched at his ruffled hair and tried to shake the fatigue off his body. Dark circles rimmed Warren's eyes; he looked as though he had slept in his clothes. That was one of the perks of working at home. Nobody cared how bad you looked.

"Breakfast coming right up," Warren offered through a yawn and a pasted-on smile. "You sleep okay?" he asked with a glint to the obvious.

"The entire night."

"No pain?"

"No."

"No any...thing else?"

"No."

Warren made no attempt to hide the relief pouring out of his eyes.

****

Writing intently in his notebook, Rick Walker took over most of a lavish, leather loveseat. The sultry secretary behind the desk a few feet away typed happily away on her computer keyboard, occasionally lifting her eyes to the detective. Her smile was slight and all-business, though it failed to conceal her interest in him. He figured it came more out of curiosity than anything else.

The ultramodern furnishings surrounding him offered his first indication as to the type of person he was waiting to see. Impressionist paintings that look like they might have been created by a chimp, reading lamps that drooped off wrought iron stems, and a tile pattern on the floor reminiscent of Alice's Wonderland all combined to generate an ambiance of a place far removed from the grime of the city outside the windows. As did the precisely placed display of magazines on the table: *Fortune, Business Week, Forbes.*

He had been waiting since nine, hiding his displeasure. It was after ten. The secretary paused momentarily when the determined click of high heels on tile became apparent.

Rick rose in anticipation.

Kate Matheson's stunning face, resplendent in corporate war paint, shot a 'who's this?' look to her secretary. Then, with a smile more plastic than her lips, she took in Rick Walker's full-muscled physique as he stood before her.

"If he doesn't have an appointment, I won't be seeing him today," she fired off with the demeanor of an executive irritated by a salesman's unwanted presence. And a rather shoddy salesman at that.

"It's Detective Walker. He's been waiting to see you," the secretary said barely above a whisper, as if she wished his presence be kept secret. She shuffled papers as she spoke in some vain attempt to appear efficient.

"Detective Walker?" Kate said with a trace of interest. Her eyes captured his and held them steadfast.

"Kate Matheson?" Rick asked, extending a hand more as a courtesy than a greeting.

Kate shifted her black monogrammed briefcase onto the desk before taking Rick's hand with a grip that surprised the detective. She stood squarely facing him with her legs in a spread stance. Her hand took hold of his with a surprisingly determined grip and not so much as a trace of apprehension. Something most unusual in a woman. Her eyes delved into his as if she were seeking to uncover his purpose. Something else unusual for a woman. Most women averted their eyes quickly when forced to confront the law.

Kate exuded the confidence and stature of the consummate executive, replete with all the accouterment of a corporate warrior, and by her determined walk, she made certain those around her knew she had no intention of moving aside for anyone. Those dazzling green eyes could smile—if they wanted to. But for now, Kate reserved her judgement of the detective.

"I won't be disturbed," Kate said into her speaker after she settled into a well-used, high-backed leather chair. There was no mistaking Kate Matheson as the owner of all that fell within her reach, and that this spacious, well-appointed office was her lair.

"So, what can I do for you, Detective?"

"I'd like to ask you a few questions about Jenny Garrett."

"I see. And this concerns her accident?"

Kate brought her fingertips across her forehead just above her eyes, moving the few strands of russet hair out of the way. Something churned behind those eyes.

"Yes."

"How possibly could I help?"

"I understand you and Mrs. Garrett are partners in this agency?"

"Correct."

"Equal partners?"

"Fifty-fifty," Kate offered with a little head nod.

"When was the last time you saw Jenny that Friday, September fifteenth?"

"Early afternoon. I had just returned from a client meeting—Simply Beautiful Cosmetics. We'd been working that account for six months at that time and still struggling to get the campaign off the ground. Jenny was working in her office. We talked for, I guess, an hour or so."

"What did you talk about?"

"Accounts, general stuff, I guess."

"What exactly do you mean by accounts?"

"Just accounts. One I was working on and one she was working on. She showed me some storyboarding nearing completion. I offered my opinion. She ignored it. Business as usual."

"How would you characterize Jenny's state of mind at that time?"

"State of mind? She was fine. Why?" Kate had turned a bit sardonic in her response.

"She wasn't upset or maybe depressed about anything?"

"Jenny? Jenny's never depressed, and it would take total devastation to upset her. Jenny's always sailed on a even keel for as long as I've known her. She's the rock at Matheson Garrett."

"And what are you?"

"I'm the wire."

"How long have you known Jenny?"

Kate paused. It was one of those things you know but have to think about to reconfirm when asked.

"Eleven years. We were at Cornell together. That's where we met."

"Ms. Matheson, how is your advertising business going?"

"You know, Mr. Walker, none of this sounds like it pertains to Jenny's accident."

"Indulge me."

"Like gangbusters. We've realized twenty percent annual growth every year since we started."

"And I take it that means you entertain a substantial client base?"

"And by entertain you mean?"

"Client lunches with around a half dozen cocktails. Extravagant dinners where the booze flows like a fountain until the client is giddy."

"So that's the purpose of this visit?"

"Ms. Matheson, to put it bluntly, did Jenny Garrett entertain any clients during lunch that Friday?"

Kate's sudden shift in her chair offered more than just a casual affront to Rick's question. He's got a lot of nerve coming in here and insinuating something like that. Business is business, and those that don't know how to schmooze, don't last long in this business. Kate thought the words but held her tongue in check. He had a lot of nerve coming in here and insinuating.

"Advertising is sales; sales is schmoozing. How far do you think we'd get ordering club soda at client lunches?"

"Ms. Matheson, did Jenny consume alcohol during her business lunches?"

Rick doled out his question with greater sternness. He was losing his patience with Kate.

"Yes. But Jenny's a social drinker. She drinks with a client, but usually nurses hers while ordering doubles for whomever she's with."

Rick said nothing. He shifted in his chair and scribbled something in his notebook. It was the first time he had put his pen to the pad.

"You're intimating Jenny was drunk that Friday night?"

"We investigate every accident thoroughly, and I take my responsibility very seriously, Ms. Matheson."

The directness of Rick's response proved unsettling.

"To answer your question, I don't know. I'll have her calendar brought in."

"Please. I really do need to understand how Jenny spent that Friday."

"You ever think of asking Jenny?" Kate asked sarcastically. The surprised look on her face meant to convey that she figured Rick to be a complete idiot.

"Jenny's memory of the accident is very unclear right now."

"You're kidding?"

"You seem genuinely surprised, Ms. Matheson."

"I am. I haven't talked with Jenny since before the accident. Warren keeps me current. He said Jenny couldn't handle seeing me. I heard she was pretty messed up. Her face, I mean."

Rick used those moments while Kate buzzed Jenny's secretary to review the set of questions he had scribbled in his notebook. Within a minute or two, the secretary delivered the calendar to Kate's desk, all the time avoiding eye contact with the detective.

"Jenny's office remains just as it was before the accident. I'm sorry, detective, can I have my secretary get you coffee or something?"

Rick slid forward in his chair. He wanted a better look at the top page with the plastic marker across it—September fifteenth.

"Nothing on her calendar," Kate quickly pointed out, as if that exonerated her partner from any wrongdoing.

Rick studied the unblemished page.

"Does that mean then that Jenny did not have a business lunch with a client?"

"Not always. If an important client calls impromptu looking for a free lunch, we jump. We never let an opportunity get away. You want to see an ad agency go belly up fast, that's the way to do it."

"What about Jenny's telephone log?"

"I'll have it brought in. Her secretary keeps the telephone log for her."

"If you please. Ms. Matheson, I'll also need a look at Matheson Garrett's financial condition."

"What? What do you mean?"

"I'd like to look at Matheson and Garrett's financial records."

"Hold on a minute. I don't see how something like that is germane to your investigation. The way I understand it, Jenny lost control of her car and went over a guard rail while driving down a hill. How can the agency's financial health have anything to do with that?"

Rick buried his excitement. His inquiry had struck a nerve in Matheson. Maybe there was something in the financial records he needed to see.

"Ms. Matheson. There's a nine-year-old girl in a coma. That makes everything germane."

Kate rubbed her fingers along the slick surface of her desk, averting her eyes for a prolonged moment. She was weighing all the implications of Walker's request. She knew pretty much what her options were at this moment and had to decide which way she should move.

"Let me tell you. We've got our problems. Our growth is a little more overwhelming than we realized. We've doubled the staff within two years. That means a hefty overhead and added expenses. If you're implying Jenny was drinking because she worried over the agency failing, I doubt that. We maintain a more than adequate reserve of working capital."

Rick felt a churning in his gut. As a result, he decided it was time to let the pot heat up before playing his final card.

"Could I ask you a few questions about Jenny's life outside this agency?"

"Sure."

"How would you characterize Jenny and Warren's relationship? Normal?"

"Normal?" Kate laughed. "Warren trades commodities. You don't have normal with a guy in that profession. Jenny's in the middle of a fledgling advertising agency. I guess their relationship was as normal as it could be under those conditions. Mr. Walker, Jenny and I spend six days a week together, but I can't say I know much about her relationship with Warren. We have very little time to talk about our personal lives. I'll say this, Jenny never really confides in me about Warren."

"Then you would be unaware of any problems between them?"

"Jenny did seem different the last few weeks before the accident, maybe even going back as far as a month before."

"Different how?"

"I don't know. Preoccupied maybe. You want to know more about Jenny and Warren, talk with Bridget."

"Bridget?"

"Bridget Sterling, a mutual friend. We were all at Cornell. Jenny spends more time with her out of this office than with me."

Kate flipped through her Rolodex, grabbed up a silver pen from its holder and jotted down Bridget's address and telephone number on a slip of paper that had FROM THE DESK OF KATE MATHESON printed in flowing script along the top.

"Ms. Matheson, I'd like to keep Jenny's calendar, telephone log and anything else that might help me get an accurate picture of those days leading up to her accident."

"Sure. Jenny's secretary is at your disposal. Feel free to contact her directly for anything you need."

Rick rose to leave, tucking his notebook in his pocket and the calendar under his arm. He thought he detected a glimpse of relief take over Kate's face.

"When do I get access to the agency's books?" Rick doled out the question in a way that limited Kate's response.

"The books? I don't know..."

Kate forced her eyes to remain on the detective's.

Rick's eyes conveyed his tenacity and authority. He expected to get whatever he wanted. Kate's uneasy hesitation sounded a blaring alarm inside his head. She seemed jolted by his request...why?

"Your complete financial records. You do keep them on premises, don't you?"

"No," Kate offered sharply, hiding her embarrassment. "They're with our accountant. Neither Jenny nor I are very good with the numbers. But give me a day or two, I'll have them made available."

"That would be fine. Here's my number. Call me when the books are ready." Rick handed Kate his card.

She stared at it for a long moment. It took every ounce of strength she could muster to keep the surprise out of her face.

"My secretary will show you to Jenny's office," Kate said absentmindedly. Her eyes never left Rick's card.

After Rick left, Kate closed her door and returned to her chair, where she shoved the papers sitting in front of her away and stared at the card.

"Special Investigations—fuck," she muttered, dialing the number for the accounting firm of Jarvison and Lewis.

8

Jenny sat propped up by pillows in bed, enjoying the sun against her face and browsing through the trades, missing more than she saw. She could hear Warren tapping away at his computer in the den. The magazines spurred Jenny's first spurts of anxiousness to return to work. But would she remember what to do? And what she might have said to clients before the accident? Did she make commitments to any of her clients that she would now not remember?

For a moment, she pressed her mind into service, trying to recapture that night at the restaurant. Nothing buoyed to the surface. It was as if that day never existed in her life. She could neither confirm nor deny anything that anyone claimed she had said or did that day. Or the days preceding it.

A total void filled her head.

The only vision she could crystallize in her mind was a meeting with Kate. And she was excited about something. Would Kate remember why Jenny was excited? And when did that memory she now clung to actually take place? Was it a month old? A year?

****

Outside in the yard, Mr. Chips sniffed over every inch of ground for the millionth time and dug with his snout through the mounds of fallen leaves. Finding nothing of interest, he returned to the porch and stretched out upon the top step with his front paws hanging over the edge, waiting for Warren to remember to let him in.

He scratched at his ear, sniffed along the crack between the boards on the porch, and went after an ant that quickly scurried to safety.

Then something changed.

A wave of icy terror fell upon the animal. His sense of imminent danger had been triggered. Chips pricked his ears. A terrible threat swam through him. The dog sampled the air swirling down from the trees. Not there. He pointed his snout toward the door.

Inside the house.

Chips issued a deep guttural growl. The hairs at his nape stood rigid. Mr. Chips bounded for the door, his yaps turning quickly to fervent braying while he scraped wildly at the wooden door frame.

****

Jenny's eyes fluttered out of focus on the page. She, at last, succumbed to her fatigue. She was pushing it and she knew it, thinking if she forced herself to work harder, she would recover much sooner. When she put the magazine down, she heard Chips whimpering from far away.

Jenny closed her eyes for a moment to refresh them.

When she opened them, the pellucid specter of herself hovered at the foot of her bed.

Jenny sucked in a breath, building a scream. The graven image, only a few feet away, was undeniably her and radiated its own pale glow, appearing to be solid, yet at the same time, translucent.

Jenny tried to swallow, but phlegm choked her throat and blocked her scream.

A battered, bloody hand rose to extend a lacerated and snaggled finger pointing at her.

Jenny stretched out her own hand as if to push the image away.

"W-W-warren!" She wanted to scream it—it came out no louder than a staccato whisper.

Downstairs in the kitchen, Chips clawed at the door until the pounding sounded like rapid machine gun fire. He yapped and barked in warning, knowing he was helpless to come to Jenny's aid.

"Wait a goddamn minute, you shit!" Warren scowled as he marched down the hall at a pace matching the rapidity of Chips' braying.

As Warren appeared through the doorway, Jenny could discern Warren's form behind the specter.

"Jenny!" he screamed.

Ruby blood oozed from the corners of Jenny's eyes, trickling down her cheeks like out-of-control tear drops. Blood gushed from both her nostrils. When Jenny opened her mouth, blood spilled out onto her night dress. It was as if she had become frozen on the bed, unable to move, unable to do anything.

The specter vanished.

"W-warren, h-help me, p-p-please!.

Warren's face paled at the sight of blood streaming down Jenny's face. He attacked the bleeding with towels folded haphazardly into compresses, pressing them against Jenny's pallid skin while tilting her head back. Moments later, the bleeding ceased.

"Jenny, what's going on?"

"S-she w-was here. Warren, please help me. I'm a-afraid."

9

Rick pressed the buzzer for apartment 602 in the Glen Oaks apartment building. A nice secure place to live amidst of an otherwise run-down strip of city. The morning's brisk north wind swirled discarded newspapers into tornadic circles along the sidewalk. Rick would rather have spent his Saturday morning at home, doing anything but thinking about this case. But he realized there wasn't much for him around the small apartment he called home, and working kept his mind off the fact that another year was passing and he was still alone.

He shifted, buzzing again. One more buzz, he thought, then he was out of here. This case was turning into a ringer anyway, and Rick held little hope of learning anything worthwhile. They would probably never really know what happened that night.

"Yes?" a tinny timid voice asked over the intercom.

"Ms. Bridget Sterling?"

"Yes."

"Detective Rick Walker, I'd like to talk to you about Jenny Garrett."

"Oh. Sure, I'll buzz you in."

A short clanking elevator ride later, Rick rapped on the door with the 602 painted on it. When no immediate response came, he placed his badge before the peephole at a distance where it would be in focus to the occupant inside.

First a deadbolt receded, then the lock on the door handle clicked and finally the sound of a sliding chain came. The door opened without the slightest hesitancy.

Rick had to force his eyes to remain on Bridget's sparkling blue orbs. It took all the will power he could muster to avoid the fluorescent orange Spandex top that stretched across well-rounded and otherwise unfettered breasts touting soft nipples that played for his attention.

Bridget's frame had all the markings of having been sculpted by an artist. Though she was a slight woman, the same age as Jenny, she completely over-whelmed anyone who came into her view. She wore Spandex shorts that began at a tight, exposed mid-section and smoothed like silk downward to where inviting thighs took over. A sweat band held her hair in check.

Rick had to work consciously to overcome the impression that he was ogling her.

"Sorry, but I live alone, and I don't like to open my door unless I know who it is."

"I fully understand."

In those few steps that it took to move from the foyer into the living room, Rick took in the breadth of Bridget's life. Doing so also took his eyes off what remained engraved inside his mind. Her furnishings were as lavish as she was beautiful. Bridget was undoubtedly a woman who liked to surround herself with very nice things.

"Yes, Detective, Jenny and I went to Cornell together, and we've been best friends ever since," Bridget answered in response to Rick's initial question.

Bridget straddled the arm rest of a chair while Rick sat on the sofa. Her lush black, shoulder-length hair had been secured in a French braid. She took a long drink from a bottle of spring water and used the towel around her neck to wipe away the beads of sweat accumulating on her forehead.

Rick waited, admiring the way other sweat beads trickled down her honey-colored flesh.

Temptation filled his head. Temptation almost impossible to quell.

"I'm sorry. I just finished my Tae-bo workout. A minute later, and I'd have been in the shower."

It was obvious Bridget worked out habitually. Her lean silky legs disappeared under the Spandex shorts. It also became obvious to Rick that Bridget's smile was more than just perfunctory.

"Do I know you?" Rick asked, his eyes testimony to the confusion in his voice.

"You might," Bridget teased with that melting smile.

"On a billboard maybe?"

"Detective, you flatter me."

"I'm sorry, this must sound real hokey."

Rick returned to his notebook to relocate the question that Bridget's smile had caused to evaporate from his mind.

"I'm teasing," Bridget chimed, reaching out to brush his forearm in a playful way. "Exotica perfumes, about a year ago. I did a few magazines and billboards. The product died before we could get to television, though one spot did air during the late night movies."

"Yes. You wore that..."

"Skintight black leotard, lying on a huge velvet pillow, exuding a million dollars worth of sex appeal."

"That's it. You're the Exotica girl."

"You remembered. I didn't last very long. It seems the perfume's scent turned out to smell more like animal sweat."

Bridget smiled pleasantly enough and her lively eyes sparkled when she spoke. She answered Rick's questions, though at times, appeared puzzled by their implications.

"I thought Jenny just had an accident. It sounds like you're trying to say she was at fault."

"It's routine. Have you spent much time with Jenny and Warren together?"

"You mean before the accident? Jenny isn't seeing anyone now. I understand there were scars," she said, her voice trailing off as if revealing a confidence.

"Yes, prior to the accident."

"Yeah, I guess. We get together at least a couple, three, maybe four times a month. Jenny was the one who got me that gig as the Exotica girl. My career was a real struggle before that. Now I've been working pretty steady ever since. But nothing as big as the Exotica gig."

"Would you characterize their relationship as happy?"

"I guess. I mean they rarely fought when I was with them, if that's what you mean."

"Does Jenny drink?"

"Jenny, drink? No. Jenny only drinks when it's expected of her."

"Has Jenny ever indicated that she was unhappy or having problems?"

"No...well...I guess. I mean lately, before the accident, it seemed like Jenny wasn't herself."

"How do you mean?"

"I don't know. Jenny is normally perky and full of life. She thrives on challenges. But she seemed preoccupied about something."

"She ever confide in you what that might be?"

"She never went into detail, but I think it had to do with her and Warren. Mind you, she never said her marriage was in trouble, but she did intimate to me that things were less than perfect in Camelot, if you know what I mean."

Rick had to mask his surging interest.

"In what ways?"

"She didn't get specific. But you want my opinion?"

"Very much."

"I think they were having problems. Jenny spends sixty hours a week at her agency. You can't neglect a man like Warren for very long before he starts to look for something better, you know what I mean?"

Bridget smiled temptingly. A smile that crawls under your skin and takes you over.

Rick found himself staring at those soft eyes in a way that was not strictly business. The lingering silence made it seem as if Rick had run out of questions.

Bridget rose, pulling the towel away from her neck and throwing her chest out in such a way that forced Rick to notice her pert, hardened nipples through the thin material.

"That's just my opinion. Call it an unspoken language. There's just something in the way they acted when they were together over the past few months that seemed out-of-kilter with the cosmos."

Rick sensed that maybe Bridget knew more about that unspoken language between people, especially the opposite sex. She was using it on him right now, whether she realized it or not.

"Then Jenny never confided in you as to what the real problem might have been?" Rick asked, holding strict eye contact in an attempt to overcome his attraction to Bridget, attempting to maintain his professionalism.

"No. And that tells me it must be very serious, if she kept it from her best friend."

Rick rose. He was very close to Bridget. He felt her breath on him, and swore he could feel the warmth radiating off her skin. She lingered, in no hurry to distance herself from him.

"Anything else?"

"No."

Bridget stepped back to show him to the door.

Rick's sixth sense kicked in. Something seemed wrong with this picture, though at the moment all he could do was make another careful pass of the surroundings before making his way back to her door. Rick paused for a moment as if he wanted to speak, using the tactic to try again to hone in on the incongruity that altered his senses. Why did he suddenly feel as if he were missing something here? There was something out of place, yet his eyes couldn't latch on to it.

"What is this all about, anyway? It was an accident wasn't it?"

The question forced Rick back to Bridget.

"My investigation's just routine. Oh, one more question."

"Yes?"

Bridget had her hand on the door handle, but kept the door closed when Rick mentioned more questions.

"Is there anyone else who might provide me with information about the Garretts."

"Not that I can think of. Is there something wrong? I mean about Jenny's accident?"

"State law requires we make a full and complete investigation regarding any accident that involves serious injury."

"Serious injury?"

"A nine-year-old girl is still in a coma."

"Oh. I never knew."

10

Kate arrived, hurried and late, at the Riverfront Towers apartments on the lower east side. She fumbled with her keys, her heart racing, before unlocking the door. Once inside, she immediately kicked off her shoes. A puckish smile spread like a wild fire across her face. She sampled the air, picking up the inviting scent of his Nautica men's cologne.

This time she remembered to switch off her blasted little beeper, then plunked it into her purse, which she tossed haphazardly onto the bureau in the foyer. A devilish excitement tugged at her now yearning pleasure spot when she detected the faint drone of impassioned voices emanating from the bedroom. She knew she was already beginning to become wet.

Damn she was late.

Kate entered the bedroom to find young, sculpted, pliable Kevin naked and splay-legged on the bed half-hidden and half-exposed beneath the sheet. His shoulder-length chestnut hair, still wet from a shower, had been hastily slicked back, giving him that famed Antonio Banderas look. Her eyes went right to her reason for coming. It appeared as if Kevin had been limbering up in anticipation of her.

Kate shed her clothes as if they were on fire. They weren't—but her passions were. Just seeing him poised in innocence for her made her want it even more.

To her right, the moans of women in the throes of orgasm pulsed out of the television speaker. Kevin had some porn orgy movie going. And after a mere glance at it, Kate returned to her task of getting naked. The sight of his now awakening erection sent her heart into palpitations.

Kevin set his glass of scotch on the night table and smiled while he turned to make his manhood more prominent to Kate.

That is exactly why you're enamored with Kevin, Kate told herself. His was the biggest thing she had ever had inside her. And she had had many over the fifteen years since she surrendered her virginity in the back of a decked-out van. And as a special bonus, it turned out Kevin's manhood was bigger than his brain. All the better for her. He was trainable.

"I saved you one," he said, angling up a mirror like a serving tray. A thin, even white line pointed directly at Kate.

"Ten more minutes and I was going to do it myself."

"Always so impatient, Kevin."

By now all that remained were her panties, which Kate slid out of, noticing she stained them with her excitement.

"You're forty minutes late!"

"Sorry, baby," Kate offered. She slid under the sheet and let the tips of her fingers smooth slowly over his tool. "I couldn't shake old man Kingston. Looks to me like you kept yourself occupied, anyway."

Her eyes bounced from Kevin to the television screen, where a man and woman were bucking in wild, and vocal, copulation.

"I love the way you do that," Kevin said, indicating the small screen.

"Then don't spoil the moment by scolding," she cooed, breathing heavily against his cheek before letting her tongue wisp into his ear. "You'll just have to punish me for being bad."

Neither wasted time nor movements as they began working on each other's pleasure spots with the skill of seasoned surgeons. Their genuine moans of pleasure overshadowed the poorly dubbed versions coming out of the television.

Though lean and muscular, Kevin was callow when it came to business, just two years out of college. Yet he had an untapped well of sexual energy with a nature prone to exploring uncharted territories, and he took guidance without becoming bitter; though Kate, at times, thought him more a lap dog than a student lover.

Kate needed Kevin as her release when the pressures mounted at the agency. With Jenny out indefinitely now, she needed him more and more with each passing week. Theirs was a relationship more of lust than love, at least for her. He fulfilled her need to escape into the salacious fantasy that consummate sex offered. And, for the most part, he made sure she was satisfied before allowing himself to blast off.

Kevin's impatience toward her proved so far to be his only flaw. But he made up for it in repetitions. The man was a machine that performed on command; like those modern robots used in manufacturing. Feed him fuel and he performs.

After reaching her third climax within the hour, Kate curled up in Kevin's eager arms, squeezing his dark nub between her fingers and strumming the tips of her nails lightly over his hairless chest. Kevin responded in kind, fondling her breasts, hoping shortly to go for a fourth.

Jenny had never once questioned why Kate insisted on using Jarvison and Lewis as their accounting firm. Kate assumed Jenny never even suspected that Kevin here did more than just maintain the agency's books.

A thick down comforter, rich in floral colors, kept their legs cozy, while outside rain pelted the window pane. Their bodies so close together took care of the rest. After Jenny's accident, Kate would have gone mad had it not been for Kevin's massive woman-pleaser.

"I need a little favor, Kevie," Kate cooed, working her hand expertly down under the blanket, while flicking at his nipple with her wet tongue.

"I should have figured. Lately, the only time you fuck me is when I'm supposed to do something for you." Kevin shifted his weight to flop himself into her waiting hand.

Kate began kneading gently, lovingly.

"The police are investigating Jenny's accident."

"So?"

Kevin closed his eyes. He moaned as Kate began a slow slide from his nipple down the center of his washboard stomach, leaving glistening saliva to mark her trail. Kevin's hand left her breast, slid down along the curve of her soft hip and sought the velutinous nest between her legs.

The flames of re-awakened passion roared inside him. Once more, he thought, and this time before she can withdraw it in time, then it's back to the office.

"The detective wants a look at the agency's books."

The fire died, doused by Kate's words. Kevin stopped, opening his eyes round and wide.

Kate worked him harder.

"What for?"

"Just routine."

"It's not just fucking routine, Kate..."

"So? You said you could take care of things. You said I wouldn't have to worry about..."

Kevin's face had become ashen. His mouth went suddenly as dry as cotton. He had difficulty swallowing.

"What?" Kate asked, feeling Kevin deflate in her hand despite her efforts.

"Fuck."

"You said it would be all right. Kevin?"

Kevin pulled away from her, leaving the bed.

"I said I could hide it from your partner. I said we could put in places she would never think of questioning."

"So?"

"So? The fucking cops are a helluva lot smarter than your partner."

"Kevie..." Kate said, taking his hand and pulling him back onto the bed, so she could grab hold of his tool.

"You're a good accountant and great with this magic wand. Why do you think I insisted you be assigned our account? You think I wanted old man Jarvison humping me? You'll take care of it for me. I need to turn the books over to the cops, or I'll start looking suspicious."

"Suspicious about what? Kate, this isn't..."

Kevin stopped mid-sentence. Kate positioned her face over his mid-section and began to work on him.

"I'll take care of..." he moaned in ecstasy.

11

Jenny went through the next three days without seeing the apparition. But she found no peace—even its absence plagued her. Was it an hallucination like Dr. Rosenstein said? Or could there really be a spirit of herself tormenting her? Tomorrow she was to see Rosenstein again. He would help her cope. Jenny wondered how he would explain away the hemorrhaging when she last encountered that specter.

And then there were the voices. They came without warning, lasted only a second or two, and never offered her more than a few seemingly disjointed words. But each time they raced through her head, she stopped all activity at that moment so she could write down those fragments she recalled.

"*Pump the bag, hurry... The pressure's falling below...*"

She found if she concentrated on what she had heard, she could even differentiate between the voices and concluded they were neither hers nor Warren's—nor anyone else familiar to her. One thread, though, common to all the voices was a driving sense of urgency. Panic filled each word.

Even seeing them on paper delivered up no explanation for their continuing troublesome presence in her mind. Troublesome, though, seemed an inappropriate description, since they startled her each time they popped into her head. It felt as if people had suddenly appeared beside her and were shouting into her ears.

After a magnificently attempted dinner of Fettuccini Alfredo that turned out overly dry because it had been Warren's first attempt at such a dish, Warren left to run an errand. He promised to be back as soon as possible and forbade Jenny from doing anything that might prove overly taxing on her.

Jenny was tired, but not fatigued. She was tired of flipping through the magazines and cable channels. She was tired of sitting in bed most of every day. She reflected gratefully on the fact that she had a career; it spared her the mundane life of game shows, soap operas and old movies.

But what about when they began their family? The thought popped into her mind as if a genie had suddenly appeared out of a bottle. What about a family? Why did that pop into her mind? Were they planning a family?

Something hidden behind dark recesses in her mind peeked out when she thought about plans for a family.

Jenny hiked up the television volume to drown out those spooky spurious sounds every old house makes. She reasoned that if she couldn't hear it, then it wasn't there, and she needn't be frightened by it.

Warren had hesitated about leaving her alone. She could see it in his eyes before he left. But Jenny had convinced him she would be all right. They had to live a normal life; it was wrong to fear every minute of every day. And besides the spirit appeared while he was here in the house anyway, so it wasn't like he was a deterrent to the thing.

Mr. Chips rose abruptly.

Jenny tensed.

The dog began to whine.

"Not now, Chips, I'll let you out later."

But Chips never once looked back at Jenny. Instead, he planted his front paws and stared at the open bedroom door. Suddenly, he began backing away—inching toward Jenny.

"What?"

Icy terror seized every muscle in Jenny's body. Chips didn't need to go out. Chips...

Jenny looked up.

"No, please, God no..."

The dog issued a low, vile growl. Then he launched into braying with maddening force. His lips curled back to expose white fangs, and he flattened his ears, though he never advanced toward the open doorway.

Jenny's heart pounded out of control inside her chest.

Should she run? Where could she go to escape?

First the hideous face bloomed, all mangled, empty and lifeless. Then the ragged body materialized in the room. It lasted a moment—unmoving—staring sightlessly at Jenny.

Then Jenny screamed!

****

Dr. Rosenstein sat beside Jenny as she lay on her bed. Seconds later the injection began to work its soothing magic. Jenny's trembling hands fell limp at her sides; and her eyes glassed over as a result of the medication.

"I'm telling you, Mr. Chips saw it, too. The dog was terrified and refused move from my bedside. This can't be an hallucination."

"Just relax, Jenny. Let the sedative work. Try to put the experience from your mind for right now."

"But...Mr. Chips..."

Sy patted Jenny's hand soothingly until she finally succumbed and closed her eyes. Despite her efforts to fight the drug's intent, her muscles lost rigidity.

"How do you feel now?"

"Just...great," Jenny said with no hint of spirit on her ashen face.

Sy remained close until Jenny drifted off into a light sleep. Even then, he convinced himself to remain a minute longer, withdrawing a few steps from the bed. Such an emotional upheaval could overcome even a potent sedative.

"Why did...Mr. Chips...growl?" Jenny asked, her eyes still closed, her words buoying out of her slumber.

"The technical term, Jenny, is anxiety transference," Sy whispered. "Not unusual between people and their pets. Your dog was reacting to your actions. Just let your mind drift into sleep."

"Anxiety transference?"

"You're fighting the sedative. Mr. Chips was only reacting to your overt fear. Trust me, he had no idea why he was growling. Just a reaction to your hallucination."

"It wasn't an hallucination."

Moments later Jenny fell silently asleep.

Sy retreated to the door and turned back for one final check to assure himself she was really asleep, then switched off the light and left Jenny alone.

"Well?" Warren asked anxiously after Sy closed the bedroom door. His cigarette quivered in his fingers. He clung to the ashtray in his other hand as if it were all that were keeping him above water.

"I've given her something to sleep."

"Fine, but what about her hallucinations? She's a wreck. I found her curled in the corner of the bedroom whimpering and crying. She trembled so badly, I... What the hell is going on?"

"I don't know. Could be side effects of the drugs. It could be...more serious brain damage than originally thought."

"What if it doesn't go away? What am I supposed to do for this? She's getting worse. She's convinced that she's being tormented by a ghost of herself."

"I think for the present, Warren, we should explore the rational possibilities. The drugs will eventually fade away, though there could be an occasional flashback. But, if the brain is irreparably damaged, rigorous therapy is our only recourse."

****

Jenny pulled herself out of a shallow sleep to the dull morning light falling in through her window. The gray sky outside threatened rain. She was combing her hair in bed when Warren arrived with breakfast.

"You look very beautiful this morning, Jenny. Sleep well?"

"Very well," she said with a glint in her eye.

Jenny seemed different this morning. She devoured her breakfast with determination and more than her usual vigor. Her facial gestures telegraphed that her mind was churning over something.

"Warren, I know what I saw. Rosenstein is wrong."

Her words were anything but confused or distraught. Jenny spoke them coolly and with rational control.

"Jenny, please, can we take this thing one step at a time? Rosenstein wants to see you in a few days. We can talk to him about it then."

"I'm telling you, Warren, Mr. Chips saw it, too. Even though it terrified him, he was attempting to protect me from it."

"Jenny, would you be okay here with Carla from down the road?"

"Why?"

"I have a meeting. It's been postponed twice and if I reschedule again I'll lose the client for good."

"But..."

"Jenny, I've tried. I have to meet with him today. It won't take long, I promise."

"Can't you meet with him here? Can't he come here to see you? Tell him you're taking care of your wife."

"I don't think that's a good idea under the circumstances."

"Okay. Then I'll be fine."

"Carla offered to come over and stay with you. I could take you to her place. Get you out of here."

There was an ominous tone to Warren's *here.*

"You didn't?"

"No, it's nothing like that. I just asked if she would keep you company. It's a very important meeting. I can't put it off."

"I can't, Warren. I can't let her see me this way. How long will you be gone?"

"Until early afternoon. Maybe two at the latest. Jenny, you have to get over the scarring. You can't hide forever."

"Okay, fine. I think that will be all right. But could you reconnect the telephone for me? I'd like to make some calls."

"You up to it?"

"Warren, I'm better. I'd just like to talk to Kate and begin getting back into the flow."

"That's great, honey."

Warren left, replaced by Carla and Randy, her four-year-old terror. Jenny, however, wishing to avoid the unwanted superficial chitchat and having to deal with the little monster, asked that her door be closed so she might make a few business-related calls and grab a nap.

Carla offered to sit with her. But Jenny refused. Since Carla was ten years older and a housewife with no ambition, they had nothing in common. She said she'd be right down stairs, if Jenny needed anything. And she emphatically promised to keep Randy away from Mr. Chips, who decided to make himself scarce since the little terror's arrival.

As soon as the bedroom door closed, Jenny pulled the telephone to her lap. She knew what she had seen—it was no hallucination. She knew Chips had experienced it along with her. That vision was real and physical, and most importantly, had been standing right there in her room.

After two hours and at least forty telephone calls, Jenny had come up empty. What she needed was someone familiar with this type of situation. A paranormal investigator. She knew they existed; she'd seen enough of those Fox Network television specials to know that much.

Her tenacity, however, did not go unrewarded. It had gained her the telephone numbers of two organizations involved with paranormal phenomena. Neither expressed any serious interest in her story. But that could have been because her stutter made her come across more like a crackpot than a sane and rational person.

However, one kind old gentleman by the name of Carlisle Schuller, who headed up a branch of the Center for the Scientific Investigation of the Paranormal in Santa Fe, New Mexico, offered Jenny the name of a young man working under a grant at New York State University in Albany. Her claim had at last fallen upon one sympathetic pair of ears.

Jenny's first call to Dwight Mackenzie ended up on an answering machine with a warbled announcement. The voice offered nothing more than confirmation of the number, then requested a detailed message and promised someone would return the call.

Yeah right.

Jenny doled out her brief message that was well-rehearsed to eliminate all but a trace of her stutter. She found if she concentrated on each word before she allowed it to exit her throat, she could deliver a few sentences without the stutter stomping out her attempt.

Hope sprouted inside her. Jenny napped with telephone under hand, waiting for that promised return call.

12

Rick buttoned another button on his coat to stave off a cold November wind that seemed insistent on wreaking havoc with his hair. He stood alongside his captain, Jason Rawlings; the two waited at the end of an expansive and deserted parking lot.

Horace Dugan approached with clipboard in hand and the kind of smile a ten-year-old uses to arouse parental suspicion. He shivered, underdressed for the weather in a light blue police windbreaker and no hat to protect his head.

"Gotta do this before the rain," Dugan said, glancing up at a crowded slate sky that seemed to be hovering over them.

"This better be damn good," Rawlings scowled.

"Camera's rolling?" Dugan asked back over his shoulder to a man at a video set up on a tripod.

"Rolling," came back.

"What's this about?" Rawlings asked Rick.

"Beats me. Dugan just said to be here."

Dugan, a slight man unhappy to have entered his fifties, waved a knuckled hand in a circle over his head. His pale lips offered a smile to Rawlings and Walker once more. But he released one of those 'this better work' sighs as he watched the maroon Taurus accelerate.

"Just watch."

The three tracked the Taurus as it accelerated past them twenty feet distant in the middle of the lot.

"Notice the blacktop is free of water and ice," Dugan narrated as a way of recording that fact and lending credibility to that which was about to take place.

"I hope you're taking your best shot, Dugan," Rawlings scowled with that Show-me expression laid out across his face. Even the hot coffee he held failed to put a thaw in his icy mood.

No one spoke. The car wound its way at thirty-five miles an hour through a snaking course of fluorescent pylons. When the vehicle finished the course it made a wide turn and rolled to a stop in front of the three men.

"Ta-da!" Dugan said.

"This is what we're freezing our asses off for?" Rick said.

Rick and Rawlings exchanged a look of disbelief. Even Rick had become irritated by the mystery surrounding Dugan's insistent demonstration.

"Now, you've seen the car take the turns at thirty-five miles per hour. Simple enough. Everything is perfectly normal," Dugan said to Rick and the captain as he continued to shiver.

Rick shot Dugan an uncertain glare.

"Yeah fine. Can we get this thing to the point?" Rawlings snarled.

Dugan always used theatrics. This was his time under the bright lights, and he wasn't going to let anyone leave the theater until his performance was over. He even made sure he got it on tape.

But as melodramatic as Dugan was, he was also rarely wrong, and everyone in the department knew it. When Dugan put his passion into something, you could be sure there was more than mere speculation involved.

"Pop the hood," Dugan commanded the helmeted driver behind the wheel.

"Funny thing about this particular design. I personally think the engineers didn't fully understand the effects of weight distribution on front wheel drive."

"Can we keep this thing moving?" Rick pressed.

Dugan proceeded to point out to Rick and Rawlings with both words and hand gestures exactly how the front stabilizer strut is mounted to the frame. In particular, he identified a single fulcrum bolt securing the strut to the top mount.

"Gentleman, watch and take notes." Dugan's words carried a ring of confidence with them.

Rawlings remained unimpressed.

Dugan held up his hammer like a magician's wand.

"Voila!"

He tapped the bolt. At contact, the hexagonal nut securing the steel rod to the mounting frame flew out from beneath the hood, hitting Rawlings in the shoulder.

"Sorry, Cap. That's it, gentlemen," Dugan announced proudly. "Now watch."

Rick and Rawlings exchanged one of those Dugan-has-finally-flipped looks.

With the hood locked down, Dugan circled his finger overhead and sent the driver back onto the course.

"You'll notice right off," Dugan said over the engine acceleration, "that there are no adverse handling effects, and as you can see, the car performs initially just as it did before. The driver is completely unaware of the change in the vehicle's structural integrity."

"Yeah, yeah, yeah. If I get sick from this you're gonna pay, Dugan," Rawlings muttered.

After a 180 degree turn, the Taurus sped up to its designated thirty-five and entered the lane of pylons.

At the first hard right turn, the vehicle spun into a doughnut. Inside, the driver whirled the wheel, trying to regain control. The Taurus swerved side to side, taking out every pylon that had been set up. The car traveled more than thirty feet before the driver's expert braking and wheel control could return the vehicle to a safe and sane position.

"You see, Rick, Cap, once the strut mounting disconnects from the frame, the car becomes uncontrollable. Any turn at a speed greater than twenty brings about the result you've just witnessed."

"So, you're saying what?" Rick asked.

"I'm saying you're going the wrong way with the Garrett investigation. I'm saying someone tampered with the woman's car that night."

"Wait a minute," Rawlings cut in.

"You're trying to sell us on that?" Rick imposed.

Dugan removed a length of threaded steel in a plastic bag. He tossed it to Walker then planted his hands at his hips.

"Bingo. I'm saying someone sheared the bolt on the Garrett car. Whoever did it knew the car would go out of control."

"This is pretty wild," Rick said. Then his expression changed. He examined the metal in his hand. There was evidence of saw marks on the end of the shaft.

"You see how half of the metal is broken clean off, but the other half has jagged saw marks."

"You confirmed that?" Rawlings shot in, now suddenly intensely interested.

"Cap, you think I'd risk your wrath bringing you out here if I weren't sure," Dugan said.

"You're saying the Garrett woman was set up to die in that accident?" Rick asked.

"Take that car, shear the top off the mounting bolt, and put it on a winding downhill road, and you've got a guaranteed crash. When the brakes are applied, which is the driver's instinctive response, the car goes spinning out of control. Our driver's an expert, and as you can see, it took at least five car lengths before he brought that ton of steel back under control."

Rick looked at Rawlings, who shifted his gaze off the metal and now stared at the vehicle and the sprawled pylons.

"I'm telling you, Ricky, my boy, someone wanted the Garrett woman to die in that crash." Dugan handed Rick the hammer and another plastic bag with the threaded remains of a bolt like the one used in the demonstration.

"Did you get all of it?" Dugan asked over his shoulder.

The cameraman signaled his thumbs-up.

Dugan signaled the driver to wrap up the demonstration and the three started back toward the building.

"Dugan, how the hell did you come up with this anyway?" Rawlings asked.

"The right side of the vehicle sustained all the major damage. So why would the left strut have separated so cleanly from the mounting? When I inspected it closer, I saw the cut marks."

"How would someone possibly have known about the condition you've just shown us?" Rawlings asked.

"Your average Joe wouldn't. But a sharp mechanic knows that the fulcrum for all the weight is on the two front struts. A collapsed strut shifts the center of gravity and voila! You're out of control. No, you don't have to be a physicist to figure out that this is a better way to kill someone than the old method of cutting the brake line. But it's relatively impossible to bring on a collapsed strut at will, so the next best thing is to allow it to break out of its mounting."

"How confident are you in this?" Rick asked.

"My reputation's on it. You just saw what happened out there. If the Garrett woman panicked when the car went into a spin, she'd never recover in time.

You want my professional opinion after thirty years of investigating car crashes? You got one slick killer out there. But he failed the first time. By all rights, the Garrett woman should never have survived. And from what I understand, she nearly didn't. If I were you, Walker, I'd be worried that the joker is going to try again. But this time, what's her name, Jenny, isn't likely to be so lucky."

"Are we going to be able to make an attempted murder charge stick?" Rawlings asked.

"Everything here, along with my written report, is going to the DA. I think you can take this into court if you can build a case behind motive and opportunity."

Rawlings narrowed his eyes as he watched the vehicle inch its way back toward them. Then he, himself, examined the threads encased in plastic.

"And you recovered this from the Garrett car?"

"Yes sir."

"I'm convinced, Rick. Bring me motive and opportunity, and we'll put the bastard away."

Rick's smile melted away the cold that had gone all the way to his bones.

****

A ten-thirty phone call brought a perplexed Warren out of the den. He stood in the doorway to the bedroom, scratching at the hairs on his neck.

"Jenny, it's for you." He sounded surprised. "A Dwight Mackenzie."

Jenny reached faster than she should have and winced from a slight pain while she snatched up the receiver.

"Hello."

"Hi. Dwight Mackenzie returning your call."

"Is this the Dwight Mackenzie that investigates paranormal phenomena?"

An unusually long pause filled the line.

Upon hearing that, Warren took up the chair in the bedroom and fumbled with cleaning his glasses.

"Yes."

Jenny took a deep breath, and concentrated on her rehearsed lines; praying she could control her stutter and avoid frightening Dwight off. She began her explanation in as detailed a fashion as possible.

When she finished, Dwight asked a few clumsy questions that seemed to indicate less than total enthusiasm about what Jenny had just related to him. But at the same time, neither did he say he had no interest in her story either. And best of all, he hadn't hung up on her.

"Then you will help me?"

"Ms. Garrett, it's not a situation where I can help you. I investigate what I deem to be occurrences that lack a critical foundation in modern science. Events unexplainable under the laws of physics or nature. I'm not a ghostbuster. I don't scare away ghosts."

"I'm sorry, that's not what I meant. I would just like someone to..."

"Ms. Garrett, would you be willing to meet with me at the university? I would be willing to at least go through a detailed interview before deciding whether I should move forward with a formal paranormal investigation."

"Paranormal mumbo jumbo," Warren said under his breath. He searched his pocket for his cigarettes, but when he realized they were back in his den, he stuffed his hands inside his pockets.

"Thank you, yes. Can I come there tomorrow?"

Warren offered a stoic nod of agreement.

"Tomorrow would be fine," Jenny repeated for Warren's benefit.

"I'll be in my office between one and four. Come to the Psychology Department located in Wilford Hall. My office is located on the lower level in the west wing, room 128."

"The shit just wants money," Warren mumbled as he left the bedroom.

13

Rick waited in the anteroom to Rawlings's office with a stack of files in hand. He felt completely unprepared for what he was about to do.

"Looks like it's ass-reaming time again," Detective Ed Perkins said in a low tone as he passed Rick.

Old 'Perky' Perkins had told Rick he was crazy for even looking twice at the Garrett case, warned him from the get-go it would get nasty if he took it on. The complete lack of physical evidence is always the first sign of a ringer. Even with Dugan's report, pulled out of thin air a la David Copperfield, there was little, if any, chance they could make anything stick. Rick, however, loved a challenge. In return, he offered old Perky no more than a faint smile.

Mentally, Rick lined up his arguments, knowing he would have to cross every t and dot every i if things were to go his way. Even after his interviews with the principals involved in the case, he had precious little to go on.

The Jenny Garrett interview proved the shocker, though. Rick never dreamed she would be unable to remember the days or weeks leading up to the accident. Now he was going before the captain with little more than his original supposition. What had changed from day one to day sixty-three, based on

Dugan's findings, was that he was looking for a killer rather than a yuppie driving under the influence.

Rawlings motioned Rick in as a junior grade detective exited. It was his time now. Rick opened his files, sat across from Rawlings, and positioned his papers so the captain could read the reports from his chair.

Rawlings, surprisingly, waved off the paperwork.

"I just want to know what you turned up to justify the supposition that the Garrett case is really attempted murder."

"I wish I had more to offer."

"We always do. That's why we get the tough stuff. Talk to me about witnesses."

"Right now, only the woman driving the car that was hit."

"And she says?"

"She says the Garrett car crossed the line out of control as it came around the bend. After the car hit hers, it caromed over the rail and down the hill."

"And Garrett says?"

"Nothing. She still claims no memory of the accident."

"Any other witnesses?"

"None. The other driver reported that she thought she saw a car immediately behind Garrett's on the hill. But no one has ever come forward."

"Do we have a case? Is there anything we can show the State's Attorney?"

"I didn't have a case when we went in on the Baby McAllister death. Everybody said SIDS. You trusted me then. I turned up evidence that the mother had killed her own baby. You've got to give me time to work the principals."

"Who are the principals?"

"At this point, the husband. There's a long shot with the business partner. But I'll need time to uncover the information to know the truth."

"Maybe the truth is: she just did a dive over the guard rail with her car because she had been sucking down martinis at dinner."

"And maybe the truth is someone tried to kill her. And failing the first time, he may just try again. Let's face it, it'll be much easier to have a case once we have a dead body."

Rawlings's hair-trigger temper began rising to the top.

"What's the status on the little girl?"

"Still comatose. Doctors are saying the kid may be brain dead. May never come out of it."

"Great. And we have to walk away."

"You want my gut on this? I think Dugan's right. Everything so far indicates the Garrett woman's not a drinker. If she wasn't drunk behind the wheel, she either lost control on her own, or the car went out of control as a result of tampering."

"You got motive?"

"Not yet."

"How about opportunity?"

"No...but I just started working this new angle."

Rawlings leaned back into his chair, signaling a willingness to listen.

"I'm not totally convinced about any of this," Rawlings added.

"Cap, let me have a shot at this. I don't turn up a motive, we'll call this one a ringer and bury it."

"You got two weeks to make me smile, or we call it an accident, pure and simple."

Rick accepted what Rawlings was willing to give and collected up his files. He walked out debating whether what he had just said was good or bad.

****

Warren harbored sufficient doubt in his own mind that he agreed to drive Jenny to the university. He would lose a whole trading day, and that might very well cost him dearly. But if this trip meant Jenny could gain peace of mind, it was worth every dollar he lost. He bantered back and forth whether Jenny could handle a two-hour drive, but upon arriving, he was surprised at how well she held up. Though he attributed that to the reason for the trip in the first place.

The only difficulty in the drive came when a teen changing lanes without signaling forced Warren to brake hard. In a panic, Jenny braced herself against the dash, digging her nails in until her knuckles paled, despite the fact there was no imminent danger. At first, Warren thought Jenny was going to pass out; her face had turned a ghostly pallor and her breathing seized, preventing her from inhaling. Warren witnessed the terror in her eyes. He expected it would be a long time before Jenny would be ready to get behind the wheel again.

Pillows employed to cushion her in the passenger seat eliminated much of the discomfort that sitting for a long period would have brought on. Jenny's eyes contained a melange of relief and anxiety as they crossed the busy congested campus to locate Wilford Hall.

Warren and Jenny blended well amongst the hoards of students flowing up and down the walks between buildings. Most avoided eye contact with the two, though a few stared curiously at Jenny's face. Jenny decided it was something she had to deal with and turned her eyes elsewhere in response to their stares. If she could deal with strangers looking at her, she reasoned, it wouldn't be long before she could face her friends staring at her. Just being there brought back memories of their own college days. A time she sorely missed now. The toughest thing to face in college, she recalled, were finals. At the time, she never dreamed she'd be doing what she was doing now.

Jenny occupied a hard wooden bench outside Dwight's door in an out-of-the-way corridor. The journey to get to this point had exhausted her, but adrenaline kept her from feeling the fatigue or the pain.

Warren paced. Not a minute passed without him confirming it on his watch. Time. To a trader, time is money and opportunity. Wasting time is like pissing away dollars. He had to tell himself he was doing this for Jenny and she was worth every ulcer he got.

The translucent glass pane on the door had no lettering on it, unlike most of the other office doors they passed. Only the painted number 128 appeared near the top center of the glass.

Warren paused to rest for a minute, leaned against the wall, but started again, growing angry over driving so far to be stood up by some psychobabble fruitcake flake. But when Jenny looked up at him with eyes that begged for his patient indulgence, he smiled and tucked his frustration deeper into the shadowy recesses, hoping to hide his growing fury.

Occasionally, passing students glanced at them with a curious interest, but no one approached the door they waited beside. Jenny reasoned those who gave them the once over must have known whose office they were waiting by.

"This is stupid, Jenny. This guy's probably some yo-yo who could care less about you. Why don't we just leave?"

"Can't we hang on a while longer. He said he'd meet us here."

"Sure. And what do you think is keeping him?"

"I don't know, but I'd like to wait another fifteen minutes anyway."

"He's already twenty minutes late."

"But we came this far."

"He's probably chasing a ghost," Warren muttered, unaware of how caustic the words were to Jenny. Insensitivity had usually been something Warren kept in check.

But if Jenny refused to let the pain of her healing body deter her, she would certainly refuse to allow Warren's callous remarks dampen her spirit. Nothing would force her to deny what she had seen. Nothing.

However, she did have to spend the next ten minutes convincing herself to remain. Maybe Warren was right; maybe this was nothing more than a fool's quest. This Mr. Mackenzie may never show up.

As Warren came about in his holding pattern to pace back in Jenny's direction, a studious, sandy-haired young man, not much older than the students in the building, strolled down their corridor as if he were in no hurry to arrive at his destination. Actually, he acted as if he were in some parallel world, the way he mumbled to himself as he walked.

The afternoon sunlight reflecting off his glasses placed white circles where his eyes should have been. As he approached the door, he scratched at his scraggly adolescent beard with one hand and pulled out a ring of keys with his other.

The surprised look on his face was evidence enough that he had either forgotten or dismissed their appointment.

"Hi, Jenny Garrett, right?" he asked pleasantly enough. He wore faded corduroy slacks and a plaid shirt complete with a knit fabric tie; exactly what you'd expect from someone claiming to be a paranormal investigator.

"Dwight Mackenzie?" Jenny asked, taking Warren's arm to steady herself as she rose uneasily to her feet.

"Sorry I'm late. I got tied up with administrative matters. Let's go inside."

Inside, sitting before a scratched up old desk, Jenny told her carefully rehearsed story—she had two hours in the car to smooth out the stutters.

Dwight listened. When she finished, Dwight asked Warren, who had remained dutifully silent during the exchange, what he might like to add to Jenny's story.

"Not a thing. I see nothing; I hear nothing."

"Ms. Garrett, yours really is quite a remarkable story. Are you absolutely certain that this ghost you're seeing is of yourself?"

"Absolutely."

"There's no room for doubt? Could it just resemble you in some ways, like hair style or similar facial features?"

"I'm sure. It is me."

"Ms. Garrett, I have to be perfectly honest with you. While your story is quite fascinating...I'm not certain there exists sufficient grounds for me to pursue a full-scale paranormal investigation."

Warren shifted. Mr. Dick Head was obviously just jerking Jenny around with his paranormal crap.

"Look, if money's a factor here, I'd be willing..." Jenny started.

Warren was quick to seize Jenny's arm with a firm hand. Their eye contact was brief, however.

"Ms. Garrett...Jenny...it's not money, per se. My work is fully funded under a university grant. It's just that there exists almost no supporting case histories where a person was experiencing a recurring paranormal exchange with their own spirit. And I don't believe we're talking about astral projection here."

"Astral projection?" Warren asked, feeling as if he were being carefully sucked into something by a seasoned charlatan.

"In simple terms, it's when the astral body detaches from the physical body and the person goes through what's called an out-of-body experience.

What Jenny has told me sounds completely different."

"Look, Mr. Mackenzie, we didn't come here for some canned psychic phenomena bag-O-bologna. Jenny is seeing a ghost of herself. It has appeared before her more than once or twice. The goddamn thing is haunting her. Will you investigate it?" Warren forced in, as if he needed to speak for her.

"Is it a malevolent spirit?"

"Do you mean is it trying to hurt me?" Jenny took over.

"Yes."

"I don't think so. But how can I be certain?"

"Has it communicated with you in any way?"

"No. It appears. I see it, but it has made no attempt to speak with me in any form. Will you do something?"

"It's not possible for me to give you an answer right away. But I will review the information you've provided, check with other sources, and let you know within a month or so if I will be looking into what you've told me."

All the air left Jenny. She composed herself, the pains in her head came crashing in like angry waves against a rocky coast. She had endured so much to get here and now within the span of thirty minutes, this investigator had shredded her gossamer hope.

"Thank you. I really do appreciate your time," Jenny said.

Their handshakes were cordial, but Jenny sensed a peculiar indifference from Dwight. Why, if he were in the business of investigating these things, would he hesitate? Did he think she was just a crackpot?

Jenny reviewed every word he had said. He seemed to take particular interest in the fact that Jenny had been in a recent automobile accident. Would he, like everyone else in the medical profession, try to pass this off as part of the healing process?

The moment Jenny and Warren left the office, Dwight jumped out of his seat and danced around his chair with the excitement of a teen who had just landed a date with the prettiest cheerleader on the squad. Then, he extracted a formal-looking manila folder from his desk drawer and opened it. The university had tendered official notification that they were declining his application for grant renewal, citing a lack of substantial data in his field as the cause, and further citing that his work no longer served any useful purpose to the academic milieu. Like it ever did, anyway.

Dwight, however, boiled the three paragraphs of administrative rhetoric down to a single word: money. He was staring at a polite pink slip on university letterhead...unless he could come up with something of substance.

There remained only three centers in the entire United States investigating paranormal phenomena, and Dwight's center had been on an endangered species list for the last year. Up until an hour ago, he believed his extinction was inevitable. Now God had given him a chance to justify his funding, and just maybe, win another year out of the university. Ms. Jenny Garrett really had no idea of what she had just done. Even if she were just a crackpot.

14

Rick sat over his desk as outside day faded into night. His fluorescent desk lamp, bent over like an ostrich, sprayed white light over the clutter of reports and printouts.

His challenge sat before him on the desk. Uncover the motive. Find a reason for someone to want Jenny Garrett dead. Did she have something in her past that warranted a murder attempt? Rick doubted it. More likely there was another reason; a reason even Jenny herself might be unaware of.

Rick bounced back and forth between various sets of bank records that, when combined, represented five years of business transactions. Before long, a pattern began to emerge. Warren Garrett made it an almost regular practice of overextending his credit to keep his trading business afloat.

It appeared as if Warren's business was again in a deep cyclical trough—deep enough that one or two consecutive bad trades could plummet him into bankruptcy. This guy was a gambler far beyond the scope of the average gambler, who habitually bets on races, sports, cards or dice. Warren regularly bet everything he had against the price of corn or oil, or the Japanese yen or German mark.

And it seemed that for the last six months, he'd been losing.

On the other hand, every cent of Warren's money could be legitimately accounted for. He wasn't dealing drugs. He wasn't into loan sharks, and as far as Rick could tell, Warren couldn't possibly be involved in any kind of money laundering scheme for organized crime. So, it would appear as if there was no dark shadow in Warren's ear whispering, '*Give me my money or the pretty little woman has a terrible accident.*'

However, the paper trail illustrated clearly that Warren was falling deeper and deeper into red ink. At one time a year go, Warren had over four hundred grand in his bank account.

Rick only dreamed about money like that. His ex-wife popped into his head as he stared at the numbers. That was the kind of money it took to make her happy. Something Rick knew he'd never see in his lifetime.

But lately the cash flow had changed directions and as quickly as it flowed in, it was gone. By scrutinizing the Garretts' banking records, it became obvious that Jenny was, in fact, the sole provider for the household. Warren's luck had turned to dust in his hand and his sporadic gains were constantly used to offset a seriously mounting debt load.

Rick jotted down all the places where the Garretts wrote checks of any substantial size. All appeared innocuous enough—at first. At the same time, he uncovered that the Garretts paid hefty insurance premiums. From the size of the premium, Rick 'deduced that a million dollar policy was probably in effect. He could confirm that in the morning.

But other things also didn't add up. Rick scratched his head over inordinate sums spread around several jewelers in town in the previous year. Why would a guy plummeting into debt be so free with his cash for jewelry? Of course, no purchases had turned up for at least the last six months.

Good old Warren had slapped three mortgages on their home—thereby eradicating any equity he could ever hope to gain between the present and sometime into the next century. He only stopped there because he had squeezed every cent he could out of the property. Easy to see why Warren's creditors might become nervous.

As he stretched in his chair to shake off fatigue, Rick felt no great sense of sleuthing accomplishment. Even the Keystone Cops could see Warren would gain from Jenny's death. A million in insurance right now would put Warren back in the black and erase a ton of burgeoning debt. If Jenny had died in that accident, Warren would have turned his business around and left himself with a hefty reserve. But why risk murder when he seemed to have the moxie to accumulate significant wealth using his own brain? From the records, Warren had traded himself out of massive debt twice in the past four years.

Was the money a sufficient motive? Would Warren Garrett murder his wife for the insurance? Been done before. Why should Warren be any different than any other greedy shithead slob?

Warren's business had been in a tailspin for months. It seemed possible, at least to Rick, that a string of good months could erase Warren's debt and set him back on solid ground. So why risk murder...unless...you could be certain of getting away with it. And Warren's string of bad months had yet to come to an end.

Rick left Warren as suspect number one on his list. But he knew he needed real, hard evidence showing Warren wanted to kill his own wife, and had the opportunity to tamper with her car.

15

Dwight Mackenzie huddled beneath the porch's overhang, hoping to be spared, at least slightly, from the driving rain that pelted him while he rang the doorbell to the Garrett house. The building's impressive size and century-old architecture, replete with what had to be fully restored gables, caused him to raise a brow as he listened for sounds of life inside. He also liked the sense of rural ambiance the landscape created despite having other houses in the surrounding area. It became obvious that the Garretts had a meticulous sense of symmetry in their lives.

After the second unanswered ring, he regretted not having called first. He figured Jenny would at least be home, since she was supposedly still convalescing from her auto accident.

At last Warren answered. Dwight couldn't help but wonder if Warren's delay hadn't been intentional. Maybe he just wanted the rain to soak him through before letting him in. Warren's face fell in obvious disappointment at Dwight's appearance. It had only been four days since their meeting at the university, and Warren never expected to see Mr. Paranormal at his doorstep.

"*Hold on to your checkbook*," Warren murmured to himself as he motioned Dwight into the foyer with a wave of his hand.

"Please confine yourself to the carpet in the foyer until you have a chance to drain off some of the rain," Warren said in a voice as level and stoic as a servant.

Mr. Chips issued a threatening growl from between Warren's legs. The dog, however, never advanced.

Offering a beaming smile and a friendly hand-shake, Dwight quickly made peace with the animal. After one sniff, Mr. Chips allowed Dwight to pass unchallenged. With wagging tail nub, Chips offered his own greeting by sniffing at Dwight's heels as he walked.

"I'd like to do a follow-up interview, if I could?" Dwight asked.

"Suit yourself. I'll get Jenny for you. Living room okay?"

"I believe Mrs. Garrett said she saw the apparition in her bedroom? I'd rather do the follow-up there."

"Fine. This way."

Dwight waited at the bottom of the stairs while Warren went up to announce their visitor. Leaning back some so he could take in the full breadth of the living room, Dwight whistled softly at the furnishings, and while he waited, he couldn't help but wander into the living room.

Very impressive," Dwight said when Warren descended the stairs only to pause near the base.

"Which part of 'please remain on the carpet in the foyer' did you not understand? I don't think you can even comprehend the cost of that Persian rug you're dripping on."

Dwight skipped an apology and hastened back to the carpet at the base of the stairs.

"He's not getting a dime," Warren muttered to himself as he showed Dwight up to Jenny's room.

Jenny sat in a chair staring blankly out the window at a sky leaden and dreary. Her hair had been hastily brushed but still lacked any indication of primping. She looked pale without the make-up she had worn at their first visit. But Dwight still found himself staring at her eyes. The rain pelted the glass while a stiff north wind tousled the branches back and forth, occasionally bringing them to scrape across the window pane in a screech that resembled fingernails raking a chalkboard.

"Look who's here," Warren offered with mock surprise, "Mr. Ghost Buster."

Dwight shed the remark as he had done a thousand times before. Only those who had really witnessed a paranormal encounter ever took paranormal investigators seriously. To everyone else, they were crackpot charlatans out to bilk people out of their money. Only the faithful shall believe. And for most, only seeing was believing.

There was no way to gain public respect without first demonstrating some physical evidence. All Dwight carried in his water-soaked briefcase was a stack of interview forms—blank interview forms—and a tape recorder.

Presenting as professional appearance as one could under the circumstances, Dwight scanned the bedroom, cataloging how the light came in through the window, and noting the door's location relative to the bed. The room was spacious enough, with angles that could allow shadows to distort reality.

After his carefully measured scan, Dwight set his briefcase on the bureau and removed the forms along with the pocket tape recorder.

"Hope you don't mind?" he asked as he waved the machine. "It's required."

"I don't."

"Good. Can't make a case without it."

"Please, make yourself right at home," Warren remarked sardonically. "Have you eaten? Perhaps I could fix you some lunch?"

Jenny's face had flashed a glimmer of hope at the sight of Dwight. Warren seemed to be working hard to stomp it out. She could only hope Dwight was willing to listen.

"What I'd like to do is conduct a more in-depth interview here, if you don't mind. It will be rather dry and technical. But I must also advise you that this doesn't mean anything. This interview will help if I have to justify my investigation."

"S-sure, I u-understand," Jenny said, though brimming hopefulness filled her eyes.

Dwight found himself immediately attracted to the way the light played off her blue eyes when she smiled. He thought about how pretty she must have been before the accident. Terrible how a small scar in the wrong place could spoil such beauty. He busied himself with his forms while those thoughts ran through his mind, attempting not to stare at her disfigurement. Despite all efforts, Dwight's eyes went to her scar.

Jenny put her hand to her mouth, noticing Dwight's stare.

Dwight shifted his eyes back to his form.

"How long will this take?" Warren asked with a sudden rising interest.

"An hour or so. Maybe two, tops. It depends."

"Great."

Warren's remark brought a raised brow from Dwight.

"Jenny, I want to make a trip into the city. You'll be okay with Mr. Mackenzie here, right?"

"Sure Warren, but won't he need..."

"Before you go, I will also need some information from you."

"Why? I see nothing; I hear nothing."

"It's just general background. I can get it later."

Warren kissed Jenny gently on the forehead and hiding a relieving smile, made a hasty exit.

While Jenny left her chair for the greater comfort of the bed and the propped pillows placed behind her to sit upright, Dwight opened his notebook, switched on the tape recorder and brought the chair next to the bed.

"Are you comfortable?" he asked.

"Sure. That's where I saw her first," Jenny said, anxious to begin. She pointed to the space the chair had previously occupied beside the open bedroom door.

Dwight rose, returned the chair to its original position at the far wall and measured the distance with a compact 25-foot tape measure he pulled from his pocket.

"And you were where you are now?"

"Yes."

Dwight measured the distance a second time, this time more accurately from Jenny's position, and jotted the finding in his notebook.

"And you said it was the middle of the night?"

"Yes."

"Was there any extraneous light in the room at the time? Wait before you answer, I need to get the header on the recorder first. Jenny Garrett interview, November tenth, Nineteen Ninety-eight. We have to record everything you say, so don't worry if you sometimes forget details. I go through the tapes later and get everything in order. I'll provide you with a complete transcript, for the record."

Dwight fumbled between his folder and his notebook. A growing excitement emanated from him. Though he sought to hide it, it became infectious. A second later, he had the folder back in order and open, and he quickly sketched the room's layout.

"Okay. It's the middle of the night, and you saw the apparition there. Was there any extraneous light?"

"None."

"Door open or closed?"

"Ah...closed...no open a crack."

"No light coming in from the hall?"

"None."

"What about the window curtains?"

"Closed."

"Completely?"

Jenny nodded.

"Then how could you see it?"

"I just could. I could see the outline of the body clearly. I thought it was Warren the first time I saw it."

"Did it radiate light of its own?"

"Not really light. But I could see it."

Dwight was busy writing, indicating Jenny's location relative to the chair. In a pitch dark room, at a distance of thirteen feet four inches, Jenny Garrett saw an apparition sitting in her chair.

"Where was Warren at the time?"

"In the den....I guess asleep."

"He doesn't sleep with..."

As Dwight said it, he realized how awkward the question was. For a moment, he wished he could take it back.

"Warren sleeps in the den...until I've healed more."

"So then, you were alone in the room. And you thought it was your husband sitting in the chair?"

"Yes."

"Where was your dog at the time?"

"Downstairs. He sleeps in a cage in the kitchen."

"Then he's not free to roam the house at night?"

"No. Why?"

"Could *he* have been sitting up in the chair that night?"

"No. I know Warren put him in his bed for the night and closed the cage door."

"Can you hear him if he barks or whines from his cage?"

"I don't know."

"Did you hear him that night?"

"No."

"Jenny, you said earlier the dog became agitated, growling and shaking the last time you saw the apparition."

"Yes. He was beside my bed like he is now."

"But during the previous sightings here in the house, which you say were two, the dog did not act in anyway unusual."

"Both previous occurrences were at night. Mr. Chips could have reacted...but wait. There was another time. Mr. Chips was outside in the yard. He began scratching at the door. I screamed when I saw it. But I distinctly remember Mr. Chips raising a ruckus."

Dwight jotted a note to himself to check the door.

"Could you allow your dog free run of the house for a while? If he does sense the spirit's presence, he could help corroborate your story. Or, at least, act as early warning."

Dwight was spellbound as he wrote feverishly during the two-hour interview. When they finished, Warren had still not returned. Dwight said nothing while he packed his briefcase, telling Jenny only that he would let her know as soon as possible what he intended to do.

He did, however, offer to remain with Jenny until Warren returned. He felt ill-at-ease leaving Jenny alone in the house, and he needed to talk to Warren anyway.

"What would happen next, if you decide to investigate further?"

"If I decide to go ahead with this, I'll bring in some very sophisticated equipment. I'll wire the upstairs for audio, video, infrared and magnetic flux detection. Then we wait and hope that the ghost returns and we can get some kind of reading on one or more of our instruments."

"Has that ever been done before?" Jenny asked, uncomfortable with what she had just heard.

"Actually, a couple of times in the last year alone."

"And?"

"I wish I had more to offer in the way of hope. Jenny, if you want to nap for awhile, I know this must be exhausting for you, I'll nose around the house to get a feel for the milieu. I'll be downstairs until your husband returns."

In the kitchen, Dwight confirmed the scratch marks on the outer rear door. He had no way of knowing when the scratches had been left. But at least on the surface, they tended to corroborate Jenny's claim that the dog may have been scratching at the door like she had said.

For the present, Dwight switched to his *wait-and-see* mode. Wait to see what happened in the next week or so.

Dwight meandered from room to room looking mainly for any sign that might indicate Warren and Jenny were trying to perpetuate a hoax against him. People will do some pretty weird stuff in search of that elusive fifteen minutes of fame. The house's third story had nothing but vacant unused rooms. The second story contained the three bedrooms and the den, of which the master bedroom, a guest bedroom and the den showed signs of use.

In his wanderings, he descended into the basement using the staircase located near the rear of the house. A light switch on the pole at the bottom of the stairs switched on two incandescent lights hanging from the joists thirty feet apart. They provided barely sufficient light to walk the expanse and Dwight now wished he would have brought a flashlight with him. The exterior walls were the original walls built a century ago from mortared brick, and despite evidence of recent repair attempts to seal the old walls, water seepage found its way through the joints. Not enough to leave standing water, just enough to let the home-owner know his repair job had failed.

What Dwight sought, as he picked his way around crates and boxes stacked head high, was a source of water rising up from below the foundation. A signifi-cant number of previous apparition cases he had the opportunity to study detailed sources of open water coming up through the sub-foundation. And it seemed an inordinate number of 'haunted houses' were close to streams or rivers, neither of which, at this point, influenced the Garrett case.

Though the light in the northeast corner became almost totally absent, Dwight bent down to check a crack that zig-zagged across the floor. He probed with a finger to determine if water had filled the crack.

Then a scratching sound captured his attention. It sounded as if it were originating on the other side of a stack of boxes to his left. Dwight stretched to get a glimpse around the boxes where the light was a bit better.

A hand to his shoulder brought him up and swinging.

"Easy, Mr. Ghostbuster. It's just me," Warren said, backing away.

Dwight just knew Warren had come down the stairs silently so as to intentionally startle him. What a fun guy.

"You find anything?"

"Nothing."

Dwight moved quickly back into the light and toward the stairs. Warren followed him up the stairs and back to the door to Jenny's room.

"So your statement is that you've neither seen nor heard anything that Jenny has claimed took place in this house," Dwight said before entering Jenny's bedroom.

"You got it exactly right. And if you're thinking you can scam us for money..."

Dwight ignored the remark, pushed open the bedroom door and forged into the bedroom.

"So, any revelations?" Jenny asked.

"I must say I am impressed with your house. If anything, it matches a little too closely to Hollywood's vision of the proverbial haunted mansion."

"If you *were* going to investigate, what would that entail?"

"A series of scientific measures would have to be put in place."

A quick sidelong glance confirmed to Dwight that Warren was clearly against the idea, and without his cooperation, any serious investigation could become easily compromised, and thereby useless in the scientific community.

"Why do I have a feeling you're going to tell me you're going to be staying with us."

"Worse actually...I'd be staying in this bedroom."

"Wait a minute...where's Jenny supposed to sleep during this?"

"Right where she sleeps now. We disturb as little as possible during our investigation."

Warren crossed to Jenny on the bed and took her hand into his. She liked the coolness of his skin against hers. She wanted to speak but could only look up at him.

"This isn't going to work. You're not going to be in this bedroom when my wife is asleep."

"I have to. I have to monitor the equipment and make certain the investigation is not compromised."

"I don't like this, Jenny. I don't like this one bit."

"It'll be all right, Warren. You're going to be in the next room."

"Well, you have some time to think about it. I've got everything I need for now. I will be in touch one way or the other."

Jenny knew in her heart Dwight would be back. She could see it in his eyes. A childlike fascination took over as he listened to her describe the encounters. He believed her—really believed what she had said.

Before leaving the Garrett house, Dwight made a slow deliberate walk through each room on the main floor. Nothing appeared out of place. Dwight silently realized that each of Jenny's 'sightings' occurred while Warren was in the house, and at a precise time when Warren was occupied out of Jenny's sight.

16

Rick returned to his desk after a lunchtime bitch session with Perkins and stared at the official papers spread from end to end. But he saw nothing. His mind had drifted into a spiral and, as a result, nothing was happening inside. The lights were on, but no one was at home.

There were at least three things he should be doing but found himself doing nothing instead. The Garrett case had become mired down in credits and debits for both Warren's trading business and the Matheson Garrett agency.

"Detective Walker, someone to see you," a round plum-faced policewoman said, poking her head into Rick's office.

To Rick's surprise, Bridget Sterling's lissome body stood just behind the policewoman's round one. He rose clumsily, knocking his knee against a partially open desk drawer. It took all he had to keep from screwing his face up into a grimace.

"Ms. Sterling, please come in."

The policewoman's eyes telegraphed her disgust at Rick's behavior: *you-typical-male-animal.* Even Rick realized he was acting a little like a schoolboy.

"Please, sit down."

"I hope you don't mind. You said I should contact you if I thought of anything else about Jenny."

"Sure, but you could have just called."

"Oh, that's okay. I'm on my way uptown to a photo shoot, and I figured it was just as easy to stop by. Did I do wrong by coming here?"

"No, no. This is fine, great."

"Good. If you'd rather I called instead, I guess..."

"No."

Rick waited, realizing his tie was probably crooked around his neck, his hair must be a mess from being outside in the wind, and he had garlic in his lunch. Without checking, he hoped he had not spilled anything from lunch on his shirt. In the silence, Rick searched his desk drawer for his breath mints; though taking one now would only look obvious.

Bridget waited.

"Just getting a pen," Rick said.

Bridget handed him one she removed from the top of his desk.

"Ready now."

"After you left that Saturday, I began to think more about the time I've spent with Jenny and Warren. There was one thing that Jenny did confide in me. It's rather personal, so I mean, I wouldn't want...you understand what I'm saying?"

"Ms. Sterling, anything you give me remains strictly confidential. We're not interested in gossip, only in making sure we have all the facts surrounding Jenny's accident."

"I don't think this could have anything to do with Jenny's accident, except maybe that it might have weighed heavily on her mind."

"Sure, I understand..."

"Jenny said she was worried about Warren."

"Worried about Warren in what way?"

"I guess Warren's business is doing badly. Warren trades things, like money and crops, and things like that."

"Commodities."

"Yes, Warren trades commodities and Jenny said she was worried because I guess his trading hadn't been going good for awhile. He was losing, I guess, a lot of money doing it."

"When did she tell you this?"

"Maybe a month before the accident. No, more like two months before."

"How did Jenny tell you that?"

"What do you mean?"

"How did she sound when she said it. Was she distraught? Was it more like just as a matter of information."

"She was worried...nervous. I guess Warren deals is large sums of money and he was..."

"Was what?"

"Borrowing heavily. Jenny said they were getting very deep into debt."

"Did she say anything else?"

"No. That was it. I hesitated in coming to you because I didn't know if something like that was important to you."

"Everything is important in an investigation. You never know how pieces are going to fit together until you look at all of them."

"Well then, I'm glad I came in."

Bridget's smile had a way of stealing attention.

"Ms. Sterling, I'm glad you came in, too. With that I mean."

Bridget rose, smoothing the black v-neck knit dress she wore which clung to her hips as if it had been painted onto her body. The soft exposed flesh made looking at anything else impossible.

Rick stared as he moved around his desk and walked Bridget to the door of his office. He stopped there.

So did Bridget. She turned to him and smiled.

Rick felt her warmth reach his body. The heady scent of her perfume swirled inside his head. He mustered every ounce of will power to keep from reaching out and touching her.

"Just go back through the double doors with the exit sign over them."

Perkins walked up to Rick the moment Bridget began walking away.

"We still on for Haloran's tonight?" Perkins asked. His eyes were riveted to the undulating flow of Bridget's curvaceous body as she departed.

"You bet." So were Rick's.

"Ten says she turns back," Perkins added.

"No takers," Rick said.

At the double doors, Bridget gave Rick one more quick look and a departing smile.

"You know who that is?" Perkins asked.

"Exotica perfume."

"Are you *doing* her?" Perkins asked in a hushed tone.

"She's part of the Garrett investigation."

"No shit. She's definitely an all-nighter. Why don't you introduce me? If you're not going to do her, I will."

"Not on your life."

"Pull your tongues back into your mouths, boys," Policewoman Schurer said as she passed. But neither Rick nor Perkins made any move to return to their respective duties.

****

Rick liked Haloran's. It had a quiet subdued ambiance. The walls were plastered with nostalgic mementos from the sixties and early seventies, and the steaks were better than any other place he had eaten. But the best reason was that Haloran's wasn't a cop bar where the uniforms hung out. Rick spent twelve to fourteen hours a day with cops; the last thing he wanted to do when he unwound was hang with a bunch of cops bitching about law enforcement. And at Haloran's, nobody paid attention to you.

Perkins arrived before Rick, took a table just off the main thoroughfare and nursed a scotch and soda while he waited. The place seemed more populated than usual for that hour of the night. Usually the dinner crowd was gone by nine.

When Rick arrived, both ordered their usual: 22 ounce porterhouse steaks, medium rare, hold the salad—salads are for wussies. They talked briefly about their cases, using each other as a sounding board for ideas. This time was usually spent as an informal brainstorming session or bitch session, depending on the mood of the detectives. Seemed lately they spent less time brainstorming and more time bitching.

Old Perky and Rick only handled the off-the-wall cases where evidence was absent and suspects were more like phantoms than real people. They were considered the best of the best in solving unsolvable cases. However, such distinction did have its pressures. And pressure needs to be vented on occasion.

Rick had been looking for a way to vent his pressure for sometime and still had not found relief.

Perkins liked Haloran's because it attracted more than an average share of young single women in the area. The place wasn't a pick-up bar nor a meat market. But six months earlier Perkins had met a fox at Haloran's. The relationship lasted three dates. A record for Perkins, considering he had an attitude most women objected to. Now he returned, hoping to repeat.

As a rule, most women avoided cops. Oh, they're great for chitchat and a meal, maybe even a movie, but the profession had so many debilitating stigmas that a detective was a fool if he thought he could convince a woman he was normal by any measure of the word.

Rick was half-finished with his steak and had just locked a piece between his teeth when his eyes caught Bridget's as she moved through the place with a flowing grace. Her smile seized Rick's eyes, and she altered her path to take her directly to his table.

"I tell you, the look on that scumbag mother-fuck..." Perkins was saying when he noticed Rick wasn't listening.

"Good evening Detective, never imagined I'd be seeing you here."

Rick rose clumsily, chewing down his food behind his napkin, and stumbled for the right thing to say.

"Ms. Sterling..."

"Can't you call me Bridget? I mean this is purely a social environment here."

"Hello Bridget."

Perkins was doing everything but punching Rick in the gut to remind him he was there.

Finally, Rick figured it out.

"Bridget, this is Detective Perkins."

"He your partner?"

"No. But we have worked cases together."

Bridget's eyes gave Perkins no more than a cursory going-over, then they were back on Rick.

The noise level in the restaurant rose around them, forcing Bridget to lean closer to Rick to be able to hear.

"You come here for the food or the circuses?" Bridget asked, clearly hoping to stretch their encounter.

"A little of both I guess."

"Would you like to join us?" Perkins forced in, though his request hardly penetrated Bridget.

That moment lingered between Rick and Bridget.

"No, thank you. I'm meeting someone. It was nice seeing you, Detective."

Bridget left their table in search of her own.

"Boy, you are one smooth operator," Perkins said after Bridget had faded away.

Rick returned to his meal, never once looking back over his shoulder at Bridget. He didn't have to.

Perkins gazed her way every few minutes, offering regular updates as to Bridget's status. She sat alone, nursing a glass of wine under the light of a stained-glass fixture over the booth.

Bridget consumed Rick's mind, but he refused to let Perkins know that. Instead, he inquired about a homicide investigation Perkins was predicting would end in a ringer.

"You haven't heard a word I said since that Sterling chick came in," Perkins said.

They had finished their meal, an after-dinner drink, and a second cup of coffee, and still Bridget sat comfortably alone in a booth at a point furthest from where the detectives sat.

Perkins had to force himself to remain in his seat instead of going over to talk to Bridget. Unconsciously, he smoothed his hair with his fingers as if he were preparing to walk over and take the place beside her in the booth.

"It's been forty minutes, and she's still alone."

"So?"

"So..."

"She's...just..."

"Look, if you're not going to try to put the salami to her, I am," Perkins injected.

"No...it's not that."

"Is she a principal in the Garrett investigation?"

"No. She's a friend to the Garrett woman."

"Not germane in any way to your investigation?"

"No."

"Then she's fair game. Man, what are you waiting for?"

"Come on, Perkins, you know better than that."

"Hey, just say the word, and I'm out of here. I figure either she's been stood up, or she's waiting for you to come over."

"What's makes you think I'd do that?"

"Let's see, you've been divorced now for three years...you haven't been out with a woman in over six months. Am I right? Don't bullshit me. Am I right?"

"Right."

Perkins rose, downed the rest of his drink, handed the check over to Rick and winked.

"You pick up the bill, and I just ease on out of here like nothing has happened, so you can go over there and at least give it the best shot you've got. You are looking at a once-in-a-lifetime shot. I suggest you take it."

With that, Perkins nodded toward Bridget on his way to the exit. He never looked back.

Rick ordered another scotch, neat, and with that to steady his nerves, made his way to Bridget's booth. One side of his brain told him to walk away; the other side told him to go for it.

Bridget's soft eyes moved up to his and held them as if she had hypnotic power. The corners of her mouth turned up into a slight smile. Her lipstick glistened in the soft light falling from the fixture overhead. The way she shifted in her seat placed more of her exposed flesh under the glow of the light.

"Your night not going well?" Rick asked.

"No, I guess not."

"Have you eaten?"

"Not yet. I was supposed to have dinner with a friend, but I guess she isn't going to show. Sometimes photo shoots can drag on forever. Would you like to join me?"

"Sure. And I promise no questions."

Rick slid into the booth beside Bridget.

"Great."

****

Jenny lay awake in the darkness, her eyes staring vacantly at the ceiling. Warren had left her more than an hour ago and the den had fallen silent shortly afterward.

Jenny feared she had hurt him when his good-night kiss failed to ignite any passion in her. Warren was so warm and caring, yet she felt no desire inside when they kissed. The thought of lying with him in the bed now sent a quiver through her body and icy bumps along her skin.

In the late hour, the house took on a funereal atmosphere. Jenny listened to her breathing—slow and steady. She felt her heart beating.

Strands of moon glow that found their way through the drawn window curtains played off the mirror and the bedroom walls. They allowed the illusion of sight amid the pitch-dark night. Jenny could pick out the empty chair in the corner. The furniture held her eyes as if she expected it to begin to move by itself.

Overhead, the house creaked, as outside a nasty wind soughed against the roof. Noise made Jenny skittish. Even though the bumps and groans were as much a part of this home as was the plaster and pipes, they still unnerved her. The creaks and cracks that came from the hundred-year-old wood had always been there, and over the years Jenny had conditioned herself to tune them out. Until now.

Could the noises be from...

Jenny refused to allow fear to control her.

Jenny's heart began beating faster. An icy chill swam through her.

The wind suddenly fell silent.

Jenny feared being alone, and at the same time, feared what Warren would think if she begged him to join her in bed—not to share love, but to fend off something only she had witnessed. Something that might ultimately be an hallucination.

Then she heard her breathing again. It rose and fell like waves lapping gently against a shore. In and out. The gentle rhythm gave her comfort. But the night fueled her growing terror.

Then Jenny held her breathing...but the sound of air moving in and out continued.

17

With a slap of her hand along the wall, Bridget flicked on the living room lights, kicked off her heels, and tossed her coat over the nearest chair.

"How 'bout that nightcap?" she asked. She was already in the kitchen, removing the bottle of Chivas Regal from a cabinet.

"You like it neat, right?"

"Sure, but I don't think I should..."

"Just one. And I promise it will be short."

Rick ambled into the living room, settled on the sofa, where he thumbed through a portfolio of Bridget's poses that had been left prominently on the coffee table. Rick couldn't remember seeing it there during his last visit. He stopped and caught his breath at a shot of her in black, lacy, high-cut panties while she crossed her arms nimbly over her breasts in a coy attempt at modesty. His mind refused to leave the picture.

"How long have you been a model?" he asked. His heart began beating faster. Even though he flipped further into the portfolio, his mind remained stuck on the one displaying her nakedness.

Unable to turn off those detective instincts inside, Rick picked up traces of stale smoke. It must have attached itself to his clothes at the restaurant.

"Five years. But I don't really count my first year. I hardly worked."

Rick forced himself to close the portfolio. He then sauntered over to a high stool at the end of the breakfast counter. Standing face to face with Bridget as she poured, he caught her fragrance, Exotica. As the fragrance blossomed around him, his hormones urged him closer to her, commanding him to reach out to brush her skin. Her warmth swarmed over him, clouding his mind with thoughts of her in that photograph.

"How long have you been a detective?" she asked, clinking ice cubes into her drink.

"A detective for six years, but on the force for eighteen."

"Gee, that makes you..."

"Much older than you."

Bridget smiled impishly.

"Not that much," she toyed.

Her eyes sparkled when she looked into his. Her lips were soft and pink like rose petals.

"You ever married?" she asked.

"Long time ago. At least it seems like it."

"She didn't like being married to a cop?"

"No, she didn't like being married to me."

"Oh."

Bridget handed him his glass. As she did, her finger slid across the back of his hand. There was no mistaking that the contact had been intentional. She held her glass out to meet his.

"Here's to...whatever cops drink to."

"How 'bout to your success."

Rick took a sip, keeping his eyes in line with hers. The scotch made her lips glisten in a naughty way. She was truly a fantasy in the flesh, standing before him, beckoning him with her eyes. He never considered asking himself why. He only knew if this was his moment, he had to seize it at any cost.

Rick felt his heart pounding as he set the glass down. His mouth had gone dry. At thirty-eight, he never thought he'd still be clumsy at this. He sought words until he realized he needed no words. He had to act.

Bridget set her glass beside his and looked up into his eyes. She was offering herself to him, sending him all the right signals.

Rick couldn't say no.

Her kiss became the spark that set everything inside him on fire. There was urgency in their embrace; a need they shared in common. Rick worked his hand down her curves—stopping at nothing, wanting everything.

Bridget employed her body with the same precision a surgeon applies his scalpel. She knew exactly where to touch to draw out Rick's pent-up passion.

Something emerged. Something Rick had locked away inside years ago. He never thought he would be pulling it out for another woman. He never thought he would be holding someone as beautiful and as sensuous as Bridget Sterling in his arms.

Bridget's hands worked him to a fevered pitch. She lifted her dress so she could wrap her legs around his buttocks.

Their breathing came in gasps, flashing like wild fire over the otherwise silent apartment. Rick had abandoned all control. His hands sought to make her hotter, more excited than she already was.

"Oh, Officer Rick, what a big gun you have," she whispered.

She assisted him when he fumbled to get beneath her panties, responding maddeningly to his intimate intrusion and his driving animal passion. Then in a delicate whisper, she begged him to take her to her bed.

Rick left her lips to breathe, sucking air deep into his lungs as he carried her out of the kitchen. He had no doubt this was going to be an all-nighter.

****

Jenny listened to air moving in and out, knowing it came from another.

She checked the clock. It was after midnight. She shifted her upper body to reach the lamp without having to stretch. Pain punished her and forced her to recoil once the lamp was switched on. She sought to penetrate that darkness beyond her bedroom and focus on the source of the sound.

"Warren?" she called.

No response. The sound, however, grew more persistent.

"Warren, is that you?"

The hall beyond her door was a black curtain.

Outside her window, a limb scratched the glass.

Jenny jerked back. She could hear heavy footsteps, someone moving about in the den.

"Mr. Chips? Warren, come on."

The footsteps grew steadily closer, along with the sounds of breathing—breathing that was not her own. Something was in the hall, nearing her room. Jenny fixed her eyes on the door. Her mouth went suddenly dry. Why wouldn't Warren answer her?

****

Mr. Chips lifted his head out of his shallow sleep on the sofa; something he enjoyed previously only when Warren was out of the house and had forgotten to lock him in his cage. The dog turned immediately toward the stairs, pricking his ears.

The tapping had fooled him into thinking Warren was working in the den. But there was no way Chips would have slept through the front door opening and besides, Warren would have swatted him off the sofa before going upstairs.

Chips sampled the still air. Nothing. He whined when he heard Jenny's voice. But the last thing he wanted was to give up his warm corner of the sofa. This had been the only time in months he had been able to lay up there untouched by Warren's wrath. But still she called him again.

****

Jenny's thoughts turned morbid. Had someone broken into the house, killed Chips, and was now ransacking Warren's office? She was helpless here in her bed. Her eyes moved quickly to the bathroom door. It had a lock. She'd be safe in there.

But before she could move, she saw it.

The spirit bloomed into existence, filling the open doorway. That hideous face was clearly her own. It wore ragged, grimy clothes. The presence stopped, rotating its head ninety degrees until the two black sockets bore down on Jenny.

"No...please...no..."

Jenny's heart surged inside her chest. Her breathing came in wild gasps.

The spirit's mangled hand rose and leveled a crooked open hand menacingly at Jenny.

"No please!" Jenny forced out of her raw throat. Without words, Jenny knew inside what the ghost was attempting to communicate.

The spirit slowly floated around to face her. It moved through the doorway and approached her bed. The face sent off an eerie glow as it fell within the light of the lamp beside the bed.

"No, p-l-e-a-s-e."

****

Chips rose to all fours. *It* was up there. The thing that had terrified him so—was up there. So was Jenny. He knew it was up there. He knew it was...

****

Shivers shuddered through Jenny's terrified body. The image lifted a hand and reached out for her. The bottomless sockets looked straight at her as if they could somehow see. Jenny felt the coldness of death precede the hand edging closer to her own.

She leaned away from the oncoming hand, and at the same time, she tried to slip out of the bed to get to the bathroom.

She screamed when it shifted to block her way.

Mr. Chips bounded off the sofa. He had to help. He had to do something to protect Jenny from that thing. The stench of rotting flesh flowed down the stairs like a thick blanket of fog. Chips padded up the stairs firing off an aggressive growl of warning.

As the dog reached the last stair, he saw the thing beside Jenny's bed. Jenny was struggling to escape.

Mr. Chips was a stride from the entry. His lips had receded to expose fangs poised to tear into flesh.

Suddenly the chair beside the door flew over, knocking the door closed.

Chips crashed headlong into the wood. Yipping in agony, braying in anger at being isolated from his master, Chips clawed fervently at the door.

Jenny watched the door bang shut. Chips had been trapped outside. The spirit stood over her bed reaching down. It issued a vile lament as Jenny sought to evade its outstretched reach. She felt lifeless flesh take her arm.

Then the cigarette lighter from her night table— Warren's lighter—sparked once, then twice. A sallow flame shot up and ignited her flannel sleeve.

"No!" Jenny screamed with a strength and anger she never knew existed inside her. In a flash of light, flames spread to her bed and leapt to the nearby lamp shade.

Jenny rolled off the bed, hearing the smoke alarm blaring in the hall outside her door. Despite the burning agony, she rolled back and forth on the floor to extinguish the flame on her arm.

The spirit vanished, leaving Jenny in a room filling with smoke.

She felt numb except for the instinctive drive for survival. Risking more burns, she tossed the burning lamp out the bedroom window, feeling a rush of cold night air sweep in around her. Then she smothered the blanket, grabbed it away from the dying flames, and also flung it out the window.

Warren saw the flaming lamp arc out the bedroom window and plummet to the ground as he turned the corner. He slammed the pedal to the floor and screeched to a sideways halt on the front lawn just before the stairs.

It took precious seconds to unlock the door.

Warren threw it back with a crash and assaulted the stairs two at a time. The bedroom door was closed with Chips bouncing off it in a frenzy. Warren threw the door open to find Jenny in the corner, struggling to get the mattress from the bed.

He moved her away, and in one motion, pulled the mattress from the frame and forced it out the window into the night-enshrouded yard.

Below, warbling sirens filled the night. Red and white emergency lights danced across the face of the house as the first engine company arrived. Men in yellow suits raced up the stairs and into the smoky bedroom. But the fire had been removed. All that remained now were smoldering remnants.

On the lawn outside the bedroom window, firefighters dragged the mattress and debris away from the vulnerable structure and doused it repeatedly.

Inside, Warren held a trembling Jenny while a paramedic cut away her sleeve to attend the burns on her arm and hands.

"You were very lucky, ma'am," the paramedic said. "Your flame retardant clothing protected most of your arm. It could have been worse."

The burned flesh was right now the furthest from Jenny's mind. She felt no pain, only a terror that wormed its way like a plague into her heart. The spirit had attempted to kill her!

"What about there?" the paramedic asked, indicating the blood stains over her abdomen.

"My wife's recovering from an auto accident," Warren said.

"I'm okay. It's just my arm."

"Do you want to go to the hospital?" the paramedic asked when he finished bandaging the arm. He began re-packing his instruments into his case.

"No, I'm all right. It's just my arm that was burned. I'm all right."

"Ma'am, I suggest you see your doctor, just to be safe."

Jenny's eyes went to Warren's.

"Where were you? How come you weren't here?"

"Jenny, baby, I'm sorry. I just ran out for smokes. I ran down to the gas station on Willis Ave. I was only gone maybe ten minutes."

"Warren, she was here. She tried to kill me!" Jenny kept saying in a whisper, while men removed the window curtains, bed frame and anything else touched by the fire.

Warren tried in vain to comfort her.

The house, now quiet, reeked of smoke.

While Jenny rested on the rollaway bed in the den, Warren met with a fire department supervisor downstairs on the front lawn.

"Your wife was very lucky to be awakened so quickly. Usually it's too late. Another minute or so and this whole place would have gone up. Oh, and rest assured Mr. Garrett, your fire alarm system is working. The Honeywell central station dispatched us when they got the alarm. I guess it pays to put in the best."

"I'll be sure to thank them. I don't understand why Jenny..."

"Your wife was smoking in bed. My men found smoking materials on the floor near where the fire broke out."

"My wife doesn't smoke. Those were mine from earlier."

Warren thanked the fire marshal again for their quick response, then raced up the stairs to be with Jenny.

"Jenny?"

"Warren, listen to me. It's not what you think. I was sleeping when noises in the den woke me up. I thought it was just you. I didn't know you weren't here. But it wasn't you, it was her. She was here!"

"Jenny, this is crazy! Dr. Rosenstein said this vision is nothing more than a hallucination."

"Damnit Warren, hallucinations don't set you on fire! She was here. She kept Mr. Chips out. She tried to kill me. Don't you understand?"

Jenny could no longer contain her tears.

"She set me on fire. She..."

Jenny winced from the pain, choking down a torrent of tears.

"I'm not imagining this. There is a ghost of me in this house. It tried to kill me tonight."

"Jenny, I'll call Rosenstein. He'll come right over. Please try to relax. He'll give you something to help you sleep."

"Warren, I want Dwight Mackenzie. Tell him what happened. He needs to know that the ghost tried to kill me tonight."

A short while later, with Jenny resting on the cot in the den, Warren sat in his overstuffed chair in a completely dark living room, hiding behind the smoke from his cigarette. The air was thick with the odor of charred wood and smoke. He blamed himself. He was supposed to be here. He was supposed to make sure she was safe. These things were not supposed to happen.

As Warren tamped out his cigarette, he sought another from the pack beside him—the pack that had taken him from the house. It was then that he realized he had gone into her bedroom earlier. He was hoping to find a cigarette, but the pack on her night stand was empty. Why didn't he remove the lighter and stick it in his pocket?

Upstairs, Mr. Chips stationed himself outside the den door. The dog had refused to leave even when Warren offered him his favorite Liver Snaps treat.

Finally, Warren withdrew the card from his pocket, turned on the lamp and dialed the number. It was well after midnight, but Warren knew sleep would not come until he made the call.

"Mackenzie."

"Yes. Who's this?"

"Warren Garrett. We need to talk."

"I'm listening."

"I don't know if you can help, but..."

18

Morrison's grim face let Jenny know he was anything but pleased to see her so soon after her discharge. Displeasure poured out of his stone face and less than gentle eyes. He said nothing as he inspected the burned tissue on her arm.

Jenny complained of moderate lower abdominal pain that radiated out from her healing incision. And the burn on her forearm was a matter for concern.

While a nurse waited silently near the door, Morrison opened Jenny's gown and gently probed the immediate area surrounding her scar. One corner of the incision had split open, accounting for the seepage of bright red blood onto her clothing. Even after all this time, Jenny still refused to face the hideous sight.

"You want to tell me about it?"

Jenny hesitated, scrambling to line up the words in her mind before offering them up. How could she possibly tell him the truth?

With two fingers, Morrison pressed a sensitive area.

Jenny winced and shifted to ease the pressure.

"Well, it would appear that most of my hard work is still intact. You may have just overextended a healing muscle. I don't think this is cause for alarm. But

137

you still haven't told me how you got that nasty burn, or why I'm having to re-examine you so soon after discharge."

"A freak accident," Jenny offered up feebly. "I...dropped a flaming lighter on my sleeve. The material caught fire before I could get it out. In the flurry to extinguish the flame, I strained something."

"Well, you see, there's another reason to pitch those blasted cancer-sticks once and for all. You'll live a lot longer."

"I don't smoke. Warren's the smoker. I was using his lighter to light a candle on my nightstand."

"I see." Morrison raised a brow. "Is that to suggest that there is romance..."

"It suggests nothing."

The dejection in Jenny's voice smothered any spark of relief that might have ignited in Morrison.

"Jenny, be patient. Warren will come around."

"I'm n-not s-so s-sure."

Jenny's sudden regression to her stutter caught Morrison unguarded. His face released more of his surprise than he would have wanted known.

"W-what?"

"I would have thought the stutter would have faded by now. Do you want me to arrange for therapy?"

"N-no. I'm fine. I j-just stutter when I'm n-nervous."

"What are you nervous about? You know, you have to take care of this walking miracle." Morrison indicated her body. "I do marvelous work, don't I?"

"I'm just having sort of a p-problem."

"A problem? Sounds ominous, maybe you'd better tell me about it."

Morrison closed Jenny's gown and stepped to a side table, where he began recording his findings into her records.

"Dr. Morrison," Jenny started out weakly, but strengthened with each word, "what happened to me in the operating room?"

"What do you mean? Here, let's get you up now. I'm confident you did no serious damage in there."

Jenny grimaced when a jolt of electric shock shot through her midsection.

"I mean, what really happened in there? Did anything unusual...happen?"

"Why do you ask?"

"I..." Jenny faltered, where to begin? If she told him the truth, would he believe her? She suspected even Rosenstein doubted the veracity of her story.

"I keep hearing voices inside my head."

"Voices?"

"Yes, fragments really. Parts of sentences, a few words."

"Like what?"

"There is one that says: 'the pressure...we can't...' and there's another that I thought might have been your voice."

"Mine? What did that one say?"

"Just damnit. You sounded very angry."

"Jenny, you were unconscious when they wheeled you into the emergency room. Then we put you under a potent anesthetic for about five hours while we worked on you on the table. We had a lot of patching up to do in there," Morrison said, indicating her stomach.

"But why do I hear these voices? Why are they plaguing me so?"

"I don't know."

Morrison shifted his eyes quickly to Jenny's record.

"Are you seeing someone about them? A professional?"

"Yes, Dr. Sy Rosenstein."

"Good man. I've heard of him. So how can I help?"

"I was hoping you might tell me what happened at the hospital that night they brought me in."

"Why?"

"I don't know. I just think the voices have something to do with the operating room."

"The operating room?"

The more Jenny listened to Morrison's voice, the more it convinced her that his words were somehow trapped inside her mind. They were vexatious when they arose to torment her, and then as quickly as they came, they would evaporate.

"Jenny, you were in bad shape when they brought you in. Dr. Rashad in emergency worked on you for a time before you were brought up to surgery. I was on call; I arrived within an hour of you're being wheeled in."

"Dr. Morrison, the words won't go away. I don't know what else to do."

"What does Dr. Rosenstein say of this?"

Jenny shifted on the table. She hoped to avoid vocalizing the words, as if saying them somehow gave them the air of credibility.

"He says it's trauma related. He believes it's just part of the brain's healing process."

"I'm no psychiatrist, but I would agree with him."

"Dr. Morrison, did anything unusual happen in that operating room?"

"Unusual? Jenny, you were barely clinging to life for about the first hour. We weren't sure we'd be able to save you. But we did, and you're alive and recovering. You're going to lead a normal and productive life."

"Then nothing happened in there that might explain why I'm plagued by these voices?"

"Nothing Jenny. I think you need to trust Rosenstein. Let him help you through this difficult period in your recovery."

With that, Morrison jotted a line of scribbles in Jenny's record and closed the file with a certain sense of finality.

"Our brains are slow healers, Jenny. Give yours time to mend and return to normal. And I don't want to see you in here again until your normal visit, okay?"

Morrison squeezed Jenny's hand, hoping it would ease her anxiety. Then he rose off his stool to leave.

Although she started to open her mouth to speak, Jenny couldn't bring herself to tell Morrison that she was being tormented by a ghost. He, like Rosenstein, would think it nothing more than a hallucination brought on by a healing brain. And the last thing Jenny could stand right now was more cold, clinical rationalization. She never felt more alone than at this moment.

"I'll help you dress," the nurse offered as the doctor departed.

Jenny nodded.

The nurse held Jenny's blouse without saying anything until Morrison had completely left the room and the door closed.

"You know," the nurse began cautiously, helping Jenny get her bandaged forearm into the sleeve, "there were other people in that operating room. Nurses, an anesthesiologist, and maybe even other doctors."

Jenny stared at her quizzically. What was the nurse really trying to say?

"You could talk to them."

"Would they be able to help?"

"Don't know. But I tell you this, doctors aren't gods, even if they think they are. Dr. Morrison's not perfect—nobody is. Sounds like..." She stopped with an arresting suddenness.

"What? It sounds like what?"

"Nothing. I just think it wouldn't hurt for you to talk to someone else who was in that operating room."

Holding her arms out like stabilizing rails, the nurse assisted Jenny off the table, then left the examining room. When Jenny emerged from the examination room, Morrison stuck his head out of the next office.

"I still want to see you at your regular appointment, Jenny. And leave the burn exposed to air as much as possible over the next few days."

Jenny nodded and smiled weakly. Not even Morrison was going to help her understand what was happening inside her head.

Dr. Morrison closed the door and walked over to his desk, where he tapped a business card on the surface while he listened to a ringing phone in his ear.

"Yes, Detective Walker, this is Doctor Morrison. You wanted to be contacted if anything unusual occurred regarding Jenny Garrett...."

In the reception area, the nurse suspended her activity at the desk and slid the glass window open as Jenny walked by. She held out a small card.

"Mrs. Garrett, your next appointment."

Jenny clutched the card in one hand, Warren's waiting arm in the other. When she turned the card over, a name had been hastily written across the back.

19

A sleepy-eyed Dwight Mackenzie arrived with the next sunrise. It took three trips to move all the equipment from his van into Jenny's bedroom. Each trip only angered Warren that much more.

Warren refused to help, remaining sequestered in his den after admitting Dwight into the house without so much as a good morning greeting. He wanted none of what Dwight had planned for his house and for his wife. Yet there was nothing he could say that wouldn't devastate Jenny.

While Jenny watched with a child's fascination, Dwight set up a menagerie of monitors and instruments, each designed to track one particular aspect of Dwight's intended investigation. One by one, Dwight removed them from steel-case cocoons, all marked DELICATE INSTRUMENTS, where they were kept safe from jostling in transport. Each instrument would detect the minutest changes in the surroundings, and in so doing, provide empirical proof that a ghost was, indeed, presenting itself before Jenny. Or so that was the theory behind the planned paranormal investigation.

The empty cases now cluttered the floor of Jenny's walk-in closet. Her forty-five pairs of shoes had to be piled into an out-of-the-way corner for the time being. How long would all these contraptions be here? If Warren had his way, they'd be out by sundown. Dwight wanted to stay wired until he had what he came for.

By three that afternoon, Dwight had single-handedly wired the entire upper floor of the house for video, sound, infrared, and magnetic field detection. Usually, Dwight found his clients willing participants, but not so in the Garrett house. Jenny would have loved to help, but couldn't. Warren wanted to know if Dwight intended to refill the holes he was making in the walls to hold the wires.

Dwight would have liked to wire the entire house. He was concerned he might miss something significant if he didn't, but limited funds kept him from having enough sensors on hand for a completely thorough investigation. And he didn't dare ask the Garretts for money right now. That would be a sure way of getting bounced out on his ear.

Having festooned the wires overhead along the hall to prevent inadvertent breakage, Dwight checked them once more before connecting the sensors to the instruments. He knew he might very well only get one shot at this, and he needed to minimize the possibility of equipment failure or human error as a cause for his failure.

With instruments set up, tested, and calibrated, Dwight set about the task of collecting signatures. Voice, infrared and magnetic signatures needed to be recorded for himself, Jenny, Chips, and lastly, Warren. Only if Dwight secured a reading that did not match any of the inhabitants of the house could he gain evidence of another's existence here.

Warren, however, made the task even more difficult by acting as if it were a game that required him to beat the machine. If one of the machines did detect something—and no one knew the staggering consequence of that more than Dwight—but if something were recorded, Dwight would have to present incontrovertible proof that the image was neither Jenny, Warren, the dog nor himself.

Warren's callous attitude, however, did much to spark Dwight's suspicions. If Warren were the one tormenting Jenny through the use of some sick perverted trickery, the last thing he would want in the house was a means of exposing his deeds.

After taking a baseline set of readings on all the instruments, Dwight switched them to the monitor mode and left to return to the university, promising he would be back before nightfall.

"I'm not feeding him," Warren scowled, setting a dinner tray hard onto the bed before Jenny. Then he caught himself, took Jenny's hand and kissed her gently on the forehead.

She seemed worn-out and depressed, despite the presence of Dwight, who seemed to be the only one taking her seriously.

"It's only for a few days," she apologized.

"I still can't believe I'm allowing this whole..."

"Warren, please."

"Jenny, I can't believe you're going to allow him to sleep in this room with you. This whole thing is crazy. There's no such thing as ghosts!"

Warren finally abandoned all reasonable discourse and stormed out of the room, stomping down the hall like an angry child. In doing so, he left Jenny no opportunity to respond. Something she needed desperately to be able to do. She needed to vocalize her feelings. Above all else, she need someone to listen.

Jenny's cries found their way into the den, where Warren sat staring at a computer screen of scrolling green numbers. And every number that slid by was bad. He had lost sixteen thousand dollars today because Dwight had innumerable times diverted his attention away from what he had to monitor.

"Fuck," Warren muttered, slamming his hands down on the keyboard in frustration. If he didn't get a grip on things soon—very soon—everything around him would come crashing down. He snatched up the telephone and dialed.

****

Rick decided the time had arrived for him to become acquainted with Warren's living habits. Morrison's surprise phone call put an edge on Rick's suspicions about the Garrett household. It was very difficult to buy that Jenny had become suddenly accident prone. An accidental fire could be yet another way for Warren to eliminate Jenny without finding himself indicted for murder.

Rick had to hope his surveillance would turn over some physical evidence that could be linked to a motive for why Warren might want to murder his wife. There was little doubt in Rick's mind that Warren had opportunity.

Captain Rawlings's memory lasted only so long; as did his good graces. He was again pushing Rick to either make his case or close it out once and for all. Given a few days to mull over Dugan's demonstration, Rawlings was drifting away from the analyst's theory of attempted murder. If it remained beyond proof, why pursue it?

Heat was coming down on the captain from the police commissioner to get the department's statistics up. And the best way to lift the numbers was to shift manpower onto cases that could be solved quickly and leave the *ringers* to collect dust. For Rick, it may very well boil down to a numbers game. The higher the percentage of solved cases, the better the section looked to the top brass. Wasting time on a long shot like the Garrett attempted murder case would hurt the section's numbers and, possibly, Rawling's chances for promotion.

The argument that the killer might try again had been the only reason Walker remained on the Garrett case. Now an 'accidental fire' could indicate that Rick needed to continue his investigation. However, that implied that the killer was such a klutz that he failed in a second attempt. Would there then be a third attempt or would Rick's continued interest in the case send the killer into self-isolation? If Warren suddenly took to the highway, that would be proof enough in Rick's mind that he had focused in on the right suspect.

Right now, Walker cared about one thing: making certain Jenny Garrett's *accidents* did not turn out to be the cause of her death.

Walker requested Vicki Chandler be reassigned to the case. Rawlings laughed him out of the office and told Rick he had to go it alone. Chandler was tied up working a child abuse case that had far-reaching political ramifications. No one could be spared. No one.

A recent rain left the grassy fields surrounding the Garrett house glistening in the moonlight. The brightness, however, afforded Rick precious little opportunity to blend in with the neighborhood. As a result, Rick parked down the road from the Garrett house, and as he sat there, he drank tepid coffee while waiting and hoping for something to happen. He went into this surveillance having little or no expectations.

Within two hours of his arrival, activity perked him up in his seat.

A plain blue van pulled into the Garrett drive, parking off to the side as if to remain out of the way. The overhead porch lamp shed sufficient light for Rick to discern the driver as a scruffy-looking male, in his late twenties with sandy-brown hair.

Rick noted the visitor's arrival time and license number, but paid it no attention until Warren departed fifteen minutes later.

The late hour left little traffic on the road, so Rick delayed his start until Warren safely turned the corner. Then Rick followed at a safe distance, hoping this was more than a trip to the market. He'd almost forgotten how mundane surveillance could be. A partner to talk to would have been nice.

Warren stopped at the market.

While he waited, Rick rummaged through his pockets for change. Before he could leave his vehicle and get to the soda machine, Warren came through the automatic doors with a half-full bag in hand. Warren then continued down the road to the pharmacy, and afterward, pulled back onto the main drag. But he headed toward the city in the direction away from his house. Okay, so this was a trip to the market, but Junior wasn't ready to head back home just yet.

Rick lagged further back when he thought he might be getting too close. Traffic was sparse and even a yutz like Warren might sooner or later realize the same car had been behind him for a dozen blocks.

Rick's top priority was to shadow Warren without being detected, collect data on the guy's habits and see if anything fit into his puzzle. If Warren was up to anything criminal in nature, he would no doubt back off as soon as he saw the eyes of authority watching over him. And then Rick might never uncover the truth. If there even was truth to be discovered in this case.

The blaring neon of retail outlets reflected off the puddles on the road as Rick watched Warren's silver Saab take a hard right corner.

Had he spotted Rick? Warren's quick turn seemed to indicate that possibility.

A black Jeep Cherokee roared out of nowhere, cutting in front of Rick and forcing him to brake hard and swerve into the curb to avoid the collision. He waited until the driver completed his turn into a Seven-Eleven parking lot. Part of Rick wanted to follow the Cherokee and shove his badge down the driver's throat.

But when Rick made the right turn to fall back in behind the Saab, a freight train rambled and clanked across the road a block ahead. All Rick saw were flashing red lights on the lowered gate as he listened to the regular clanking of mostly empty boxcars.

Warren had beat the train to the crossing and, by now, was long gone. Was it just coincidence or had Warren suspected the tail and raced beneath the lowering gates to shake Rick's presence?

Minutes seemed to last forever while Rick waited for the train to pass. The moment the gates lifted, he roared over the tracks and sped on for another mile—hoping to catch up to Warren—before abandoning the surveillance. Luck was against him. He would gain nothing this night and decided to pack it in.

Part of him wanted to go on the six or eight miles to see Bridget. He pulled into the next gas station he came to and dialed her number. No answer. The other, more rational part, told him to call it a night and get some sleep. Rick decided to listen to his rational side.

****

Jenny's fatigue the following day forced her to cancel her appointment with Rosenstein. Just knowing those machines were there in her room prevented her from sleeping. Something inside her kept tugging away like a persistent child saying, *look, look here, see this.*

Warren suspected Rosenstein was relieved by the cancellation, since this was pro bono and not a billable patient for him anyway. Though Rosenstein, at the time, never put it into words, Warren was certain Rosenstein had made the offer believing, like Warren, that it was a favor destined never be called upon. Most seek professional help only as a last recourse. And the stigma attached to psychiatric help would more than stave off most.

Dwight did nothing other than sit and stare for hours at the instruments cluttering a third of the Garrett master bedroom. At regular intervals, he checked each of the machines to verify that they were continuing to function in their prescribed manner; similar to the way someone checks for a dial tone when they're expecting an important call.

Jenny slept off and on in the morning and seemed to be adapting quite well to Dwight's unobtrusive presence. Even though he was there, it was more like he was invisible.

"All quiet?" she asked upon awakening.

"Except for your husband in the den."

"Your machines are picking that up?"

"Sure," Dwight said. He angled an oscilloscope screen so Jenny could see it from her bed.

"What is that?"

"Your husband's breathing."

"You're kidding? That machine can pick of the sound of his breathing in the den?"

"Actually, there's a sensor in the den sending the signal back to the instrument. He should give up smoking."

"Pretty sensitive."

"I wired three sensors just inside the door. If you like, I can tell you when he leaves his chair."

"Can you see him, too?"

"No. I only wired the hall and this bedroom for video. I left the den alone. I didn't think your husband would appreciate Big Brother watching over his shoulder."

"He's not very supportive in this."

"I know. All we can do now is wait and hope. How are you feeling today?"

"Better. The pain in my arm is finally going away."

"That's great. And by the way, I believe what you said...about what really happened."

"Thank God. For a while I thought I was losing my mind. I mean the spirit seems too real to be a hallucination."

"For what it's worth, animals don't react to hallucinations. No matter what the learned community says."

Warren popped his head into the bedroom, glared at Dwight, then turned his attention to Jenny, his face softening into a smile.

"I'm going to the market for dinner stuff. Grilled swordfish on the Jenn-air sound okay?"

Dwight made certain to be checking his instruments during Warren's question. The more Dwight avoided eye contact, the better for them both.

"Just great. Dwight, do you like fish?"

"Ah...I'll be leaving for awhile this evening. I'm having dinner with a college friend who lives not far from here. But I'll have the instruments set to trigger on anything that happens, and I'll make sure I'm back before you retire."

Ninety minutes later, Warren returned from the market surprised to find Bridget's car in the drive beside Dwight's van. Through the window he spied her sitting on the sofa in the living room with Jenny. Jenny never mentioned that she had talked to Bridget nor that Bridget would be coming over. Progress, Warren thought as he climbed the stairs.

Warren spent a few minutes catching-up with Bridget, then excused himself to put the groceries away and return to his work in the den. Jenny never mentioned if Bridget was staying for dinner, but Warren assumed she wasn't, especially since he had only purchased enough fish for two.

Bridget repeatedly told Jenny how great she looked despite the accident, and that she would be back to normal in no time. Bridget, however, did have a difficult time avoiding the scar on Jenny's face. Her obvious attempts to avoid looking at the scar made Jenny even more conscious of her appearance.

"You seem to be getting around good. When do you think you'll be back to work?"

"I don't want to rush it. I know it must be difficult for Kate right now, but I just need more time."

"I didn't mean to make you feel under pressure..."

As Dwight came down the stairs and crossed the opening to the living room, Bridget's eyes followed him; she suspended her conversation in mid-word.

"Who is that?" she whispered with a girlish grin across her face.

Jenny stumbled to line up something plausible.

"Just a workman. He's wiring a new alarm. We've been having problems with the other one. They think it's faulty wiring."

"Are you going to introduce me?"

"To our workman?"

"A girl has to try."

As they laughed together, Jenny covered her mouth suddenly, uncertain of her scar's appearance in such a situation. Part of her wanted to reach across the sofa and throw her arms around her friend. Another part of her cautioned the wisdom of such an action. Though Jenny was baffled at why. Bridget had been her best friend since college. They leaned on each other through the hard times and laughed together through the good times. So why did it all of a sudden seem wrong to feel that way?

"I should be back in a few hours," Dwight said, bidding his leave without imposing on Jenny. His eyes never left Bridget and he lingered a moment longer than appropriate before disappearing.

"That guy even works nights. My kind of man," Bridget said with a wink.

"Bridget, you need to find yourself a husband."

"He might do."

Jenny made no further comment, and she was glad Bridget prodded no further for information about Dwight. Some things she knew she had to keep buried. She didn't think she'd ever be able to tell

Bridget the truth about her life right now. Besides, how do you tell someone that the person they just saw is a paranormal investigator looking for a ghost? Bridget was her best friend, yet Jenny knew there was no way she could confide in her about something as bizarre as that.

"So, you look really great, Jenny. And after...well before you know it, you'll be back at the grind and this whole thing will be behind you. Has Kate been by yet?"

"She stopped by briefly the other day, talked to Warren because I was asleep and said the visit wasn't for anything important. Seems the agency is keeping her hopping."

As quickly as she said it, Jenny banished thoughts of the agency from her mind. She was still struggling with a black hole in her memory, those voices that kept calling to her, and, finally, the horrifying apparition that haunted her and seemed to want to harm her. There was no way she could even consider stepping foot in the agency now.

After Bridget departed, Jenny watched the fading sun out the living room window while her mind drifted aimlessly. Her life had been so perfect before the...

Now it was a nightmare.

With her head resting on her arm, she thought about Warren's needs and how she must sooner or later face being intimate with him. The very thought of it sent a shock wave through her mind. She would have to do something, have to allow him to express himself in a sexual way before he burst. What if her body repulsed him? In the past week, he had touched her once. If the very thought of the scars turned him off, how would it be when he had to see or touch them?

"Dinner," Warren called, drawing Jenny out of her worries and back to the reality of living her life one hour at a time.

Jenny regretted having to return to her bed after dinner. That bedroom had become her dungeon. The place where she was kept away from the rest of the living world. The light and the air in the living room seemed fresher and brighter. The vitality of being in there seeped into her.

Warren dutifully cradled her in his arms, kissed her gently on the lips, and then carried her up the stairs despite her insistence that she was ready to give it a try on her own. His kiss erased all the things that had worried her earlier. He loved her, she thought. He had to, to be so patient with her.

She resolved it was time for them to make love.

"Another week and you can try the stairs," he said, setting her gently upon the new king-size bed and bringing the blanket up. When he kissed her, his hand began to gently massage her breast. His breathing inflated with the heat of pent-up passion.

"You need some, don't you?"

"Desperately."

"I don't know if I'm ready. But..." Jenny found herself saying, though inside she had instructed herself that this was something she must do.

Warren peeled back the blanket and moved his hand slowly up her nightgown behind her legs. He felt the warmth radiating from between her thighs. His other fingers took her stiffening nipple between them. Warren's breathing became urgent; his kisses trailed down from her lips to her neck, then inside her gown to her breasts.

Jenny opened herself up and shifted to allow Warren's hand under the leg band of her panties. She wanted so much to feel the excitement of their love. Could *that* be what was missing from her? Would everything fall back into place after making love with Warren?

Warren knew as his hand found her spot that Jenny was not responding to his efforts to set her afire.

"*I love you*," he whispered.

Jenny knew she was expected to give those words back. She couldn't. Something inside forbade her from saying them.

While Warren groaned in mounting ecstasy, Jenny sought to ignite the fires of her own passion. Somewhere in her mind there must be memories of the pleasures they shared as lovers. But nowhere inside could she locate them. Her fire sputtered and died, leaving her cold inside. She tried to hide her emptiness from Warren.

In his excitement, Warren worked his hand up and brushed his fingers across her scar. He recoiled as if burned.

The action forced Jenny to tense up.

"I'm sorry, Jenny. Did I hurt you?" Warren asked when their eyes met.

The awkward moment stripped him of his longing. He felt the life drain out of his erection and knew he would be unable to revitalize it now.

The doorbell's ring and Chips' subsequent barking signaled Dwight's return, right on cue.

"The *shit* is back."

Warren pulled himself from the bed and smoothed Jenny's night gown to its proper place.

"I guess it's a cold shower in the meantime," he said, returning the blanket over Jenny's body. Jenny's eyes offered an apology, though Warren sought to reassure her none was necessary with a kiss to her forehead.

Yet Jenny saw the deep disappointment in Warren's eyes. Why couldn't she say what he so desperately needed to hear? Why were those words suddenly so foreign to her? She must have told Warren she loved him a million times during their first year of marriage. Now her stomach convulsed every time she even thought about the words.

Warren was certain he would never last another day with Mr. Ghostbuster in this house.

20

After a number of delays from Kate Matheson, Rick finally had his hands on the ledgers from the Matheson Garrett agency. Had the books been turned over in a timely fashion, and had Kate *not* hesitated in responding to his request, Rick would have given the information no more than a cursory examination. But, that slight hesitancy could mean there were things in those ledgers that Kate wished to keep from Rick's eyes.

As a result, inconsistency became the target of Rick's inspection. Because inconsistency then pointed to where the books may have been doctored. And doctored books could lead him to a new suspect.

Rick began his inquiry by cross-checking gross expenses against gross revenues. Gross revenues are easily obtained through bank records. Gross expenses, however, had to be tallied from a number of different sources such as payroll, vendor invoices, etc. Initially, the numbers seemed to match and substantiate that Matheson-Garrett was, indeed, a good tax-abiding corporate citizen. No red flags rose to wave above the numbers.

The agency's revenues seemed quite high, but then again, Rick knew little about how the advertising game really worked. Their revenues did support

Kate's claim that the agency had seen a consistent 20 percent annual growth over the last few years. Of course, if expenses are steadily rising thirty percent over the same period, the company could still get itself into trouble. Too many young companies outspend their revenues under the assumption that sales will eventually outstrip expenses. When that fails to happen, debt becomes unmanageable and the company must seek alternatives to bankruptcy.

Rick finally found the focus of his initial search: the agency's annual premium to the Occidental Insurance company of San Francisco. A telephone call got him the head of accounts, where Rick learned that Matheson-Garrett had in force a fairly standard 'Partners Insurance' policy. Like all conscientious partners, it had been taken out at the agency's birth five years ago. Everything seemed normal so far.

Rick circled the pay out he had hastily scribbled down earlier given him by a supervisor. A million bucks gets fed into the agency if either partner dies while the policy's in force. The supervisor also confirmed that Matheson-Garrett was never once late with their premium.

A million bucks...flowed into the agency if Jenny Garrett died.

Rick stared at the number for a long time after returning the receiver to the cradle. Kate Matheson becomes sole owner of the agency—maybe—and takes possession of a million bucks. Even though the policy was without a double indemnity clause for accidental death, it still provided a hefty sum, making it much easier for Kate during a transition to a one-owner agency.

"So what if..." Rick found himself saying to the empty room.

Would Kate go so far as to try to kill Jenny for the money? For a reason yet unknown to Rick, he doubted Kate had the moxie to attempt murder. While she cloaked herself in corporate armor, inside she was still a woman and few women were capable of murder. But instinct cautioned him to rule out no suspect until he became convinced of their innocence.

The ledger account also listed payments to the agency's law firm and accounting firm. Rick's inquiry to the lawyer handling the Matheson-Garrett legal affairs confirmed what Rick had suspected from the beginning: there was a clause in the agency charter that guaranteed rights of survivorship to a spouse. Therefore, if Jenny died, the million went to the agency and Warren then became Kate's partner.

Rick wrote Warren and Kate's name on his pad and drew a heart around them. Anything is possible, and everything has to be checked.

Playing out a what-if scenario, Rick surmised that if Warren and Kate were romantically involved, they could eliminate the sticking point—Jenny—and fill up their bank accounts at the same time.

Four more hours of cross-checking ledger entries and innumerable telephone calls led Rick down a whole new path of investigation. No matter how hard he tried, Rick still failed to account for inconsistencies in some of the Matheson-Garrett ledger entries. Sloppy accounting? Maybe. But Rick knew to keep digging until he made his way to the bottom of the irregularities.

Rick's job could have been made easier had he been able to access the agency's accountants directly. But accountants tend to have loose lips and itchy palms. While Rick had no reason to suspect the accountants in Jenny's accident, they might very well be involved in the anomalies staring Rick in the face.

So far, each questionable entry led to a blind alley. At first anyway. But Rick's tenacity and telephone calls all ultimately led to the same place—a dummy company bank account that gave Kate Matheson signing privileges.

Piece by piece, Rick assembled the truth, despite someone's slick attempt to bury it. He finger-poked the buttons on his adding machine, then hit the key for a total.

Bingo!

Sixteen thousand dollars in the last two quarters had been funneled from the Matheson-Garrett agency account into a dummy vendor account, which then fed into a non-existent supplier account, and was finally transferred into the dummy company account where Kate had sole signing power.

Kate Matheson was embezzling from her own agency. Foolish—but a legitimate reason for wanting a partner permanently out of the way. Upon further inspection, Rick surmised that the number could triple in size.

Against the curtain of a starless night outside his window, Rick concluded that one of the accountants at Jarvison and Lewis had to be privy to the scam. There was no way Kate could hide that sort of operation for long from a conscientious accountant.

But was the money reason enough to kill Jenny?

Over a pizza and a six-pack of beer, and with a Bureau friend's help, they determined that the embezzling went further back than Rick had originally thought. Careful scrutiny eventually turned up sixty-two thousand dollars that had been funneled through the dummy companies and into Kate's account.

From Kate's bank records, Rick also determined that the money never stayed in Kate's secret account for very long. Kate was either spending the money, or moving it to another, still hidden, account. But why? She co-owned the agency. She could write herself bonuses any time she wanted. All she needed was her partner's agreement....

Exhausted and elated, Rick went home, hoping to shut the books out of his mind. But in the middle of the night, while Rick thought he was asleep, his subconscious took hold of the Garrett case facts and began shuffling them around as if it were playing with a Rubik's Cube. The more his subconscious turned a piece in his head, the easier it was to find the place where it lined up.

"Warren," Rick said, awakening with a start. "Could Kate be moving the money into one of Warren's accounts?"

Over the Sunday morning paper, Rick appraised the notion that Warren and Kate were romantically involved with each other. Rick already determined that Warren's business was in deep trouble, and maybe he was getting money from Kate to keep it afloat? Maybe they *were* lovers? And maybe they realized they could collect a windfall in insurance if Jenny were out of the way.

Two insurance policies to collect on and joint ownership in the agency. Not a bad reason to take Jenny out of the picture.

There was one way to know for sure. Monday morning he would set up surveillance on Kate and learn what she was doing with the money. If it went where Rick suspected, he might catch them in the act and put a lid on this whole case.

****

Dwight sat in a musty, deserted, and very cluttered storage room in the second basement of the University of New York library. Only Dwight and the maintenance men ever came down this far into the bowels of the building. A place long used as storage for university discards and the forgotten, Dwight had been afforded this space to store the thirty-six file boxes that made up the archives for his field of interest. Paranormal investigation never warranted premium space—being a field that few believed in anyway.

Rather than sit at the Garrett house, Dwight was here, sifting through moldering pages of paranormal research dating back to the late eighteen hundreds. This mountain of faded material had, over the years, provided the source for countless fictional ghost stories that saw the light of publication. Funny, when someone tells a ghost story and confesses it as fiction, everyone enjoys it; but the moment someone says, 'this is a true story,' people turn their backs in disbelief.

The thought of it made Dwight laugh. Readers never realized the writer had based his scary story on an actual account documented by a tenacious paranormal investigator, who believed enough in what he was doing to stick with it until he could find at least some basis for truth.

Dwight perused every article available on paranormal phenomena, all the time kicking himself for his laziness about organizing this stuff. Of course, if he lost his grant, he would have plenty of time to spend with these crumbling old papers.

His previous day's research had been fruitless, and for a time, he believed there was nothing left to uncover. But a voice inside his head urged him to persist. Turn that one more page. Open one more folder. He had only an inkling in the very back of his mind of what he sought. But he had to stay with it, for Jenny's sake.

For a moment, his mind drifted away from research and onto the way her eyes sparkled. Her skin had a heady fragrance all its own. Seeing her in his mind's eye stiffened him involuntarily. He shook off the inappropriate excitement and grabbed another thick folder out of the box beside him.

About a quarter of the way into the stack, he uncovered a third article of the kind relating to his quest. This new recurring phenomena convinced Dwight to bury his previous theory of astral projection as an explanation of Jenny's episodes. At first, he thought Jenny's astral body was separating from her physical body, then returning. However, in all documented cases of astral projection, there was never physical contact between the projection and the host.

And Jenny insisted that her image had physically touched her. That physical contact meant that the spectral form was somehow penetrating into the dimension of the living world. The thought sent a shudder through Dwight's bones.

Such an occurrence of physical interaction forced Dwight down a darker path. A path that sent an icy chill through his veins.

The phenomena Dwight now suspected Jenny was experiencing was that of a Doppelgänger—a ghostly image of herself. But beyond a concise definition, he had little else to work with.

Dwight had in hand three documented case histories of Doppelgänger sightings. Each of the claims were studied by paranormal investigators and included verification from other sources. But none of the three had occurred in the second half of this century, and none involved physical contact between spirit and host.

The Doppelgänger episodes, like paranormal research in general, were fleeting and, at best, sketchy. But out of the three studies, Dwight extracted a pattern that sent a coppery fluid into the back of his throat. He swallowed hard to force it back down as he contemplated what was emerging in the case histories.

One case in particular seemed to worm its way into Dwight's head and refused to lie dormant. A yellowed research journal published in London in 1967 contained an article near the rear of the publication that struck an uneasy chord. Written by a Dr. Wilhelm Grayworth, a renowned psychiatrist at the time, it chronicled the case of a twelve-year-old boy, Josef Lukenhan, under treatment for chronic schizophrenia. The boy, however, insisted he was being terrorized by a ghost of himself. The young lad could even describe the manifestation in terms beyond the clarity Dr. Grayworth had ever previously experienced.

In one encounter, the boy was rushed to a nearby hospital after inflicting himself with multiple slash wounds with a hunting knife. The boy, however, claimed that the malevolent ghost had attacked him with the knife.

Throughout the two years of psychiatric treatment, which took place between 1957 and 1959, the lad's terror continued unrelentingly until the death of the boy's father forced the relocation of the family to Vienna.

Dr. Grayworth used the term Doppelgänger at the time only in the sense of indicating an alter-ego personality capable of dominating the boy's psyche. Though the term was never used in the paranormal sense, it did provide valuable clues as to the actual extent of the boy's hallucinatory manifestations.

Again, Dwight realized the rational explanation for a Doppelgänger was a hallucination. And a simple hallucination could put the whole idea of a ghost of a living person to rest without any need for investigation.

Dr. Grayworth justified his rationale citing examples of cases dating back to the early 1900s; though, at no time did he give credence to the boy's claim of an actual spiritual haunting. Instead, Grayworth sought to separate the two personalities inside the boy's mind and enable him to deal with each one individually.

Young Lukenhan, on the other hand, persisted in his claim that the Doppelgänger, or spirit double, had been terrorizing him for four years. Grayworth attributed depression and delusion as the true cause for the Lukenhan boy's schizophrenic tendencies and instead tried in vain to substantiate instead his claim of a new form of schizophrenia.

Dwight scribbled a series of questions on his pad.

Were any paranormal investigations performed to validate the boy's claims? How much more documentation is available relating to this particular case? What ever happened to the Lukenhan boy?

For now, Dwight decided to contact the London office of the International Society of Paranormal Phenomena for more data. Hopefully, they would have a complete file on this case even though it was over twenty-five years ago. If Dr. Grayworth were still living, he might be able to provide bits and pieces that could assist Dwight in his investigation.

As a result of a telephone call he made before leaving the university to return to the Garrett house, Dwight learned the psychiatrist treating the boy died in the late seventies, but he had written a follow-up paper on that particular case. The center supervisor promised a complete package would be forwarded to Dwight within the next few days.

Dwight was elated—until he got into his Voyager and it wouldn't crank. Wishing to avoid losing a whole night at the Garrett house, he had the van towed and borrowed a colleague's car.

He wrestled with the information he had learned and on the drive to New Brighton, decided to withhold what he had learned until he knew more. After all, there was little data to indicate the Doppelgänger really existed in that London case documented back in 1967.

****

Jenny picked at her dinner, complaining to Warren that even though she had slept during the afternoon, she still felt exhausted.

Warren had hoped to get Jenny downstairs into the sitting room for awhile, just to offer her a change of scenery and give him a chance to relax in his favorite chair.

Television bored Jenny, so she clicked it off early and closed her eyes.

Warren used the opportunity to sneak back to his den to check on the trading day in Tokyo, then go out for some fresh air.

In minutes, Jenny fell asleep.

Like water leaking in somewhere, the voices rose out of the depths to torment her.

...get the pressure...we're...
adrenalin...the needle...hurry...

Jenny's heart raced out of control. She felt herself being pulled under, unable to breathe. Something was sucking her down an endless chasm. She snapped up in the bed.

"No," she screamed, her face stripped of life, her lungs gasping for a final, living breath.

Dwight's head popped up from behind his instruments. He rushed to the bed, cradling Jenny in his arms without thinking.

Her cold skin was soaked in sweat.

"You okay?" he asked, pressing her against him in an effort to calm her trembling body. Pulling her closer he sought to keep her warm and safe.

"Oh God..."

"Jenny, it's okay. I'm here."

"Dwight?"

"Yes. Take it easy, Jenny. Everything is okay."

Jenny's breathing slowed along with her heart. She wiped away the sweat and covered her face with her hands.

"Where's Warren?"

"Out. You were asleep. He figured it would be okay as long as I was here."

Jenny closed her eyes and swallowed hard, wanting nothing more than the peace she had known in her life prior to the accident. This torment was slowly, torturously tearing her to pieces. How much longer could she withstand this?

"You want some water or something?"

Dwight released Jenny, albeit reluctantly, once her trembling had subsided. She felt so good against

him that he wished he could hold onto her forever.
He couldn't remember the last time he held a woman
so closely. It was wrong—he knew that—yet he
wanted her. He wanted to be intimately close to her.
When her body was against his, he could feel her
heart beating. Could she feel his heart racing at their
touch?

"Was it...the ghost?" he asked.

"No. Not the ghost. There are voices in my head,
screaming in desperation. I can't force them out; I
can't get rid of them."

"What do they say?"

Jenny repeated the words as she remembered
them and told Dwight she thought one of the voices
was the doctor who had performed the surgery on
her.

"Are you sure?"

"I'm sure."

"It sounds...like you might have somehow...I don't
know how it could be possible...could you be recalling
things said in the operating room?"

Dwight was talking more to himself than to
Jenny. He had heard of cases where patients under
the knife regained some level of consciousness prematurely and were able to actually feel the surgeon
working on their insides. But the effects of the anest-
esia were still sufficiently potent enough to prevent
them from moving or making any sound. The very
thought made Dwight shudder.

Just then, a needle on one of his instruments
started scratching back and forth. Dwight and Jenny
looked first at the bedroom door, then to the instruments and monitors in the corner.

Mr. Chips lifted his head from his place on the
floor, but did nothing more than sample the air with
his snout and return to his shallow sleep. Dwight
tried to read into the dog's actions.

Turning back to Jenny, Dwight could see the
tremors of terror rising up through her body. He

shifted his gaze to his video monitors, which showed a deserted hall and staircase.

Jenny clung to his hand, refusing to release it despite the fact that Dwight rose to return to his monitors.

"It's okay. I'll be right here."

"But..."

Dwight left the bed and returned to his collection of sophisticated gadgetry. His heart was surging. His eyes swept from instrument to instrument trying to catch everything, yet still hide his brimming excitement.

"I'm getting a reading from the den," Dwight said as his hands moved across the knobs and switches on his monitors and recording instruments.

"Warren?"

"No. We would have heard Warren long before he got to the den. The hall sensors would have picked him up."

When Dwight lifted his eyes away from his instruments he saw Jenny clutching her blanket with balled fists. Her eyes never left the open bedroom door.

Stay cool, calm, and clinical, Dwight thought to himself.

A second later his excitement evaporated.

"False alarm. I ran a calibration check on the sensors. The den sensor isn't reading properly. Just a bum sensor. I need to replace it. Will you be okay?"

"S-sure...it's just a b-bad s-sensor."

Dwight flicked the overhead light on and pushed Jenny's bedroom door wide open before going down the hall.

The den was quiet and dark, just as Warren had left it before departing the house. Dwight took the handle and eased the door open. A foreboding chill swam under his skin. The handle was cold to the touch. Without further effort from Dwight, the door continued its arc until it banged against the wall. Something wormed its way deep inside Dwight. The den had taken on a different air from when he had planted the sensors in there earlier.

He quickly slapped on the light switch. The room appeared undisturbed.

Across the expanse of a cluttered desk, situated below a window so Warren could look out without having to leave his chair, the blank screen of a quiescent computer reflected his faint image. On a side wall, just inside the room, newspapers and books had been stacked on a long trestle table.

Warren put neatness low on his list of priorities. Above the table, the sword Excalibur gleamed. Flanking the blade on either side were two armor chest plates.

"A knight in shining armor," Dwight muttered aloud. He wondered if that's how Warren viewed himself. Or was that how Jenny saw him?

Dwight crossed to the desk and scanned for anything that might have triggered the sensor. Nothing. No papers had toppled from the desk to the floor. No teetering pencil had rolled off as a result of vibrations from a passing truck outside. Not one thing rose up to plead guilty for tripping the sensor. Therefore, the sensor must have just failed.

Even the night air was ominously still beyond the window; so still that no branches scraping the glass could have triggered his instrument.

For a long moment, Dwight stared out the window at the night. The shrubbery below sat like black boulders in the inky murk. During that time, Dwight thought about nothing.

"Dwight?" Jenny called out.

"Everything's all right. I'll just need another sensor from my van..."

Then Dwight realized his van was right now sitting in a mechanic's garage. He had no spare sensors on hand with which to replace the faulty one.

Dwight turned to leave, but when he did, he caught something out the corner of his eye on the long table. He went over to check it out. Setting both hands on the table, palms flat, he stared at a magazine page. The model in the picture was the same gorgeous woman he had seen at the Garrett house a few days ago.

Dwight whistled softly, his eyes lingering on the sleek curves of Bridget's body in a full-length black leotard. Her perfect roundness stole every ounce of his attention.

Suddenly, the sword sliced down, stabbing into the soft flap of skin between Dwight's thumb and index finger.

Dwight screamed as blood gushed from the wound.

The force was so great that the point stuck into the table and the blade quivered back and forth.

Dwight's scream spiked terror in Jenny. She fumbled her way out of bed and dashed from the bedroom a step behind Mr. Chips.

Dwight locked his jaw while he worked his bloody hand out from beneath the sword. He stared at the glistening blade while fumbling with his handkerchief to wrap the wound and stanch the bleeding.

Jenny hobbled to the den doorway, supporting herself with a hand on the frame of the door.

"What happened?"

"Nothing Jenny, it's all right."

"You're bleeding..."

When Dwight stepped toward her, she saw the sword sticking in the wood.

"What happened?"

"It's nothing, really. I was just reaching for the sword to get a closer look. It fell from its mounting and nicked me. Nothing to worry about. I just need to get a compress to stop the bleeding."

The uncertainty in Dwight's eyes and a discernible weakness in his voice caused Jenny to question the integrity of his explanation.

"Come on, Jenny, let's get you back to bed now."

Dwight tightened the handkerchief around the gash and then slid his good hand under Jenny's elbow to help her back into her bed.

"I'll change the sensor tomorrow."

Jenny looked back into the den expecting to see more than just the sword stuck in the table.

On their departure, Dwight scanned the den once more. Then he made sure he closed the door tightly.

21

With the morning came Warren's insistence that Jenny and he leave the house so she could convalesce upstate while Dwight remained behind to monitor his equipment and do his 'ghost hunting' in the house. Neither Jenny nor Warren put much stock in Dwight's story about the sword incident. The tip of the blade had buried itself a good inch into the oak tabletop. Warren had to yank hard to pull it free. It would have taken more than just the force of a two-foot fall to stick so deeply in the surface.

Jenny resolved that Dwight had avoided the truth about what really happened. Her ghost had caused the sword to come down into his hand. The spirit was leveling a warning to Dwight.

Warren was also certain Dwight was avoiding the truth. He hypothesized that Dwight, himself, stuck the sword into the table and intentionally cut his hand to keep Jenny from losing interest in her haunting. The guy was nothing more than a charlatan using his gadgets to suck money from them. The shit was going to be damned surprised when he found out there was none.

"You don't understand," Dwight said to Warren when he refused to budge. They were in the kitchen out of range of Jenny. Dwight actually had to take

171

hold of Warren's arm to get him to come about and listen.

"We're leaving," Warren said with finality, jerking his arm free.

"Listen, goddamnit, this spirit is linked to Jenny. That's why it appeared in the hospital and in your home. You can't just go to a motel and think the ghost won't be able to find you."

"I listened to about as much of your psycho mumbo-jumbo as I'm going to."

"I need you here, Jenny," Dwight said. Jenny appeared in the doorway, having descended the stairs by herself while the two argued.

Warren, it seemed, had completely tuned him out.

"For whatever reason, this ghost is tied to you. It is an apparition of yourself. Not only do I doubt that we can be successful if you leave here, but I believe that there's no way you can escape this thing."

"This is absolutely crazy," Warren muttered. "My wife's seeing a ghost of herself, and you're telling me that it's going to follow us wherever we go."

"No. It's going to follow her. This phenomena isn't something that's been dealt with before. We're dealing with something uncharted."

"I can't believe I'm even listening to this," Warren snapped more to himself than to Dwight.

Jenny stood there, torn between the two men in her kitchen. Warren was obviously losing patience with her. She saw it in his eyes, and felt it in his voice. And Dwight seemed more concerned about his work than her safety.

"Please, Warren, just listen for a minute. I've investigated a number of cases where people believe they're seeing ghosts, but I've never been involved in a case where the ghost of a living person is appearing before them. You see, if a ghost is a manifestation of death, then how can Jenny's ghost haunt her while she's still alive? It's a psychic paradox. It's a contradiction to say that the ghost of a person can exist while that person is still alive. At least to our conventional way of thinking."

"Conventional way of thinking? This whole exchange is ludicrous. Now Jenny must remain here while you play with your electronic Tinker Toys, hoping to prove she's not hallucinating."

"It's just until I've had a chance to monitor the environment when she's having a visitation. I'm hoping we'll pick up something that can be used to substantiate her claim."

"Or her hallucination," Warren said.

"If you wish."

Warren left the room *and* the conversation. He aided Jenny back to her bed, seeing the turmoil in her eyes that their heated exchange had brought on. If Jenny wanted to remain, then they would remain.

Dwight spent the next two nights curled up in a sleeping bag on the floor of Jenny's bedroom. For his effort, he had a stiff neck, aching back and headaches that felt like mini-nuclear explosions inside his skull. Nevertheless, his first duty upon opening his eyes was to check his instruments and hope something had gone his way for a change.

One of his instruments, the one with a needle writing to a circular disk, constantly sampled the air temperature in various sectors of the room. Another recorded to magnetic tape the magnetic fields on the entire second floor and could capture the slightest deviation from the initial settings gained during Dwight's first survey.

A third instrument with a round cathode tube that looked like a mini-television tube monitored for infrared radiation and recorded its findings onto a video recording machine set on Jenny's bureau. It had a playback capability that would allow them to view over and over anything they might pick up in the bedroom or hall.

The wires strung about rekindled painful memories of Jenny's weeks in the hospital, of the endless hours lying in that bed staring at nothing. But she had been glad to be alive. Now she questioned whether she really *was* glad to be alive.

With a flood of effervescent warmth from the morning's light, Warren served Jenny a breakfast of waffles with jam, and on his return to the kitchen, found a sleepy Dwight sitting at the table over a cup of coffee.

"I hope you don't mind," Dwight said, indicating the coffee.

"There's a McDonald's three miles down Bunker Road if you're hungry."

"Oh. I didn't think you'd mind..."

"Mind? Why should I mind? You've filled our bedroom with electronic eaves-dropping gadgets, which probably overloaded the electrical circuits up there, and you're sleeping closer to my wife than I am. Why should I mind?"

"I understand how you feel."

"Do you? Let me ask you something. And shoot straight from the hip."

"Okay."

"Do you *really* believe in this paranormal bullshit you're shoveling around?"

"You know, nobody believes in ghosts until they've seen one. Those that have—I mean those that have really encountered an image that defies all our natural laws—believe. The question is: Do you believe in your wife?"

Warren swallowed a sudden rush of guilt at the force of Dwight's question. It forced him to pause and look deeper into himself than he had for many months. The moment of silence lingered between the two. Warren sensed Dwight had not just delivered a rhetorical question.

"Have you ever seen one?" Warren countered.

"No."

"But you believe they exist?"

"Yes. I even once got readings on my equipment that pointed to the notion that something beyond what we can explain..."

"Let's just make sure you understand one thing, Bud. There is no way you are ever going to get a dime out of this. I'll put an end to it the first time you open your mouth—or your hand—for anything but a thank you."

Dwight returned to his coffee, staring for a long time at the dark reflection of two eyes.

Warren busied himself with the mess from breakfast.

"Let me ask you something else. Let's say for some cosmic reason you're right. Jenny is being terrorized by this ghost. What can you do to help her? I mean really help her?"

"Nothing...I don't know if anyone can help..." Dwight answered with deep resignation.

Jenny's scream ripped through the air from above.

Dwight was out of his chair and up the stairs; Warren was a step behind.

"What happened?"

"She was here. She came through there. She looked at me."

Warren was at Jenny's side while Dwight scanned his machines. Warren looked to Dwight with genuine concern. Jenny's body was trembling out of control in his arms.

Dwight shook his head.

"Nothing here."

"I'm telling you she was here. She looked through the wall right at me with her black eyes."

"Jenny, exactly where was she?" Dwight asked.

Jenny pointed to the corner to the left of the chair.

Dwight began sampling the air with a hand-held instrument the size of a calculator. His foot-long

probe collected samples far enough away that it eliminated Dwight's own body as an influence on the
reading.

"Nothing," he said dejectedly, after exhausting
his scan.

"Jenny, was the ghost actually in this room?"
Dwight asked in the way a physician asks a patient
where it hurts.

"What are we, splitting hairs now?" Warren shot
in.

"Yes, I mean no. Her face appeared as if it was
coming through the wall."

Dwight retreated to his equipment, rewound the
video machine and then the tape machine. While he
carefully watched the screen, he listened to a playback through his headset.

"I'm sorry, I've got nothing."

Then Dwight shifted to an oscilloscope screen
while playing back the magnetic field tape. The green
line of light remained perfectly horizontal.

"See Jenny, it was nothing. There's nothing to be
afraid of," Warren said, as if the lack of physical evidence made it so.

Jenny searched Dwight's eyes.

Dwight could do no more than wonder if he had
erred, or if it was impossible to gain tangible proof
that a ghost had inhabited this room a few minutes
ago.

"I'm calling Rosenstein. Let's get you in right
away to talk to him again."

Jenny offered no resistance.

Dwight stared at his readouts, praying to see
something he might have missed.

****

The leather couch in Rosentein's office was the one place Jenny felt most apprehensive about. But lying down was less painful than sitting.

Sy sat beyond her field of vision and asked her to stare at the ceiling. Whether she talked or not, and what she said, was completely up to her. He said it was best to vocalize anything that came to mind.

For ten minutes, Jenny said nothing.

Sy sat in stoic silence and made no movements to distract her.

"It's not a hallucination. I know that now."

"Why do you say that?"

"Because it wants to destroy me. It is bent on killing me."

"Are you saying that is how your arm came to be burned?"

"Yes. That's what I told you before. You don't believe me."

"Jenny, what do you think the ghost represents?"

Jenny was silent. What kind of response was he looking for?

Sy waited.

"Must it represent something?" she asked at last.

"What do you mean?"

"Can't it just be? Can't it just exist on its own?"

"Jenny, were you smoking that night?"

"I told you, I don't smoke."

****

Rick sat on the wooden bench outside Dwight Mackenzie's office door for ten minutes. Then he rose and paced uneasily back-and-forth amid students flowing past on their exodus out of the building. Most leveled a curious eye at a seemingly nervous man in a tie and jacket.

From the midst of the crowd, Dwight emerged and stopped at his office door, shifting a stack of books from one arm to the other.

Rick moved closer, which caused Dwight to fumble with his keys.

Dwight shot him a sidelong glance and guessed him to be an authority figure by the way he carried himself. Most likely a cop or a lawyer.

"Dwight Mackenzie?"

"What do the police want with me?" Dwight responded with his own question, unlocking the door and pushing it open. He, however, waited before starting in.

"Good guess. I'm Detective Rick Walker," Rick said, fumbling for his next line.

Dwight gave himself a silent accolade for knowing his psychology.

"I'd like to ask you a few questions."

"I'm very busy. I don't have much time. Is this about Jenny Garrett?"

"You a psychic or something?" Rick said.

Dwight motioned him in with a casual wave of his free arm.

"No. What's it all about?"

"Once we're inside."

Dwight offered Rick the chair across the desk, while he set his books on the desk between them. Afterward, Dwight slumped into his chair, and as if burdened with a great load, kicked his feet onto the corner of his desk. He lifted his glasses to sit on top of his head and vigorously rubbed his eyes.

"Okay, ready if you are."

"I'd like to know what your involvement is with the Garretts? You family, friend, or something else?"

"Something else."

"And exactly what something else is that?"

"I'm an investigator."

Rick suddenly became alert.

"And you investigate what?" Rick already disliked this Mackenzie guy and figured things could only get worse.

"Paranormal phenomena."

"Paranormal phenomena?"

"That's correct."

"So, you're saying you investigate what with the Garretts?"

"Apparitions."

"Ghosts?"

"If you prefer."

"You're a ghostbuster?"

Rick drove down the urge to laugh out loud; he could see Dwight was serious.

"No. I'm saying I investigate paranormal occurrences for authenticity."

"Okay, what paranormal occurrences are you investigating that involves the Garretts?"

"Mr. Walker, I'd like to know exactly why you're questioning me. I'm not sure it's proper that I continue to answer your questions without knowing the nature of why you're asking them."

"Don't worry, Mr. Mackenzie, it's proper. As far as I know, there is no law of privileged communications for ghostbusters."

"Jenny Garrett believes she being haunted."

"Haunted? By a ghost?"

"Actually, she claims it's a ghost of herself."

"A ghost of herself? What are you saying?"

"I'm sorry, I can see you're having trouble with this." Dwight became sardonic, "I'm saying Jenny Garrett came to me about three weeks ago seeking my help. She believes there is a ghost of herself haunting her."

"And what are you doing about it?"

"I'm investigating. What are you doing?"

"I'm investigating."

Rick was quickly tiring of Dwight's little college-boy game.

"Investigating what?" Dwight persisted.

"I'd like to stay on your investigation for the moment."

"Why? What are you investigating that is so secret? I've been painfully honest with you. The least you can do is be painfully honest with me."

"The circumstances surrounding Jenny's auto accident."

"From what I understand, Jenny lost control of her car and went over a guard rail while coming down a hill. What's there to investigate?"

"Have you found out anything in your investigation?"

"No, have you?"

"Did you know Jenny Garrett before her accident?"

"No. And I really don't know her now. This is strictly a professional inquiry into what she may, or may not, be experiencing in that house."

"Has Jenny spoken to you about the accident?"

"Only to say she has no memory of what happened, nor of the weeks preceding the accident. My primary concern is what Jenny believes she is experiencing at the present."

"Which is?"

"Where am I losing you? This isn't that difficult. An apparition of herself. She also claims that there has been physical contact between her and this spirit."

"And you believe her?"

"Mr. Walker, I believe strong evidence exists to suggest that there is some plane of spiritual existence after death. I'm just trying to find out if there exists some way of confirming that."

"How does Warren feel about your inquiry?"

"Right now he's ambivalent. He wants to help Jenny. I understand she's also under the care of a competent psychiatrist."

****

With a rock-steady arm, Warren helped Jenny out of the car and up the stairs to the front door. Her session with Rosenstein seemed to have plummeted her into a depressed state. There was a distance in her eyes; like she was trying to separate herself from Warren. She intimated with her eyes that somehow she had concluded that he was the bad guy in all this.

The improvement in Jenny's stride was noticeable, though she was still wobbly when it came time to climb the porch stairs. Only Warren's tight hold kept her from stumbling.

Think positive, Warren kept telling himself.

"You're definitely improving, Jenny," he said.

"I know. I think I'm about ready to go solo up to the bedroom, don't you?"

"I think you're pushing too hard. You still have another week before Morrison said you'd be ready for any solo activity."

"Maybe a little at a time."

Jenny smiled.

Warren kissed her, but Jenny pulled away surprised and confused. Warren pretended not to notice.

"I love you, Jenny," he whispered, as if he needed to hear it more than her.

Jenny tightened her fingers around his forearm. Why didn't she feel it? Why had it become so hard for her to say I love you? She realized she had only said it once since coming home. Was Warren trying to get her to say it? Maybe it was time to make love.

That very thought sent a shiver up her spine. But she resisted it. When Warren carried her to their bed, she would let him know she was ready to have him inside her again.

Warren pushed the front door open fully, extending his arm out in a chivalrous salute as Jenny entered unassisted.

"How about tea?" he asked as he hung their jackets in the foyer closet, then rummaged through his pockets for his cigarettes.

"Where's Mr. Chips? Did you leave him outside again?" Jenny asked.

Warren looked guilty.

Jenny paused at the outskirts of the living room, expecting Chips to come bounding off the sofa or, at least, run in from the kitchen.

"I made sure I let him in before we left. Here, Chips!"

"Did you lock him in his cage?"

"No. You know I wouldn't do that. Mr. Chips, come on boy. If that damn dog shit by the kitchen door, I'll..."

Warren stomped into the kitchen, feeding his anger with the thought of having to clean up another one of the dog's foul messes.

But he found the kitchen clean and quiet, just as he had left it.

At the kitchen window, Warren scanned the breadth of the yard, suspecting he might have forgotten about the mutt and left him out in the cold. As guilt rippled down his backbone, he glanced over his shoulder to make certain Jenny was not staring at him. With so many things to juggle, Chips remained at the bottom of Warren's list of responsibilities.

Satisfied that Chips was not left outdoors, Warren put a pitcher of water into the microwave and rummaged through the cupboard for Scottish shortbread cookies. Jenny loved shortbread cookies with tea, and after her distressing visit with Rosenstein, she'd need something to brighten her up.

"Chips, are you down there?" Jenny called from the top of the basement stairs.

Nothing.

She listened with hands planted on her hips to let the dog know she was angry. But the basement door had been closed, and surely Chips would have been scratching at it if he'd been inadvertently locked down there.

"Come on, Chips. Get out here," Warren yelled with growing concern in his voice.

"Not in the basement," Jenny said. She shifted her search upward but remained at the base of the staircase leading up.

"Mr. Chips, you up there?"

No sound came down to her.

"Warren, did you close our bedroom door before we left?"

"No, why?"

"Because I didn't either. The door's closed."

Warren stood with Jenny, gazing up the staircase. The bedroom door was closed.

"I swear, I didn't close the door on the damn dog," Warren pleaded.

Jenny felt a wave of terror sweep through her.

"Mr. Chips, are you up there?" she yelled with a melange of anger and fear in her voice.

"I'll go check."

"No, we'll go check."

With Warren's help, Jenny did the stairs one at a time without incident. They stopped at the bedroom door. Warren also noticed that the door to his den was closed—he never closed that door, not even to sleep. He was hoping though, that the den door might escape Jenny's notice.

When Jenny opened the bedroom door, a rush of cold air that brushed past her on its way into the hall. The far window was wide open. Jenny refused to go in. The window curtains luffed about in the breeze and the room was frigid.

"I didn't..."

"I know," Warren said, moving past her to the window. His chills ran to the very core of his body. And they came from other than the cold air.

Warren grabbed the window handles, stopped, and stared at the ground below. The dog's mangled body lay sprawled in the midst of a bushy copse with a thick limb impaling the animal's neck. Its tongue hung lifelessly at full extension from its mouth.

"Jenny, don't look," Warren said. But it was too late. Jenny was beside him, staring at the scene below.

"Mr. Chips!" she cried out, tears streaming down her face.

"Come on, Jenny, get away from the window. Don't look."

Warren scooped her into his arms, holding her face away from the window while he closed it one-handed.

For a time, Jenny sat under a blanket on the living room sofa, sipping tea while Warren took care of Mr. Chips's remains. He buried the dog under the sprawling elm in the garden. Chips always liked sitting under that tree and chasing the squirrels that taunted him from the safety of its limbs. It seemed only fitting he be laid to rest there.

Neither spoke when Warren returned. He reheated his tea and sat down beside Jenny. She no longer trembled, but neither would she look him in the eyes.

"Don't leave me alone in the house, Warren," she said after a long silence.

For the first time in his thirty years, Warren truly felt the icy chills of pure terror gnawing away at his spine. And he knew in his heart this was something they could never escape by running.

****

Dwight sat in the corner of the bedroom, his mind wandering in a dozen different directions at once. The instruments surrounding him remained silent. A weak glow seeped in around the window drapes while Jenny lay curled in bed under her blanket.

Dwight flicked on his red-filtered flashlight, shining the light across the face of the bank of instruments on his flank. Nothing moved. No variations in sound, temperature or magnetic field.

The hours dragged on.

"Are you awake?" Jenny's voice rose like a beacon out of the still. Her vibrations caused a needle to scratch across a rolling sheet of paper.

"Yeah. Can't sleep?"

"No."

"You frightened?" Dwight asked all of a sudden.

"No. Just can't sleep."

Dwight shifted and, at the same time, switched off his flashlight. Losing the red light had little impact on the dark room. Only the outline of Jenny's form was discernible.

"You think I'm crazy?"

"No. Do you think you're crazy?"

"No."

Dwight watched Jenny shift to face him.

"You think there's any chance you'll get something on one of your machines?"

"I hope so. But we're dealing with uncharted territory."

Silence ensued for a long moment.

"Dwight, what's going to happen to me?"

"What do you mean?"

The pause sent bile into Dwight's throat. He knew what she wanted to know.

"I mean, even if your machine picks up something, it won't help me. Nothing can help me. I know the ghost killed Mr. Chips. I know it is bent on killing me."

"Jenny, let's take this situation one step at a time."

"Dwight, I don't know how long I can last. I'm terrified. This ghost or spirit isn't going to go away. It isn't going to stop, is it?"

"Jenny, can I ask you something?"

"Can it help me?"

"I don't know. Do you feel anything different in your life since the accident?"

"Different in what way?"

"I don't know. If what you're saying is true, that there is somehow a ghost of yourself haunting you, it would seem that there must be a void somewhere? Does that make sense?"

"It could. Maybe that void is my memory loss. Maybe that's why I have trouble remembering things."

Dwight said nothing for a long moment.

Jenny considered how she had felt since leaving the hospital. There was so much different in her life that no one thing stood out over the rest.

"Anything else?"

"I...I have this feeling that there is something missing..."

"When?"

"When I'm with Warren."

"How do you mean?"

"When we got married we were very romantic. He would excite me just holding my hand. But now I don't feel anything inside when we try to be intimate."

Dwight thought for a moment. Her disfigurement could be the decisive factor.

"Could what you're saying be physical? I mean as a result of the accident."

"I don't know. But I have this strange feeling that it has something to do with those two weeks out of my life that I can't remember. Maybe there was a reason why..."

Jenny stopped suddenly as a blurry image raced across her mind. She saw Warren looking at her...in a restaurant. She watched his lips move to form the words, *I am happy*, but she heard no voice.

"I can't feel...love. That's about the best way I can describe it."

"But you can't find anything in your memory that might be the root cause for those feelings?"

"No. I just feel empty inside when Warren kisses me. Does that sound crazy to you?"

Dwight shifted, drawing the sides of his sleeping bag up around his shoulders as he sat cross-legged on the floor.

Could that be it? He wondered while he stared into the darkness consuming the distance between them. If Jenny did somehow become separated from her inner spirit, could she now be feeling the emptiness brought on by that absence in her life?

"What's going to happen to me?" Jenny finally asked, as if Dwight were some gifted soothsayer, who could look beyond the present and see, in a glimpse, the futures of those who asked.

"Jenny, nothing is going to happen to you. I'm here and I'll make sure nothing happens to you."

"Dwight, no one can help me. No one can stop this thing from destroying me, if that is what it intends to do."

"I want you to wipe that out of your mind. We are going to get you through this thing. We're going to find a way to keep you safe."

Even as Dwight said the words, his mind raced back to what he had learned about the Doppelgänger. The Lukenhan boy claimed to have endured four years of torment. How could he tell Jenny? How could he ever confide in her what he really knew?

"We'll find a way, Jenny. I promise..." As Dwight's voice faded into silence, so did his conviction.

22

Rawlings began applying pressure. Rick had to either make the link between Warren and Kate, or shelve that theory and find a fresh way to approach the Garrett case. He theorized that maybe Warren and Kate were involved and both saw the obvious advantage of having Jenny out of the way. The money would be a windfall beyond belief, and then they could be together without jeopardizing a business relationship between Jenny and Kate. If Rick's way of thinking held water, keeping an eye on Kate, and what she did with the embezzled money, could lead back to Warren. Both were still the top two on his suspect list. And they were the only two at the present.

Ensconced in his car from across the street, Rick watched Kate march from her office shortly after eleven. She drove directly to a trendy up-scale restaurant six blocks from the agency.

Rick had ample time to stuff down a hot sandwich at Caulter's, though he would never drop a ten-spot for lunch on his own. *So this was the world of the advertising executives*, he thought. Classy restaurants, eighty-dollar bottles of wine and prime rib for lunch.

From his vantage point, he watched Kate and her male client laugh it up in a corner table. The alcohol flowed as freely as the hand on Kate's thigh under the table. The only way Rick could discern this was a business meeting was by the portfolio that Kate kept referring to while they talked. There was a gentle insistence in the way she kept redirecting her client's hand and interest back to business.

Kate's style impressed Rick. She seemed to be manipulating and controlling the burly, gray-haired gentleman with a lecherous smile and an avocado texture nose. This had to be the closest thing this grub would ever get to copping a real feel from someone as attractive as Kate. Rick became so interested in her skillful defense maneuvers that he missed the telltale signs that their luncheon meeting was about to conclude.

As luck would have it, Kate deterred to the Ladies room, which afforded Rick time to exit and return to his car. As he started his engine, Kate and client pushed through the front doors.

Kate smiled endearingly while shaking the gentleman's hand and marched at a good clip back to her car. Rick pegged Mr. Grub to be high enough on the advertising food chain to warrant a little groping now and then.

It was past two, and for sure, even for Kate, the lunch hour had to be over. It was time to get back to work. But Kate sped from the restaurant in the direction opposite of the agency.

Rick maintained his safe interval, but kept her in sight at all times. He idled away the time trying to second-guess Kate's intentions. A tinge of excitement rose at the thought of Kate meeting Warren instead of returning to the agency. Maybe the old guy had excited Kate's juices and now she needed a little release. Rick knew he was falling into a fantasy and stopped himself short. His conjuring did, although, conjure up visions of Bridget naked on her bed with her arms outstretched for him.

Rick would have never guessed a second restaurant as Kate's destination.

It couldn't be hunger that drove her into the eatery. Rick performed a quick scan for Warren's car. *Please be here*, he thought, almost aloud. Could this be their little afternoon tryst? But Warren's Saab was nowhere in sight. Rick, however, refused to abandon hope.

Kate's sudden stop caught Rick unprepared. He veered through several lanes of traffic to get to the curb and prevent Kate from detecting him. She left her car with the valet.

Left with no alternative, Rick parked beside a hydrant and flashed his badge to the valet attendant on his way by.

"Make sure no one tows it, comprende?" he commanded the confused Puerto Rican valet.

This might just be the break Rick had been waiting for.

Once inside, Rick scanned the bar. Empty, save for a few blue pin-stripped suits nursing drinks. That's where Rick expected to find Kate. But he was wrong.

At the dining room's rear, where the outside light never reached, weary servers moved about, and the clatter of busboys clearing away plates and cups rose over the silence. Rick swept the main dining area with a glance that missed nothing. Kate occupied a corner table with her back to him, browsing over a menu. Rick slid into a chair at the bar in such a way as to keep her reflection in sight using a mirrored wall.

He waved off the bartender. His eyes never left Kate.

Could she possibly be eating again? Unless...she was bulimic and had purged herself and now planned to engorge herself anew.

The thought made Rick's stomach convulse. How anyone could force themselves to vomit was beyond rational thought. But maybe that's the way Kate could indulge herself so lavishly and yet maintain the shape that attracted her client's attention.

A few waitresses scurried this way and that, clearing away the lunch mess, and avoiding the lone woman studying the luncheon fare. A well-rounded, happy-faced waitress finally came over and leveled her pad.

Kate ordered, but right after, she left the table and disappeared into the ladies' room.

Something seemed out of kilter. Rick's first instinct was to wait for her return, but something inside told him to move. He was glad he did.

Kate spent less than a minute in the bathroom. Inconceivable for a woman. But Kate never returned to the dining room. Instead, without looking back, she marched out the front doors as if she were late for an important appointment.

Bada-bing!

Rick realized the anomaly. Kate's coat remained on after sitting down. Did she plan to eat with it on? Ordinarily, she would have removed her coat had she intended to stay. So why the sudden departure?

Rick paused at the front doors. Outside, Kate shoved a bill into the valet's waiting hand, slid into her car and roared away. No way did the entire exchange make sense. Why would the valet have her car waiting in idle for her? Kate's eyes never went back to the doors, so Rick remained confident his presence had gone undetected.

Inside, a young black waitress left the bathroom. Her eyes met Rick's. Guilt was writ across her face.

"Stop right there. Don't move!" Rick delivered with authority while he flashed his badge.

She seemed too frightened to move anyway.

Rick was playing a hunch. The whole set up moved too smoothly to be anything other than a buy. He brought his face inches from the waitress's.

"We have the entire buy that just took place in there on tape."

"Fuck! Son-of-a-goddamn-bitch," the waitress scowled, surrendering a wad of bills and a small bag containing eight balls of cocaine even before Rick asked for them.

God it's easy to catch stupid people. Rick thought as he called in the bust. He wondered how long it would be before the waitress would realize there was no camera in the ladies' room.

The bad news was Rick had to abandon his surveillance until an arresting officer could be called to the scene. But another piece to his puzzle had just fallen into place.

****

Restless as he lay tucked on the floor next to the bureau, Dwight pushed his sleeping bag down from around his neck. Never did he stray beyond an arm's reach of the indicators once everyone in the house had retired for the night.

There was no moon this night to bleed through the cracks in the window drapes. The bedroom was pitch black. Six feet away, Jenny slept; her breathing no more than a whisper.

Dwight thought about her instead of why he was there. What was she feeling? How could anyone, having survived such a terrible car crash and six long weeks in a hospital bed, endure the torment of what had invaded her life? It was all beyond comprehension.

How could the spirit have manifested itself in the first place? Dwight suspected the answers would lie somewhere in those dark places he had yet to uncover.

Dwight was about to turn away from that vision of Jenny sleeping—but he couldn't. Even with the scars, she was more beautiful than any woman he had ever known. The hours he spent close to her were drawing him toward something he knew was wrong. He felt something for her that he shouldn't.

It was insane to fall for her the way he was, she being married and all, but something kept telling him it was right. Finally, Dwight pulled the bag up around his head and forced his eyes closed.

The sound started as a scraping—like a mouse clawing on wood. Then it grew persistently louder; loud enough to jerk Dwight awake. He bolted upright, blinking sight back into his eyes. In the darkness, he could barely discern the bed with Jenny in it.

He stared for a long moment. Jenny never moved. Then he realized that a sound had awakened him. Switching on a penlight, he cast a pale beam upon the magnetic field recorder. The needle twitched back and forth with a voracity he had never witnessed before.

His heart thumped furiously inside his chest. Dwight felt chills crawl up his spine. Breathing became difficult. He swallowed hard as he watched his monitors.

The hall sensor was sending the machine into a frenzy.

Jenny sprang up in bed as if a rope had yanked her upright against her will. Her arms hung at her side like useless rags.

"Dwight," she trembled with undeniable terror.

"Jenny, I'm here. Don't move. I'm getting something outside your door.

"Dwight, she's here. Oh God, please help me!"

"Jenny, remain very still. What do you see?"

"Nothing."

Another one of Dwight's needles began a nervous tick.

"Jenny, is it in the ro..."

"She's in the room. She's at the door!"

Dwight raked his weak beam across the row of instruments on the table. No sounds were being recorded other than their voices; no infrared showed up on the video monitor.

"Are you sure?"

"Dwight, she's coming toward me. Please help me!"

Dwight grabbed his hand-held instrument, snapped in a telescoping probe and began vacuuming air to gather ambient temperature readings.

"She's coming toward the bed."

Despite Jenny's pleas, Dwight thrust the probe near the bed. He watched the temperature gauge plunge. At the sight, his eyes opened wide enough to be visible in the darkness.

"Jenny, I've got it! I've got it!"

Suddenly Jenny flew off the bed like a crumbled rag doll and tumbled into the chair near the door. She dared not oppose this malevolent thing that she held no power against. Her scream sundered the silence in the house.

Dwight slapped on the lights at the same moment Warren broke into the bedroom, his hair disheveled and his pajamas twisted around his mid-section.

The image evaporated in the light.

"Oh God, please no," Jenny cried, no longer able to contain her terror.

Dwight moved from the side of the bed to enter the doorway, sampling air while Warren grabbed hold of Jenny.

"She's gone now," he said.

Warren spun like a madman in a rage and took Dwight's throat in his hands. Spit accumulated in the corners of Warren's angry mouth and his eyes shot fire into Dwight's.

"What did you do, you bastard!"

"Warren, no. He didn't do anything."

The moment hung in the room.

As the rage drained from Warren's face, he released Dwight and returned to Jenny's side.

"Did you see her?" Jenny asked, once she had mustered the courage to bring herself back to her feet.

"No. But I tracked her temperature trail."

"That's how you knew?"

"Yes! Jenny, you said you felt something cold touch you in the night and when you opened your eyes, she was right at your face."

"That's right."

"This spirit is altering the ambient air temperature in whatever space she occupies at the time. I detected her presence by the drastic temperature changes. That's what you felt that night."

"This is crazy...how could she be occupying space?" Warren stammered.

"It's right here on the recorder."

"Are you all right, Jenny?" Warren said.

Jenny nodded, though she felt like someone had taken a knife to her belly and ripped from end to end.

"Look here," Dwight said, displaying for them the paper recording disc where the temperatures changes were recorded. He palmed it as if it were treasure.

"You see these spikes here? These were taken on the side of the bed where you said you saw the ghost. These variances are in excess of twenty-eight degrees. There's no way the temperature in that area would drop that much naturally. Jenny, there *was* something there."

Warren held Jenny, trying to comfort her.

Dwight dashed back to his instruments, where he began video and audio playback. Neither instrument captured anything unusual in the room nor out in the hall.

Then he began replaying the magnetic field changes on the oscilloscope screen. The green phosphorous pattern began to move. Dwight said nothing as he watched the magnetic field changes taking place on the small rectangular screen.

At first, he thought the images he had captured were his and Jenny's. But the traces showed three disturbances with a fourth appearing when Warren entered the bedroom.

"What the hell is really going on here!" Warren screamed, bursting with frustration. He was like a man who had reached the very limits of his own sanity and needed someway to crawl back into the world of the sane.

Was it possible that the spirit generated a magnetic field disturbance just before it appeared? And altered the temperature in the space where it can be seen? But why could Jenny see it when no one else could?

"This means you have proof that the ghost exists?" Jenny asked.

"This means we have a physical way of sensing your ghost's presence. I've never had this happen before. I don't know for sure what it means. I'm going to need time to study this. I have to validate my instruments before I can proceed."

Warren stared at the recording discs from the temperature meter, and even with a cursory examination, he could tell that something had occurred in the room. *If* it hadn't been some kind of paranormal investigator trick.

After Warren helped Jenny return to her bed, he left the light on but closed the bedroom door. Dwight was waiting for him in the hall.

"If you're trying to pull some bullshit on us..." Warren's voice trailed off ominously.

"I watched Jenny go flying out of bed and crash into the chair as if something had tossed her like a rag doll. You think that was some trick bullshit? You think your wife could do that on her own?"

Anger drained from Warren's eyes.

"What are we supposed to do to fight this thing?" he asked finally. There was resignation in his voice.

Dwight remained silent for a long moment. How could he possibly tell them what he believed? How could he possibly frame an explanation that would do anything besides strike terror into their hearts?

"I don't know. All I know is Jenny is right. It was there in her room."

"Could your instruments be faulty?"

"I did a calibration check at the beginning and another when Jenny said the ghost was gone. They're the marks you see here and here."

Dwight stabbed his finger at the two marks on the disc.

"I know the equipment was operating before and after the spectral sighting."

Warren's eyes held fast on the recording.

"I suggest you both try to get some sleep. I'm leaving right away to return to the university."

Dwight gathered his readings from all the instruments, and grabbing his jacket, left the Garrett house in a rush. He had broken through the invisible barrier. He had found a way of detecting a spectral presence. Now he had to document it and get help from his colleagues to understand what he had uncovered.

*****

Rick felt it the moment he walked into the squad room. It was the way people looked when he passed. They greeted him with pasted-on smiles, while their eyes telegraphed danger—*he* was in for it.

Rawlings requested Rick meet him in the conference room first thing. Rick interpreted that to mean it was time to duck—Rawlings had turned on the fan.

There was no doubt in Rick's mind that he had reached that critical juncture in the investigation: either solve it, shelve it, or close it out.

"Update me on the Garrett case," Rawlings barked with a stone face even before Rick had gotten to his chair.

But Rick came prepared with files, notes, theories and anything else that might help his position.

"Both suspects have motive and, I believe, opportunity. The husband still holds the prime spot on the list."

"And the number two is?"

"Business partner."

"Run down the husband first."

Rick's update began routinely, laying out the details of the suspect's background.

"Warren Garrett's business is teetering. He's mortgaged to the hilt and dodging flak from the banks. For the most part, the Garretts were both living off the wife's income. The insurance payoff on Jenny's death was a cool mil...."

"Solid marriage?"

"Uncertain. Jenny's memory is still a problem, and she's not saying much about their relationship."

"So what else..."

"Bridget Sterling, Jenny's friend, intimated that the marriage was in trouble. A number of people commented that Jenny was different prior to the accident."

"But you've still got nothing."

"I suspect the husband is involved with another woman."

"Proof?"

"None. Surveillance has drawn a blank."

"So, the husband's standing in shit up to his ears and boinking somebody else. Thus, he decides to off the wife for the money and the freedom. Let's move on. Number two?"

Rick shifted his file quickly and clumsily to the next section. When Rawlings switched on his indifferent gaze, Rick knew he was in trouble.

"Kate Matheson, the partner, stood to collect a million in insurance and end up with control of the agency. One of the by-products of the articles was that if one partner died, the other got controlling interest automatically."

"So? I don't see criminal intent."

"Kate's embezzling to support a cocaine habit. Goes back more than a year. Maybe Jenny became suspicious. Kate's a tough businesswoman who likes to play in a man's world."

"She like to swing something she ain't got," Rawlings said, intimating her absence of the male organ.

"Maybe Kate figured she'd pop her partner before Jenny could uncover the impropriety."

"Plausible...what's the numbers?"

"Sixty-two thousand to date."

"How'd she do it?"

"Dummy companies."

"So your theory is: she kills Jenny, erases the embezzlement and pockets a million. Hence, no more reason to steal."

"Exactly. I can even go one better."

"Oh?"

"Let's say Kate is Warren's lover. Together they plan to rig Jenny's car. Jenny dies. They get the money, the agency, and the freedom to boink each other's brains into oatmeal."

"You have any tangibles to support that theory? Have you put the business partner and husband in bed together?"

"Not yet. But Kate used Jenny's car in their business. Therefore, Kate had access to the car any time she wanted. But she had no control of Jenny that Friday. I think that's where the husband comes in. His job was to get her to that restaurant after Kate had the car jimmied."

Rawlings leaned back in his chair, gazing at the ceiling.

"So?" Rick asked. He knew the longer Rawlings deliberated, the less chance he had of winning.

"I like your theory. I can see where they might have planned the ultimate murder. But..."

"I just need some more time."

"All right, you've got another week. But I want you to nail that sonofabitch and if you can't, we close it out."

"Then give me more men."

"If you asked to borrow my wife, you'd stand a better chance of getting her over more men assigned to this case."

Rick laughed; so did Rawlings. The clock had been restarted.

"Next time we meet, show me the string tying this case together. No string, then we close this out as accidental and move on with our lives. Now that the little girl has regained consciousness and is out of danger, we're getting less pressure from above," Rawlings offered as his last words before he left the conference room.

At least something good had come out of this so far.

23

Rick stopped his Cavalier safely down the road from the Garrett house. The natural curve of the pavement kept him out of sight. He sat there for a long time, knowing what he had to do might become very painful for Jenny. But the fact was, he was out of options. Her memory loss became the one crucial factor he had failed to account for when he began his investigation. It is impossible to predict a person's reaction, Rick cautioned himself.

He pulled into the Garrett drive and parked behind Warren's Saab. This was the point of no return.

Rick just knew he had to go for it. In the back of his mind, he hoped there would be no one at home in the Garrett house—that would give him an out.

Warren, however, answered the door promptly.

"Morning, Detective," Warren said, waving Rick inside. His cigarette clung to his lips as if it had been glued there.

"I'd like to speak with Jenny if I could."

"Oh sure, I'm thinking about installing a revolving door. Upstairs. Pay no attention to the equipment in her room. It's nothing."

Warren laughed maniacally as he followed Rick up the stairs.

"How is she feeling these days?"

"Better."

Again Warren released an odd giggle.

Rick found Jenny sitting at the edge of her bed, staring blankly out the window. His eyes immediately caught Dwight's and held them.

"Am I intruding?"

"Oh no, Detective Walker. Come in. Dwight is just..."

"Ms. Garrett..."

"Jenny, remember."

"Jenny, I'd like to ask you some follow-up questions about the night of your accident."

"But I still..."

"And I was hoping to ask your indulgence in something that might help me."

Rick paused for a moment.

Dwight got the message. He slipped out of the bedroom, closing the door behind him. Warren stood just inside the room with his arms wrapped across his chest.

"I'd like you to return to the road...the scene of the accident."

"Oh."

Jenny eyes became uncertain; her skin paled at the very thought. She searched Rick's eyes. There was something in her look that ignited the detective's concern.

"It might help you recall that night."

Jenny was silent as she weighed the ramifications of Rick's request. Did she *want* to know what happened?

"Did the little girl...die?"

"No. She's out of the coma."

"Then she's going to be all right?"

"Looks that way."

At least no one had died in her accident, Jenny thought to herself.

"I realize that doesn't change your investigation, though."

"That's correct. Please, if you'll just help me, Mrs. Garrett."

Jenny looked to Warren.

"Why?" Warren asked.

"It might help her remember."

Warren stumbled for an objection. He found none that he could vocalize on short notice.

Jenny stood up and went to the closet.

"I'll get my coat," Warren injected.

"No, Mr. Garrett, I'll be taking Jenny alone. I think it might help us learn more about what happened that night."

Rick saw a sudden raw fear welling up in Jenny's eyes. She hesitated at the closet as if she had been suddenly struck by panic.

"I'll get into warmer clothes then."

"Sure, I'll be downstairs. I promise not to keep you long."

"Jenny, you don't have to go. If you're not up to it," Warren said. His tone turned cautionary.

"No, Warren, I want to go. Maybe it will help."

"I don't like this. I think we should consult Dr. Rosenstein."

Rick was sitting in the only comfortable chair in the living room—Warren's favorite—and paging through his notes when Warren came down the stairs.

Warren went right to the telephone.

"This is Warren Garrett. I must speak with Rosenstein now."

Warren glanced back at Rick while he waited.

"Yes, it is imperative. No. Tell him it concerns Jenny."

Warren rotated the mouthpiece away and turned to face Rick, who looked up in response.

"I think I should check with a lawyer before you do this."

"You feel a need to have a lawyer present?" Rick asked suspiciously.

"Yes, damnit, it's an emergency," Warren spat back into the phone.

After Warren said it, he realized he had said those same exact words before. Rosenstein must be thinking he, too, was turning into a nut case.

Rick listened while Warren explained his intent to the doctor. Rick watched Warren's face drop.

"He wants to speak with you."

"Detective Walker," Rick said, then listened while Rosenstein counseled him. All Rick understood after their brief exchange was that Jenny's condition was tenuous and that he mustn't force her to face too much this soon. Patience would yield greater results than rushing her beyond her ability to cope right now.

Rick agreed, promising to keep their excursion as passive and non-threatening to Jenny as possible.

Plainly said, Rosenstein told Rick to back off if Jenny showed any signs of extreme anxiety. Rick promised he would.

Warren's eyes burned into Rick.

"I'm still against this. I demand that I accompany her."

Methinks the man doth protest too loudly, Rick thought. What was he afraid of? Something that Jenny might remember? Something that could lead Rick right to Warren? A sudden thought wormed its way to the front of his mind. Was Warren driving the car following Jenny that night? If he was, did he nudge her enough to send her out of control and over the guard rail? Might Jenny remember seeing Warren's car in her rearview mirror that night?

"Mr. Garrett, Jenny must be free of outside influence during this process."

"And if I refuse..."

"I don't think you want to do that. I think you want to just let me do my job, so we can get this whole investigation over with. Anything you do to obstruct this case would only reflect poorly upon yourself."

Jenny descended the stairs on Dwight's arm.

Warren's face flamed over in anger.

"Warren, it's all right. I can handle it."

Warren was quick to steal Jenny's arm from Dwight.

"Will you still be here when I get back?" she asked of Dwight.

"No. I'm going back to the university. I've left all the monitors set and ready. If for any reason I don't return tonight, I will see you early tomorrow morning."

"I'm ready, Detective," Jenny said, though inside she doubted she could ever really be ready to face what lie ahead.

Jenny remained quiet, as did Rick, the entire forty-minute drive to Diamante's. The road that led to the restaurant wound and turned like an asphalt snake had been wrapped around the bulging earth. The view on the summit was spectacular, which was why the restaurant had been perched there a decade earlier.

Rick approached the building using a back road, allowing Jenny to see that stretch of downhill pavement exactly same way it appeared to her that night.

The restaurant parking lot was empty when they arrived. Diamante's opened at four and only served dinner. Rick stopped the car just inside the lot, shifted into park and opened his notebook.

"You left here about nine forty-five."

Jenny nodded, but looked away from him.

"Do you remember?"

"Do I remember that night? No."

Rick slid the shifter down to drive, accelerated, and wheeled right to ease onto the road that led back down the hill. Like a tour guide, he described his every movement as if it were that night and Jenny was the one behind the wheel.

Ahead, the road rolled down to the right at a five-degree bank and disappeared.

"I'm at twenty miles an hour right now. I know from your driving record that you were prone to excessive speed. Do you feel anything, Jenny?"

As they rounded the curve, Rick saw the glistening new section of guard rail installed as a result of Jenny's accident.

Jenny suddenly lurched back in her seat, digging her nails into the padded dash. She gasped to get hold of a breath.

"What happened here?"

Rick coasted over to the shoulder and stopped.

"I don't know. I just felt...I don't know." Jenny began to cry, burying her face in her hands.

"Jenny, tell me what happened here. You remember something, don't you?"

"I...don't know what happened. I don't know what I did. But I felt something when we came around that bend."

"What did you feel?"

"Like I was out of control."

Rick eased the car forward closer to the exact spot where Jenny collided with the oncoming car that night. There were still lingering tire marks and oil stains. However, the new section of guard rail reflected the sun like a mirror.

"Please, Jenny, I need you to look. I need you to try..."

Slowly, Jenny removed her hands from her face. It was there before her eyes. The place where she...

"Think hard, Jenny. Please. I need your help."

"I'm sorry, Detective, I just can't remember. It doesn't exist for me. Can't you understand?"

Jenny's voice took on a quiver. Tears erupted from her eyes.

"Okay, Jenny. I understand. It's okay."

Rick rolled back onto the pavement, accelerating to get down the winding road and away from the scene.

"I was just hoping you could help me, that's all."

"But why? Wasn't it an accident? Why are you so driven to do this to me? What did I do?"

"Jenny, I have reason to believe that your crash may not have been an accident."

"What?"

"Can you think of any reason why someone might want you dead?"

Rick found himself choking on the question.

Jenny's mouth hung open in disbelief. What was he saying?

"No! That's crazy. It had to be an accident."

She thought she had done something terrible that night. She thought it was her fault. Now he implied something totally different.

Rick knew he had to stop. His words were overwhelming Jenny. She stared at him as if she were looking through him. He had to wait for his words to register inside her.

"What are you saying?"

"I have to look at your case from every possible angle. Even the possibility that someone tried to kill you that night."

"I can't believe you could possibly think something like that. Who would have a reason to want me dead?"

"You're sure? Could there be something, anything, you can remember that might help us?"

"Don't you understand? I can't help you. I can't remember those days. I can't remember the night of the accident."

"Jenny, we know your car had been tampered with mechanically. Someone rigged your car to fail on this road. What we don't know is who and why. Who else used your car?"

"Warren. Kate. Even my secretary used my car when I needed her to run an errand for me."

"Who else? Anyone else?"

"I can't think of anyone else. Bridget might have borrowed my car."

"When?"

"In August...early August. She had a remote shoot and her car was in the shop, so I let her use mine and I used Warren's."

Rick shrugged. Whoever rigged Jenny's car to fail had to have done it just prior to that night. Most likely, the day of the accident or the day before.

"Did anything unusual happen during that week? Jenny, think hard. Try to remember."

Jenny's grimace told Rick she could handle no more of his questions. She couldn't remember. And Rick had played his last card.

****

As Jenny slept that night, the voices kept replaying inside her head with growing voracity. Like knives furiously stabbing her again and again, the words tormented her. Twice she awoke drenched in sweat with her heart hammering out of control. She called out for Warren, but her words went unheard. Or he chose to ignore her cry. She knew not which.

Dwight failed to return from the university, and for the first time in a week of nights, Jenny was sleeping alone in the room. Yet even in abject solitude, there was no yearning inside her for Warren.

His patience surpassed a saint's. No other man would have endured Dwight and those crazy machines for this long. So why could she not make love to Warren? Why did the very thought of intimacy send waves of fear through her?

In the darkness, she ran her hand along the sheet where Warren should have been. A tear emerged from her eye, felt but unseen in the night as it rolled down her cheek.

Jenny closed her eyes and attempted to find her way back into the soothing comfort of sleep.

But the voices returned. This time angry and snarling at each other.

Damn you, take care of the bag...

I can't get a pressure...where's the...

"Please leave me be!" she yelled at the quarreling monsters inside her head. She pulled her hair in frustration, wishing that could somehow force them out of her life.

They stopped for now. But Jenny knew they would return. They, too, slept—only to awaken again to torment her further.

****

By four o'clock that afternoon, Rick stood on aching knees, ready to abandon his search. It was cold, drizzling, and for the past five hours, fruitless. He and Dugan, along with six uniforms, had covered Diamante's parking lot nine times, and still they turned up nothing.

If the restaurant owner had his lot swept by a contract sweeper, they might have lost the single most important piece of evidence Rick could have hoped for in the Garrett case.

Even Dugan, the champion of the cause, was getting testy. He was an inside man who disliked being out in the elements more than he disliked his wife's bitter coffee. His smile had fled his face hours earlier, along with his enthusiasm and his faith that they would ever find what they sought.

"Come on, Duggie, one more pass," Rick said, folding a stick of chewing gum into this mouth. A hot cup of coffee would have tasted better right now, but that had to wait until they called it a day. Of those involved in this detail, Rick was the one who had to stay with it. He needed to find that one piece of evidence. At least, that's what he kept telling himself.

Two cars parked in the farthest corner of the lot, owned by restaurant employees inside, were the only barriers to a complete and thorough search. But one of the uniforms laid on his rain gear to search even those inaccessible places.

Diamante's was the kind of place where you went for only the finest foods and spirits. And don't forget to bring your platinum card, because you can't carry enough cash to eat there.

"How 'bout we give it up?" Dugan said, refusing to leave the side of the squad car now holding him up. He blew repeatedly into his hands, hoping to stimulate circulation back into his aching fingers.

"I think we're dead right on this one, and I'm not giving up until we find what we came here for," Rick persisted.

"And if it doesn't exist?"

"It does. You're the one who convinced me it does, remember?"

"How did I do that?" Dugan said with a genuinely puzzled face.

"Your demonstration."

"Say what?"

"What happened when you struck the top of the bolt with the hammer?"

"It popped off?"

"Where did it go?"

"Flying into Rawlings. I think I pissed him off with that. You don't think I could have planned that, do you?"

"You pissed him off all right. But until last night, I failed to realize that you were giving me a clue. The most important fact was that the head of the bolt flew off. So before going into the restaurant that night, Warren went to Jenny's car, lifted the hood and popped the bolt with a hammer. Hell, it was his car, so even if someone questioned him, it would appear innocent enough...."

"It would have went flying."

"*Exact-o-mundo*, Duggie. Warren had two choices at the time. One: search for it and remove any evidence of tampering...or two: let it go, figuring no one would ever think to go back to the scene to find it."

"Man, Walker, you're beginning to sound like a desperate man."

"Hey, it fits. Somewhere around here he had to put the final piece together for his murder plan to work. And if he did, maybe he forgot to take the most important piece of evidence with him."

"All right. One more pass. But you're buying me dinner, steak and lobster, whether we find it or not."

"Can't tonight, Duggie, got a date."

"Get out of here! I heard you were doing push-ups over some model. But I didn't believe it."

"How 'bout we find what we came here for, and I'll buy you dinner tomorrow night."

"Ten-four, it's your case, and you're the boss on this one. Hey, you two, pan out over there," Dugan yelled when the officers began to cluster and chit-chat.

Duggie abandoned his leaning post and trudged his aching feet down toward the south edge of the spacious lot of the restaurant. On any weekend night, this place was usually full and remained full until after ten.

"You think we even stand a ch..." Dugan started.

"Bingo!" A uniform yelled from the corner closest to the building itself. Without thinking, he bent down and retrieved the object that had kept them out there for so long.

"I think I found what you're looking for."

The uniform's only mistake—he was a second-year patrolman who didn't know better—was that he picked it up. Rick would have preferred it be left in its position, especially if the location bore some relevance to the case. But at least they had it. A physical link to the crime—if it matched up.

"Thank-you, God," Rick whispered.

Dugan examined it and crowed his approval.

"Bag it and let's go home," Rick said.

They had located the sheared-off head of the sta-bilizer strut mounting bolt that came from Jenny's car. Now, if it matched exactly with the shaft already in evidence control, they had a case.

"I'll go to work on it first thing in the morning," Dugan said, already tasting the steak he was going to order.

****

Rick appeared at Bridget's door promptly at seven, all clean and perky after a long, tedious day in the rain. Even though he was dog-tired, the thought of being with Bridget gave him an invigoration that erased all he had gone through earlier.

Bridget's warm smile and wet kiss removed the chill lingering from the weather. She was ready and waiting for him. With a gentle amorous squeeze, she put her arm in his as they left the building and never once hid the excitement in her eyes.

Rick felt like he was strolling on top of the world. He wanted to introduce the gorgeous girl on his arm to everyone they passed.

The restaurant, though crowded, was quiet and the light subdued. Rick and Bridget took a corner booth and ordered a bottle of California wine. Bridget giggled giddily when she drank, and Rick loved to lis-ten to her. It was the kind of laughter two lovers share in the dark in their bed. Between bouts of gig-gling, Bridget droned on and on about her latest mod-eling assignment: a boring fashion shoot for a mail-order women's fashion house. It was small potatoes as assignments went, but it paid the rent.

"You're not listening to me," she said seductively, when she noticed Rick's attention wandering off into another time zone.

"Am I getting boring?"

"No. Sorry, I'm wrapped up in other things. Go ahead, I'm all ears," he apologized and reached out to take her hand.

She surrendered it, reaching over to kiss him. But even after that, his mind still seemed elsewhere.

"I'm not wearing underwear," Bridget whispered.

"I'm sorry, what?" Rick asked, embarrassed that he allowed his mind to think about anything other than her. The worst way to insult a woman is to communicate to her that she is failing to hold your interest.

"We can go, if you want," Bridget offered.

"No. It's okay. Sometimes work gets a stranglehold on me."

"You still investigating Jenny's accident?"

"Yes."

Wafting cigarette smoke forced Bridget to cough as it drifted lazily over the back of their booth. The restaurant appeased their limited smoking clientele by providing a smoking section in one corner. The grayish streamers lingered like an ominous fog over their heads, rising as it neared the updraft of the burning candle on their table.

Bridget's eyes crossed, her mouth tightened into a thin angry line, and her hand moved, flagging down the waiter and dispersing the noxious fumes at the same time.

"Excuse me," she started, rising out of the booth to get her head above the silk ferns behind her. "Would you mind putting that vile, disgusting thing out?"

The barrel-shaped Sicilian gentleman put the cigarette back to his lips with a sinister smile and puffed in open defiance. His eyes held Bridget's in a way that let her know he had no intention of even considering her request.

"You talking to me?" he asked with a New Yorker's caustic bite.

"Yes. You, the fatass, blowing the smoke."

"This is a smoking area, and if you don't like it, you can suck squat, Toothpick Lady with the pointed head!"

"Yes, Madame?" the waiter asked with his thick French accent and genuine concern as he stepped between Bridget and the Sicilian. The waiter's eyes went immediately to the smoke rolling in over the booth.

"We said non-smoking. What the hell is going on?" Bridget said angrily. The fire in her eyes out-shone the glowing end of the cigarette.

"I'm sorry, this was all that was available. It is non-smoking. But you are on the border, so to speak."

"Yeah, so there, you peanut brain," the smoker said with unfettered sarcasm.

Rick rose out of his seat to level his badge over the booth.

"Up yours, you shit," Bridget mumbled more to herself than for the Sicilian's benefit.

"Can you move us?" she said finally to the waiter.

The smoker receded to the corner of his booth and heeding the gravity of Rick's badge, pressed his cigarette out in the ashtray.

Rick reached a hand across the table to bring Bridget back into the booth and next to him. He said he didn't mind, but Bridget pulled away, leveling a glare at the waiter.

In a nervous frenzy, the waiter tapped his pen upon his order pad while feigning an intense search across the breadth of the restaurant.

"I am so sorry, but we are full in non-smoking. I do have a table open in the opposing corner, but it is not only in smoking, it is also next to the kitchen doors."

Rick waved him off.

As the waiter retreated, Bridget leaned to Rick, "He can kiss his tip good-bye," she whispered.

When the dust settled, it was that detective's never-resting instinct rising up out of the depths that interrupted Rick. Something about that smoking incident alerted Rick's well-honed instincts. Bridget's intolerance had struck an uneasy chord. Now Rick sat there staring, trying to determine why.

"What? You'd rather give him a tip?"

"No...nothing," he said, realizing his stare was unnerving.

"I loathe cigarette smoke...almost as much as I loathe rude and condescending people," Bridget offered in response to his look.

Rick, for another long moment, remained silent.

"But...Warren smokes. That doesn't bother you?"

"Not usually. He's great about refraining when I'm with them."

"But you're friends with Kate and she smokes. Did she smoke at college?"

"Yes. Actually Warren's the one who got her going on cigarettes, if I remember correctly."

Rick sat back. Why did *that* bother him so?

"I think our friend will refrain until after we've eaten," Rick said finally, forcing thoughts of the case out of his mind and commanding himself to pay more attention to Bridget.

"Hel-lo. This is New York. You really think he'll refrain?"

Bridget wrinkled her nose.

Rick pushed and pulled on Bridget's statement, massaging it in hopes of making it reveal its hidden meaning. What was it about Bridget that now raised a red flag at her comment?

"You said Warren started Kate smoking. When was that?"

"When we were in school. We were all college 'coolies,' you know, try anything and everything at least once. Kate was dating Warren when..."

Rick leaned forward with rising interest, moving closer to Bridget. But for a reason other than what entered Bridget's mind.

"You didn't know?" she asked.

"Kate never mentioned that she knew Warren other than through association with Jenny."

"Oh no, Warren dated Kate at Cornell. That's how Jenny and Warren got together. I mean...that's not what I mean. Jenny and I met Warren through Kate."

"How long did they go together?"

"I...ah...sophomore year. Most of sophomore year. Then they broke it off."

"Did Warren begin dating Jenny right after breaking up with Kate?"

"Rick, you're sounding like a detective now."

"Sorry, it's my job."

"Oh, then this is official or unofficial?"

"I'm afraid it just became official."

Bridget pouted, delaying her answer to Rick's question. Even pouting, she was irresistible.

"They started dating a few months after Warren broke it off with Kate."

"You said Warren broke it off with Kate."

"Yeah, I guess so. I haven't really thought about that. It's been, what, six years now. Why?"

"Just routine. Kate never mentioned any romantic associations with Warren, that's all."

"Oh, we're talking about romantic associations now. Is that what we're having? A romantic association?"

"No, I didn't mean that."

"Good. Because I'd call what we're having more like great sex than a romantic association."

Rick blushed; the waiter was standing silently beside Bridget with two steaming plates of steak and lobster.

24

Deliciously hot splashing water invigorated Rick, and made him forget that he had just pulled himself out of bed after only two hours sleep. It also softened what awaited him at the precinct. He was *way* too old for something like this.

There were just too many unknowns in the Garrett investigation to make a solid case, he thought. If he just had one strong piece of physical evidence or one witness who could point him in the right direction, he could make some progress. But like so many other cases that had been handed to him, he was working on the dark side of ignorance. Now his day of reckoning loomed just over the horizon.

"Eggs and toast okay for you?" Bridget asked, popping her head into the bathroom. She waited, taking in all of Rick's lean body through the clear stall door.

She fought down the urge to drop her robe and slip in there with him. She knew, however, neither could handle more sex. Bridget was pleasantly surprised that men of Rick's age could still perform the way he did last night.

"Great," he called out.

The steam accumulating in the glass caused Bridget to remain unaware of the broad smile painting his face. Something that had long been absent from his life. Nor could she see the churning inside his head.

Rick dressed quickly and took a minute to clean his mess in the bathroom. Before leaving, he even made sure he lowered the toilet seat. Then he changed his mind, concluding that he might be trying too hard. He raised the seat back up and tossed a wet towel ball under the sink. Now that looked like the normal male aftermath of a shower.

He toweled his hair dry while strolling into the living room, his mind still ruminating over his next step in the Garrett case. They had locked down the method with the sheared bolt. If only he could connect Warren to it, he could bring him in. It would all be circumstantial anyway, but sweating Warren under the threat of a long prison term could yield a confession.

Bridget hummed in Disneyesque fashion as she fluttered about the galley kitchen wearing nothing more than Spandex. As she leaned over the stove, Rick watched her body sway with gentle seduction. The urge to touch her proved too much to resist. Rick slid his hands around her waist and gently eased her back into him, softly kissing the nape of her neck.

Bridget ceased all movement, lavishing in the thrills his lips shot into her head.

"If you don't stop, I can't be held responsible for what I might do," she cooed. "And you don't want to be late for work, do you?"

"I'm already late."

Rick released her, albeit reluctantly.

"I hope you like scrambled, that's all I know how to make. And I don't have any juice."

"Scrambled's fine. Coffee's perfect. Juice is for pansies anyway."

Rick settled in at the glass-top table, poured himself a steaming cup of coffee from a carafe sitting before him, and watched Bridget glide back and forth in the kitchen, transferring her creation from the frying pan to a china plate. She garnished the eggs with a slice of tomato and thin slivers of green pepper.

Was this a dream? Or was it real? And more importantly, how did he go about making this permanent?

"I noticed your shower's got a leaking hot water valve."

"I know. I've been meaning to fix that."

"Can't you get building maintenance up to take care of it? That's wasting water and energy."

"Well, thank you, Mr. Ecology. This is a condo. I either fix it myself, or I give a plumber my arm and leg."

"I'll fix it for you...if you let me choose the body part for payment."

"Then I'd owe you."

Her smile was engaging, yet mysterious.

"Oh..."

"I'll fix it tomorrow. I'm free for the rest of the week."

"You're going to fix it yourself?" Rick asked incredulously.

"Does that sound incredible to you?"

"I just never thought..."

"Oh, you figured with these gorgeous looks and luscious body, there's no way I can have a functioning brain?"

"That's not what I meant."

Bridget turned stern, which put Rick on the defensive—and she loved it.

"Believe it or not, Mister Macho Police Detective, I know about plumbing, electricity, and a little bit about cars."

"Get out of here."

"Swear to God. On our farm, my father believed in total self-reliance. You never pay someone else to do something that you should be able to do yourself. And my father, I think, viewed me as a boy without a penis. I learned how to fix a leak, replace a light switch, and tune up a car."

"Really?"

"Absolutely. My oldest brother and I owned a stock car for a while. He raced at a local clay track."

"*You* drove a race car?"

"Never said that. I paid half the bills and watched him drive. But he taught me a few things about cars in the process. Mainly to justify the checks I kept writing for new engines and transmissions."

"He ever win?"

"Got a third once. Then he totaled the car and I pulled out. Seemed like the only one having fun was him."

Bridget set her slightly runny egg creation before Rick and watched for his response. She detected the stoic tolerance of a lover in his eyes. She should have gone with something out of the freezer instead.

Rick smiled appropriately, but his eyes were the true harbingers of his feelings.

"They taste better than they look," she offered in defense.

"I guess I'll just have to trust you."

"Oh, I like that."

Rick devoured his eggs, using the toast as a means of absorbing some of the yoke, but his eyes were always on Bridget as she sat across from him, picking at her breakfast.

"I don't like owing people, especially a man."

"And that's important to you?"

"You live alone, you become self-reliant. I'm glad now my father forced me to be so involved."

"So I guess that means you want to wear the pants in the family?"

"Not at all. I'd be happy to let my husband take care of things. But until then, I handle my life myself."

That didn't surprise Rick.

"Now, can you get away for lunch tomorrow? We can eat in the park."

****

Rick stood at the proverbial fork in the road. Decision time. Either Kate was, or was not, a suspect in the attempted murder of Jenny Garrett. And Rick knew there would be only one way to find out for sure—sweat it out of her.

It was late afternoon. A brisk wind scattered papers and trash along the sidewalk outside, while inside the police station Kate had been placed in a soundproof room with a silent female officer standing at the door.

Rick had asked Kate to come in for some follow-up questions without revealing to her any inkling of his real intent.

Kate was completely blindsided when Rick placed her in what he called the witness room. She knew from the movies that witnesses don't get locked into interrogation rooms with guards. She lit a cigarette without asking for permission, assuming it was allowed by the ashtray on the table.

Between puffs, she kept her arms folded across her chest in a cold, unapproachable way, keeping her back to the policewoman. In time, her determination softened and she fumbled with her cigarette, tapping it incessantly on the rim of the ashtray.

Rick remained alert for telltale signs from behind the mirror. He wanted to let her stew for a while before starting. Each minute alone broke down her resistance by an equal amount. Though he suspected it wouldn't take terribly long to break her down.

Kate had been sitting for more than an hour and had given up on badgering the policewoman for information.

The room's silence seeped into her very core. Only Kate's own thoughts kept her from raising a ruckus. What the hell was all this about anyway? She was tired of waiting. She took to checking her watch every few minutes. Time was vitally important to her, and this detective was definitely pissing away plenty of it.

Circles rimmed Kate's eyes, her cuticles were battered and red, and her attempts to hide her nervous tremor failed miserably.

Time to go.

Rick entered with a file folder and a hard edge to his face.

"I'd like to know why I've been kept waiting for more than an hour," Kate demanded, checking her watch, then noticing Rick's cold, level eyes.

"Sorry about the delay," Rick offered placatingly, then he set the folder down on the table before him. He eased his chair closer to Kate, deciding to invade her personal space right from the outset. He hoped it would cut down his interrogation time. Kate already exhibited the first signs of cracking under the pressure.

"Why am I here?" Kate asked, rising out of her chair. This was to be no follow-up interview and she knew it.

"Please, Ms. Matheson, just relax; we'll get this over as quickly as possible."

"Get what over with?"

"I just need to ask you a few questions."

"About what?"

Rick withheld his answer. Instead, he paged through his file, rolled a stack of sheets over the top, and then began clicking his pen repeatedly.

"Ms. Matheson, if you don't mind my saying, you look a bit ragged today. Are you sleeping okay?"

Kate combed her fingers through her hair, reaching into her purse for a mirror.

"You think it's easy keeping a struggling agency afloat? I'm handling both mine and Jenny's accounts. You know how long she's been out?"

"Of course I do."

"Great. So what is this about? Can't this have been handled at my office, where I could have been working while I was waiting for you?"

"I don't think you would have wanted this done at the office."

Kate rubbed her hands together in a nervous way. Her throat turned cottony and dry. She struggled in a vain attempt to clear it.

"Can I get you some water?"

Rick motioned the policewoman. She left and returned a minute later with a pitcher and a cup.

"Thank-you, Chatty," Kate said.

The ice water soothed her throat, but did little for her nerves.

"I really demand to know what this is all about."

"I think you know what this is about."

Kate took to fidgeting with her purse. She wrapped the straps around her fingers in order to avoid Rick's eyes and conceal what they sought to reveal.

"I'm sorry, Detective, but I haven't the foggiest fucking idea what you're talking about."

"Well, Ms. Matheson, we should start with embezzlement. You know, taking money that is not properly yours. Stealing."

"Are you serious?"

"Very. But having said that, what I really want to talk about is cocaine. Because I think that's where the embezzled money goes."

Kate feigned surprise, while at the same time trying to hide the guilt rushing out of her eyes.

Rick had hit the right nerves. Now all he had to do was force open the spigot and let Kate reveal her involvement in Jenny's accident. A momentary triumph coursed through his veins.

"But that's not what I really want to talk about, either."

Rick allowed Kate a moment to react. He deciphered the confusion in her eyes, and it sent a sick rumbling through his gut. That one sustained look chipped away at his confidence.

"What I really want to talk about is Jenny Garrett's accident on September fifteenth."

"What has that got to do...with anything?"

After Kate spoke, her mind began to assemble the insinuations harbored within Rick's statements.

"Embezzling is a serious matter. But not as serious as attempted murder."

"Attempted murder!"

"Now that I've got your full attention, Ms. Matheson, let's talk. Where were you on the evening of September fifteenth?"

"I...ah...I was at the Concord hotel."

"For how long?"

"The entire night."

"And someone can confirm this."

"My boyfriend. But you're insinuating that I had something to do with Jenny's accident."

"When was the last time you drove Jenny's car, prior to the fifteenth of September?"

"I don't know..."

Kate paused, racing through her memory in search of something that seemed trivial to her. From Rick's granite expression, it was vitally important to him.

"We shared the cars. I drove hers when I needed it, and she drove mine."

"When was the last time you drove Jenny's car?" Rick hammered the question into her.

"At least two weeks before the accident."

"You're sure?"

"Sure? I never really thought about it."

Rick notched the burner to high.

"You can stop me at any time and we'll wait for your attorney."

"What? You're accusing me of having something to do with Jenny's accident?"

"The problem is, Kate, it was no accident, and *you* know that. I just want to know how you set her up."

"How can I know that? I had nothing to do with anything."

Kate clung to the edge.

"You want me to believe that? And I'd really like to believe that. But there's that ten-grand-a-month coke habit you're supporting by stealing from your own advertising agency. I think you know damn well what I'm talking about," Rick said, smoothing the wrinkles out of each word as he spoke them.

"No, I don't," Kate stammered. She began to cry.

"You're in way over your head, Kate. You knew the only way out was killing Jenny for the insurance."

"You're fucking insane. I'd never try to kill my friend for money."

"No, what about for the coke? You'd kill her to keep the nose candy coming, wouldn't you?"

"Never! You're crazy. Jenny had an accident. It was just a bad accident."

Kate's tears ripped at Rick's insides. He wanted to back off, but knew he had to press until he got to the truth, regardless of the hurt it caused.

"Who's the boyfriend, Warren Garrett? He the one you've been banging?"

"What? Warren?"

"Yeah, I know you were lovers in college."

"Warren's a self-centered jerk off. He always was and always will be. You think...I was in bed with Kevin Murphy at the Concord the night of the accident."

"Then he'll give you an alibi. Give me a number and we can clear this up right now."

Rick shoved a paper and pencil under Kate's hand.

She stabbed the pencil onto the paper, scribbling numbers.

"Top one's the office."

"You just sit tight, Kate. We'll make a phone call. Now might be a good time to contact your lawyer."

That line always got to them. If Kate *were* holding anything back, she'd surely cut loose before calling her lawyer.

Kate wiped away tears but never left her chair. The passing minutes were like a high speed grinder on her nerves. What if Kevin...

Minutes passed. Kate contemplated every one of Rick's accusations. Finally, Rick returned with a tired, somber face. His eyes revealed nothing. He sat down next to Kate, pulling his chair closer to hers.

Kate tried to read into his mind, uncover his thoughts. She felt her heart hammering inside, and the sweat rolling down her back. She needed more water.

"Convince me you didn't know Kevin Murphy no longer works for Jarvison and Lewis."

"What?"

Kate's eyes widened in fear. Breathing became difficult.

"He skipped. Up and quit his job two days ago. We're trying the home number. I hope for your sake he's sitting right next to the phone."

Rick said no more. He just sat there, staring at her while he twirled the pencil on the table.

A few minutes later, a uniform entered and signaled Rick.

Rick's eyes and face turned glacial. His breathing became very light.

"You didn't know Kevin Murphy's home phone has been disconnected?"

25

Jenny lounged on the sofa, her mind as carefree as the sparrows fluttering in the trees beyond her windows. The late afternoon sun warmed her as it poured into the living room. She loved being out of the bedroom, even if it could be only for brief periods of time.

Occasionally, the sounds of Warren at work in the den drifted down to her. He had truly been wonderful since her accident. Only once in awhile did he complain about the effort it took to care for her. Never once had he said it was too much. He really did love her. So why couldn't she love him back? What was missing in her that kept her from feeling the way she did before the accident?

But then how did she *really* feel before the accident? There were those fleeting images that aroused suspicion and confusion in her head. Was there something lurking in her past that now remained buried by layers of amnesia?

She tried to focus on that night. For a brief moment, she saw herself in the restaurant. Warren sat across from her.

Of course, I'm happy, she heard him say in her mind. Yet she was uncertain that he meant it.

Fatigue began to overwhelm her, drawing her toward sleep. It felt glorious to be out of that bed, and moving around the house; even if it were limited to just sitting in a different location.

But she knew she must end it. She must return to her bed and rest.

Jenny endured a slight muscle pull when she rose from the sofa. She contemplated first the effort required to get up the stairs, and second, the need for Warren's assistance.

Warren was busy; she could hear him conversing on the phone while at the same time pounding away at his computer keyboard. He sounded upset. His trading must be going poorly today.

Jenny sized up the stairs. She could do it. She felt stronger today than yesterday. She had to challenge herself. It was time to give it a try on her own. Time to demonstrate to Warren that she was really back to her old self. The very thought muddled her mind. Only a dozen stairs to reach the top. Just take one stair at a time.

Beyond the reach of Jenny's ears, within confines of her bedroom, a needle on one of the instruments began scraping across slow-moving paper. First tiny spikes appeared. Then the needle twitched more rapidly, recording large spikes of activity.

Warren also never heard the sounds. A telephone conversation consumed him. And before leaving, Dwight had forgotten to set the alarms on his monitors to trigger on adverse activity. Though, for Dwight, it mattered little now. He had the evidence he believed he needed to make a mark on the world of paranormal phenomenon.

Jenny paused at the base of the stairs. So far no more than minor discomfort. She gazed up, the way a rock climber sizes the sheer granite before making his ascent.

"You can do this. Handrail. One step at a time."

It looked easy.

She resolved that now was the time to scale the mountain alone—to demonstrate that she was ready for that next plateau in her recovery. Negotiating the stairs unaided would surely be a feather in her cap.

The first three stairs came and went. On the fourth, Jenny stopped. But not because of pain or discomfort. An icy chill swam down to meet her, wrapping itself around her like a swirling winter wind that had come to whisk her away. The chill ignited terror deep within.

She could do this, she cautioned herself. She could make it to the top alone. Her reward would be a nap in her bed.

Jenny sucked in a breath and attacked the next three stairs with determined strides. This time a wrenching pain constricted her midsection. She winced, vacuuming in air to fill her lungs and knowing she could go on. Three more stairs. Her chest muscles were like boa constrictors, slowly tightening to make further breathing difficult.

The stabbing discomfort forced Jenny to pause momentarily, and to consider calling for Warren's aid. Then she decided to try another stair or two. If she could just make it to the second floor, she would take a well-earned rest.

Ice froze her veins as she stared at the second floor hall. No sounds drifted out of the den. Warren had stopped tapping at his computer. Maybe he was writing, for Jenny could detect a faint scraping.

With two stairs still before her, Jenny felt the presence. She turned to look behind her, sensing the ghost in her wake.

"Warren!" she issued in a terrified cry.

As she came around, a hand pressed against her chest.

Jenny toppled in a reverse somersaulting action down the stairs, her scream rising up to shake the house.

****

Jenny awakened on a cold table with a white sheet covering her from neck to knees. Warren sat at arm's reach, gripping her hand so tightly she thought her fingers would go numb.

"How we doin', honey?" a smiling, embarrassingly overweight nurse asked, examining the contusion on Jenny's forehead.

Jenny could not even muster the strength to respond.

"Dr. Morrison will be right in. So just relax."

Morrison offered only a perfunctory greeting when he arrived. Jenny could see the disappointment in his eyes. He closed the curtain around his patient, asking Warren to wait in reception while he performed his examination. The nurse retreated to her position at the foot of the bed.

After peeling back the sheet to expose Jenny's entire midsection, Morrison poked and prodded around her stomach from a number of different angles. He seemed more concerned with her facial responses than anything else.

"Well, I don't believe you did any damage in there. But we can't always be sure. Jenny, what happened this time?"

"I slipped and fell while going up the stairs."

"How many stairs?"

"At least six."

"Were you alone? Why didn't Warren help you?"

"Warren was there, but I wanted to try it myself. I thought I could do it without help."

"Jenny."

The doubt in Morrison's tone made Jenny uneasy.

Morrison probed further with heel of his hand. He pressed with greater force—as if he wanted to punish her for failing to heed his advice. Though in reality, he needed to work deeper inside her to make certain nothing had breached as a result of the fall.

"Any bleeding of any kind?"

"None."

"That's a good sign. Any pain in the lower abdomen?"

"None. Well, a little."

Jenny flinched when he pressed firmly with one hand over the other into her lower right quadrant.

"Jenny, I wish you wouldn't..."

"I'm all right, right? I didn't re-injure myself, did I?"

"I'm a little concerned about this area here." He indicated her lower right quadrant. "I did some fancy stitching in there, and I don't like that it's tender. I'm not taking any chances with this. I'm admitting you overnight."

Jenny mustered the beginnings of an objection.

Morrison's paternal finger silenced her.

"Just to be safe. If any internal bleeding develops, we can go in immediately to staunch it. Is that okay?"

Jenny frowned.

"Best to be safe," Morrison cautioned, taking her hand into his.

"If you say so. Warren can go a day without me. He'll probably like a break from playing nursemaid."

"Okay then, I'll call for a bed and have you transferred up. I'll let Warren know. You just lie there and let my people take care of you."

Warren launched out of his chair the moment Morrison emerged from the examination room.

"How is she? Is she okay?"

"I think so. Exactly what happened, Warren?"

"I don't know. She tried climbing the stairs by herself and must have fallen."

Morrison raised a brow, but said nothing while he scribbled his observations into Jenny's records.

"I'm admitting her overnight. There's some tenderness and swelling. I don't want to take any chances. You can go in and stay with her until we can get an orderly to move her."

Warren nodded.

Morrison watched with concern as Warren headed for the examination room.

****

Rick sat at his desk in the deserted squad room with his head in his hands. A cold cup of coffee and a half-eaten sandwich remained from his supper an hour before.

For the fifth time, he went over every detail of his interrogation of Kate Matheson. So far, he had almost nothing to link her directly to Jenny's attempted murder. Embezzling was hardly sufficient motive for murder. However, the insurance money gave Kate motive, and she possibly had opportunity if she had used Jenny's car shortly before the accident. And she currently had no alibi for that Friday night when she could have gone under the hood of Jenny's car while it sat in the restaurant parking lot.

How easy it all seemed to Rick now. Borrow the car a few days before the planned accident. Cut the bolt halfway through with a hack saw and wait until the moment arrives. *Ping!* Snap off the bolt head and watch the festivities. Warren could have set up the restaurant days in advance. Once the car is rigged and ready to go, Warren gets Jenny to the place, Kate makes the final tap and voila!

Rick could muster no rational reason to cross her off his list, but on the other hand, he was still without any physical evidence linking her to the accident, and his attempt at extracting a confession had failed.

His telephone rang. Rick hesitated until the fourth ring. He really just wanted to go home. Or rather stop to see Bridget. The last thing he wanted now was to get involved in anything else.

"Special Investigations, Walker," he said, though his eyes and attention remained riveted on the spread of reports in front of him.

"Detective Walker, This is Dr. Morrison, Jenny Garrett's doctor. She's had another accident."

Rick shifted his attention to the telephone.

"Warren brought Jenny in an hour ago with bruises and contusions. Says she fell down the stairs. I'm keeping Jenny overnight for observation."

"Thanks, Doc. Thanks alot."

Rick's mind churned. He stared out the window for a lingering moment. Jenny fell down the stairs. Could Warren have assisted Jenny's fall? Was this another attempt on her life?

Rick snatched his coat off the back of his chair. When presented with a golden opportunity, he had to take full advantage of it.

****

Rick doused his headlights and rolled to a stop three houses before the Garrett place. Lights illuminated both the first and second stories of the house. He had to hope he had gotten into position in time.

He lowered the volume on his police radio, turned the FM radio volume up and tuned to a classic rock station. Then he settled into his seat for what he hoped would be only a short wait. It boiled down to luck and tenacity now.

Rick's wait dragged on for two hours. But then Warren left the house, roaring out of the garage in his Saab and disappearing around the corner. Rick gave him plenty of distance, but not so much that he might lose him again.

Warren first stopped at the hospital, where like a dutiful husband, he spent an hour with Jenny.

During that time Rick ran in and out of the hospital snack bar, where he purchased a hamburger that he choked down in his car along with a cup of hot coffee. At first, he thought Warren's intent might be to remain overnight with Jenny. But promptly at nine, Warren exited the doors and returned to his vehicle.

26

Jenny eased out of bed, wrapped her fuchsia robe tightly around her waist and began a slow stroll out of her room. This might be the best opportunity she would ever get, so she knew she had to make the most of it. Answers to questions that had plagued her since awakening from the accident could very well be somewhere in this hospital. At the very least, she had to try to find them.

Jenny stopped first at the nurses' station, leaning slightly against the counter for support, but making it appear as if she were casually waiting rather than holding herself up. Her face hid the pain ripping through her abdomen.

"Can't sleep, Mrs. Garrett?" a sour-looking Filipino nurse asked as she sat in her chair catching up on paperwork, which she then placed in various medical charts. She offered up no more than a sidelong glance, as if to indicate that Jenny's presence was an intrusion.

"No. I feel fine. I still can't see why Dr. Morrison wanted me overnight."

"Better to be safe. Insurance pays anyway. Might as well enjoy. Besides, we don't want anything happening to you. Doc Morrison worked too hard putting you back together."

234

"You know about me?"

"Know about you? You're our miracle girl. We're all thoroughly familiar with your case. Morrison briefed us before he left. Did you think the *doctor* was going to take care of you?"

"No, I just..."

"We know everything about you."

"I was wondering then...could you tell me something of what happened that night?"

The nurse stopped what she was doing and stared up at Jenny.

"What do you mean?"

"I mean...I don't remember most of what happened to me. I have a black hole in my memory."

To humor Jenny, the nurse pulled the Garrett chart from the stand beside the telephone.

Jenny shifted, masking her discomfort while the nurse scanned the stack of charts and doctors' notes that filled her file.

"Not much to tell. You came in with severe head trauma, a number of fractures and internal hemorrhaging."

"What happened to me...I mean after I got here?"

"Honey, you were initially treated by a third-year resident in Emergency. Morrison was called in almost immediately to do the surgery. You were in bad shape."

"Why Morrison?"

"Surgeon on call. We keep three surgeons and a complete operating room staff on call twenty-four hours a day."

"How long was I in the operating room?"

"Honey, you sure ask a lot of questions. Most of the night. Says here you were brought in at ten fifty-one and entered surgery at eleven forty-seven. I guess they had to stabilize you before they could take you up."

"Would that say if anything unusual happened in the operating room?"

The nurse glanced away from the chart, looking quizzically into Jenny's eyes.

"What do mean, unusual?"

"I don't know. It's just I hear these strange voices in my head. One of them is Dr. Morrison's. I was just wondering if something might have happened in there."

"What kinds of voices?" the nurse asked, now focused entirely on Jenny.

"There's one that sounds like...'the pressure...we can't...we're losing her.'"

Jenny witnessed a transformation in the nurse's eyes. They betrayed anything the nurse might say to dispute those voices. She knew something by the way her face changed. She had heard of this before. Jenny was certain by the way the nurse reacted.

"There's another one I sometimes hear...it's a woman's voice. She's panicked, yelling that they can't do anything."

The nurse shrugged and returned to the chart. She flipped through the sheets of doctors' notes, honing in on those dated the night of the surgery.

"Says here Alma Carter was the nursing supervisor on duty. She monitored you in the operating room. You could talk to her. She'd know exactly happened during your surgery. I'm afraid there isn't anything more in the notes I can tell you."

"Thank you so much. Do you think she might be on duty now? Maybe I could talk to her while I'm here."

"I'll call and check."

Jenny waited. The nurse dialed the surgery station. There seemed to be a change in the nurse after she learned of Jenny's voices. She maintained a more guarded stance toward Jenny's inquiries. There had to be some meaning behind the voices inside Jenny's head. But if someone on the hospital knew something, would they ever reveal to her the truth.

"Sorry, Alma's off tonight. Check with hospital administration in the morning. They might be able to help you."

****

Rick knew in a minute he had latched on to something when Warren turned west instead of east upon leaving the hospital lot. Warren had no intention of returning home. At least not right away. Rick hoped this would be his break.

Warren's route appeared well-planned, as he stopped at a liquor store and then at a drug store before heading across town. But as the surrounding buildings became familiar, Rick began to feel as if his stomach were being sucked down into his intestines. This was not where he wanted to be taken. This was turning bad fast.

Rick had to face what was churning up out of the dark recesses of his mind when the Glen Oaks Apartments came into view. At first, he told himself that this trip was an innocuous one. But little by little, he faced the truth. Rick broke off his surveillance to turn down a side street as Warren slipped into the underground parking garage. Coincidence?

Rick knew better than that. Warren was seeing Bridget. Rick no longer hoped it was strictly an innocuous visit. His mind began churning, reassessing all that he knew about the case. What had he missed? How had he let himself be duped?

Midnight came and went. Rick was dead tired and dying for a cup of hot coffee. But none of that mattered now. How could he have fallen for her the way he did?

Warren and Bridget. It made sense now. It all made sense now. The odor in her apartment that registered in the back of his mind on his first visit. A stale cigarette odor that, at the time, meant nothing. Yet, if Bridget demonstrated so much concern about her body, why would she pollute it with cigarette smoke? She loathed smoking. Rick realized that the odor could have been left behind by Warren or Kate. He recalled now seeing no ashtray with cigarette butts in her apartment.

Bridget's willingness to offer up incriminating bits and pieces about Warren now made a little bit more sense.

By two in the morning the street was deserted, except for a shaggy mutt scavenging through the dumpsters. All but a few of the apartments in the building were blacked out. It was then that Rick realized Warren was at Bridget's for more than a quickie—this was going to be an all-nighter.

****

The hospital administration refused Jenny's request for the surgical nursing supervisor's number, and even denied her follow-up request for the woman's next scheduled shift. But after only a few minutes on the telephone, Jenny had both the woman's number and address. Maybe Alma Carter could shed some light on why Jenny was being tormented this way.

Warren arrived shower fresh to find Jenny anxiously waiting to leave. She seemed more alert and excited than she had been over the past days. Jenny insisted they make a stop before going home. Somebody had to help her understand why her life had turned into such a nightmare.

27

Jenny insisted that Warren remain in the car, and noticing the determination in her eyes, he complied without question. He just had to let her run her course and work through whatever had risen anew to disturb her.

"Don't be too long, *please!*" Warren begged, concerned that the time he was wasting here was going to cost him dearly on the commodities exchange. Each tick of the clock meant money going into someone else's pocket rather than his own.

A graying Alma Carter with a plain, serious face welcomed Jenny into her living room once she realized exactly who Jenny was. She remembered neither Jenny's name nor her face. But she would never forget the woman in the car wreck and what had to be done that night to save her.

"You look well, considering all you must have gone through that night," Alma said.

"If only you knew the whole of what I've been through," Jenny mumbled, more to herself than to Alma. And it appeared Alma's hearing must be fading. Either she didn't hear Jenny or chose not to respond.

The surgical nursing supervisor was a stout woman with a reluctant smile worn thin over her

many years. She could be demanding and cold when
the situation called for it, yet sensitive and compas-
sionate as well. There was a moment of hesitation
before Alma agreed to talk with Jenny about that
night. It seemed to Alma that a Pandora's box could
be opened by discussing what happens in the confines of an operating theater.

Alma first confirmed that she had been in the
operating room the entire time. All of the nearly six
long and arduous hours, as was every other member
of the surgical team. The collective sigh of relief when
the operation was finally over proved overwhelming
in itself.

"I don't know what I can tell you," Alma said, sipping tea on her sofa while Jenny sat beside her. She
had offered to make tea for Jenny, but Jenny refused,
wanting to keep their exchange brief and focused on
why she had came to her in the first place.

In minutes, Jenny realized that Alma's voice was
another of those trapped inside her head. There was
no mistaking that she was the one who seemed to let
her panic slip into her voice during moments of cri-
sis.

"I just need to know if anything unusual happened in the operating room."

"What do you mean, unusual?"

Alma shifted in her chair to put more distance
between her and Jenny, setting her tea cup on the
table before her. But rather than to face Jenny, Alma
stared into the cup.

Jenny sensed her question had dredged up something. Something that Alma knew and hesitated to
tell her.

"You have to understand. You were in very bad
shape when they wheeled you in. Dr. Morrison took it
as a challenge to save your life. That's the worst way
to have to perform. What else might you mean by
unusual?"

"I don't know what I mean. But I can tell you this: your voice is locked inside my head, and I can't get it out. I was hoping you could tell me..."

"There's nothing I can tell you."

Alma's words took on a sudden defensive edge. She refused to meet Jenny's eyes. She wanted to let sleeping dogs lie. But Jenny wasn't about to cooperate.

"'The pressure's dropping too rapidly...'did you say that?"

Alma turned to Jenny. Truth was written in her stare.

"You..."

"Did you say those words?" Jenny demanded.

Alma moved to the sofa, sitting right beside Jenny.

"Yes. Dr. Morrison was barking orders like a mad man. There was internal bleeding all over the place. He was having a hard time stopping it. I was holding a clamp in each hand when we started to lose you. He screamed at the anesthesiologist, but before anyone could react, you flat-lined on us. I was looking back at the BP monitor at the time, and I did say that the pressure was dropping too rapidly."

Alma needed to pause.

Jenny needed to know more.

She watched Alma's mind churning behind those dull green eyes, excavating the difficult memories of that night and bringing them to the surface.

"The surgeon did everything he could—your heart had stopped. But Dr. Morrison wouldn't quit. He desperately massaged your heart back to life. Missy, he never once gave up on you. That's why you're here now. He never once gave up on you. Jenny, you were gone for more than eight minutes. We were no longer certain that even *if* you came back, you'd be normal. You know what I mean?"

"By gone, you mean I was dead?"

"Yes. And usually the risk of damage is very great...but you made it back and you're normal."

"Normal? My life's a nightmare."

"I mean you're still able to function."

"I'm not a vegetable."

"Dr. Morrison was yelling orders to everyone, and we were doing the best we could."

"You're saying that I died on the operating table?"

"For eight minutes. While you were dead, Dr. Morrison fought to keep your heart and brain alive. Nobody thought he'd bring you back. But he did. He got a pulse and your pressure came back. And now you're functioning."

"I just don't know if he brought all of me back."

Alma stared at Jenny with the most peculiar expression.

"What do you mean?"

What Jenny thought at that very moment was far too wild for even Alma to be able to understand. And Jenny was living with it now.

Silence hung between them for a long moment; so long that Alma's mind reacted to the implications of the silence.

"There was no negligence, if that's what you're thinking," Alma added sharply.

"What? No, certainly not. From what you've told me, the only reason I survived is because of Dr. Morrison's efforts."

Jenny rose and pulled her coat closer to her. She felt a tightening in her throat. She had crossed over. In that operating room, she had crossed the barrier separating life from death. The chill working through her came not from the drafts in the old brownstone house—it came from what was spreading into every corner of her mind.

"You said you heard other voices?" Alma asked when Jenny seemed to be in a trance.

"Yes. But they're just fragments. Bits and pieces that before now made no sense to me."

"Jenny, you're saying you can remember what went on in that operating room? Were you conscious during the operation?"

The very thought sent icy shivers up Alma's spine.

"No. I couldn't have been. I don't know what I'm saying. I only know I have these voices clamoring inside my head, trying to get out."

"My God."

Alma Carter said no more.

At the door, Jenny thanked her for her candor, then walked carefully down the steps to return to the car. Something inside her mind had registered what had happened in that operating room when she died.

"Jenny, you okay?" Warren asked, seeing her ashen face.

Jenny just wanted to go home. She had to call Dwight. She had to tell him what she had learned— for eight minutes she had been dead.

****

Dwight sat in a lonely corner of the university library with a copy of the complete case file for Josef Lukenhan. It had been left to molder for the twenty odd years that had passed since Dr. Grayworth initially recorded his observations.

From the myriad of psychiatric jargon, Dwight learned that for more than three of the four years that the boy claimed to be terrorized by the Doppelgänger, no one had given the boy's story the slightest credence. Instead, they attached to his condition every possible variation of psychiatric terms known at the time.

Dwight worked chronologically backwards until he reached the point where the boy had fallen through the thin ice covering a pond on the family's farm. He was trapped beneath the water for an unknown period before the father pulled him out and revived him. Miraculously the Lukenhan boy suffered no lasting side effects, probably due to the fact that the freezing water reduced his body temperature rapidly. He did, however, exhibit a sudden and dramatic shift in personality.

Once a boy of bold resources and exuberant spirit, Josef turned into a timid shell of his former self, suffering from almost continual depression. It wasn't until a year after the accident, after Josef attempted his first suicide, that Dr. Grayworth began treating the boy.

Dwight scoured each page, dissecting each sentence for clues, even nuances, of similar paranormal encounters. Dwight's own depression set in when he reached the end of the case file without uncovering any information pertinent to his particular case. Luckily, he had yet to reach the last of the case notes.

It seemed, in a subsequent follow-up documented nearly a year after the boy's death, another psychiatrist in Vienna completely reversed Grayworth's position. Just before the boy's suicide, Dr. Vaullen-Schmidt began investigating the possibility that the boy had been, in fact, haunted by something from the next dimension.

While analyzing the boy's latest suicide attempt, Vaullen-Schmidt realized that it had been quite literally impossible for the boy to have self-inflicted some of the wounds that nearly took his life. Yet there was no other explanation other than suicide for the wounds in the first place.

A fellow colleague and medical practitioner to Vaullen-Schmidt demonstrated that the knife's angle of entry was such that the boy's wrist would have to have been turned completely backward. It was then that Vaullen-Schmidt suspected the boy might have been telling the truth all along.

In her final entry into the Lukenhan case file, Helena Vaullen-Schmidt wrote that a Doppelgänger could have possibly been terrorizing the boy, and that Josef's final escape from the torment—suicide—had not been a suicide after all. Vaullen-Schmidt stated in her conclusion that young Josef had contended all through his treatment that he would never find peace until the Doppelgänger killed him. It very well may have been the only way to end his torment.

Perhaps the boy had been right, Vaullen-Schmidt wrote as her final remark to the case.

Though the learned community scoffed at her conclusion, none could provide evidence to disprove her claim that the wounds were not self-inflicted.

Dwight stared at that final sentence in Vaullen-Schmidt's report for a long time. Three cases of reported Doppelgänger sightings, and in all three cases, the conclusion had been the same: suicide. The victims in all cases sought death as the only way to be free of their torment. But did they, in fact, take their own lives? Or did the Doppelgängers ultimately succeed in destroying the hosts from which they had become separated?

Dwight shuddered. A footfall not far from him brought a jolt. He swallowed hard at the implications of this thoughts.

Like Josef, Jenny might have been right all along. Maybe her ghost was trying to kill her. Maybe her ghost *must* kill her to pass into the next dimension. Now Dwight knew the ending. Jenny's ghost would never relent until Jenny was dead. There could be no escape. There would be no peace in her life.

****

Jenny sat on the sofa while Dwight sat across from her on the chair. Each had their own story to tell. Warren was quick to seize the opportunity. He had left when Dwight arrived, promising to return in time to make dinner. Jenny offered to cook, but Warren insisted she just do nothing until he returned.

"We couldn't have discussed this over the phone," Jenny started. There was so much to tell, she was unsure how she would get it all out.

"Before you start, here's the number where I'm staying."

Jenny looked puzzled as Dwight handed her a piece of paper.

"A friend's. He lives less than an hour from here. It's easier than driving back and forth to the university. Keep the number by your phone."

Jenny waited until Dwight returned to the chair.

"You've uncovered something new?" Dwight asked, secreting away what he himself had learned hours earlier.

"Unbelievable. I spoke to a nurse who was in the operating room the night of my accident. She told me...I think this might somehow help make sense of this whole situation. She told me that I died on the table."

Dwight's eyes became wide; he moved forward in the chair.

My God, what was she saying, Dwight said inside his mind.

"They were having trouble controlling the bleeding when my heart suddenly stopped. The nurse said Dr. Morrison massaged my heart for eight minutes trying to bring me back."

"Are you certain of this?"

"The voices I hear are the doctors and nurses in the operating room. Alma Carter, she's the surgical nursing supervisor, confirmed saying one of the phrases I repeated."

Dwight rose from the chair. It all became so clear, so terrifyingly clear. He sat down beside Jenny and enveloped her hands within his.

"Do you realize what you're saying?"

"Not fully."

"When you died, your spirit left your body. It began the journey to the next plane. But the doctor brought you back. Somehow your spirit became trapped outside your body."

"How can that be? How can I be alive if my spirit...I don't even understand what I'm saying."

Dwight released her and began pacing. The facts of the Lukenhan case flooded into his mind.

"That's why the Doppelgänger haunts you. Your spirit is caught between worlds, so to speak. It can't pass on to the next dimension because you're still alive. And for that same reason, it can't return to your body..."

Dwight became suddenly silent. The Lukenhan boy had drowned, only to be revived by a loving father. Somehow his spirit must also have become trapped between worlds. Dwight could see the unmasked terror rising up into Jenny's eyes as she considered the implications of his statements.

"If what you're saying is true...then the only way the spirit can go anywhere is to..."

"Kill you," Dwight said, barely above a whisper.

"Oh my God."

Jenny began to hyperventilate; the room started to collapse around her with a burgeoning force. How could she...there was no way to ever be free of this.

"The Doppelgänger has no alternative but to kill you. It will remain trapped between worlds as long as you're alive. In a sense, it can never find peace as long as you're breathing."

Jenny buried her face in her hands, releasing a rush of tears. Her sobs became audible.

"I have to kill myself..." she muttered.

Dwight dropped to his knees before her and cradled her in his arms, feeling every muscle in her body tremble under the shock of what she now understood.

"Don't say that! I won't let anything happen to you. There has to be something we can do...."

"I can't oppose this terror. I can't win against this thing!"

"Jenny, wait. Just hold on. There's got to be a way."

"How? What can we do? The ghost is going to torment me until she kills me. Then she will find peace."

"We don't know that for sure. Maybe there's a way to exorcise it."

Jenny pulled her face up. Dwight was serious.

"I don't know of anything else we could try," he admitted, realizing that he, himself, was being drawn in to accept the inevitable.

Despite his own desires, Dwight released Jenny and returned to the sofa, keeping Jenny's hands locked tightly in his. Words carried no weight anymore for Jenny Garrett. Nothing could be said or done to change what she must do.

"What do you feel different in your life?"

"What do you mean?"

"I mean some part of you has to be missing, I need to know what that part is."

"I don't know. The only thing I'm no longer sure of is my love for Warren."

28

Since Jenny had not heard from Kate in more than a week, she assumed the agency was working well during her recovery. Knowing she might never be able to involve herself in the agency again, Jenny felt relief at the thought that some things could go on without her. There was too much happening to her that kept her in an almost constant state of angst. Dealing with people right now would be too much for her to handle. Of course, assuming is always a bad thing.

Rosenstein's therapy would be all but useless. Delving into her childhood in the hopes of uncovering the source of her 'hallucinations' would be fruitless. Jenny had all the answers she needed. She felt a sinking in her stomach each time she even thought about going in for a session. She was resigned to the fact that nothing earthly could be done to help her now. But what did that actually mean?

She also knew her involvement with clients would only worsen her emotional state and further erode her professional relationship with those that trusted her. During their last conversation, Kate had said she was more than happy to take charge and hold things together until Jenny felt ready to return. Jenny wondered how Kate could feel about having to hold the agency together herself from now on. Maybe Kate could even find a new partner?

That was until the following Monday morning. Kate called and mysteriously asked to see Jenny immediately. When Jenny inquired as to why, Kate remained evasive, and there was an undeniable undercurrent of nervousness in her words. Kate insisted on a face-to-face meeting.

Warren seemed excited about Kate's imminent visit. It meant an afternoon out without worrying over Jenny. Lately, Warren had shown cracks due to the strain. His eyes had become dull and lifeless recently and he carried on with his household duties without so much as a smile. He knew nothing of what Dwight had told her and what she had learned in her visit with Alma Carter. She didn't believe Warren could handle it. For the first time, Jenny contemplated suicide while she waited for Kate. Warren would grieve, but in time, he would go on with his life and find someone new. The thought sent shock waves rumbling through her. She cast aside everything. Warren would find someone new. *Warren would find someone new.* Why was that causing such a shudder through her? The words seemed to trigger some spark of a memory.

An image flashed across her mind. It raced by too quickly for her to grasp it. But she glimpsed enough of it to realize it had to do with those missing days in her life. Warren…somebody new.

Jenny's obsession with the voices, the ghost, and her marred appearance had kept Warren from straying from Jenny's side for the past three days. He needed a break from the stress. Even Dwight had been spending more time away from the house now that he had gained his precious evidence. Since their last discussion, Dwight seemed more reserved. He checked his equipment regularly but said little when they were together.

The doorbell brought Jenny back to the moment.

Warren showed Kate in and made sure Jenny had everything she might need close by. Then he excused himself without further pleasantries and promptly disappeared.

Jenny situated herself on the sofa with her feet up and her back supported by a large pillow. Though physically comfortable, mentally Jenny wondered why Kate needed to see her so urgently.

Kate's ragged eyes betrayed her worry and distress. A worry that consumed her mind until she appeared spent. She had become terribly thin over the past weeks and she appeared lethargic as she sat in Warren's chair across from Jenny.

The tremor in Kate's hand while she lit her cigarette alerted Jenny that something was terribly wrong with Kate.

Kate's voice oozed anxiety when she asked how Jenny felt, how she was recovering from the accident and when she might be back to work. Neither broached any subject that might turn painful.

Until Kate suddenly asked, "are you aware the police are investigating your accident?"

"Yes, a detective's talked to me a few times for information about what really happened."

"What have you told them?"

"Nothing. I still can't remember that night."

"They're saying it wasn't an accident."

Jenny remained level and calm.

Kate appeared shaken at speaking the words.

"Warren hasn't said anything to you about it?"

"No, Kate. What are you trying to say?"

"The police think someone tried to murder you."

"And?"

"They consider me a suspect."

Jenny weighed her words. Her eyes never left Kate's, though a haze of smoke obscured Kate's. It seemed Kate's hand trembled with greater force now.

"They've had me under surveillance..."

"Why should they suspect you?"

Kate paused, suddenly lost for words. She swallowed the smoke from her last drag, using it to steady her before continuing.

"Please hear me out. I don't know if I have the courage to go through with this."

Kate rose.

"Go through with what? Kate, what are you saying?"

The words forced Kate to turn away in shame. Her life had turned to such shit. She hovered on the brink of totally falling apart before her best friend's eyes.

"Jenny, I've been...embezzling from the agency."

Jenny's face released genuine surprise. Never had she once felt Kate capable of doing anything dishonest or anything that could harm their friendship. They had been friends since college. How could Kate betray her this way? Then, in the ensuing silence, Jenny tasked her brain to recall those lost days. Had she uncovered Kate's improprieties? Had she confronted Kate with the truth?

"How? But more importantly, why?"

"I have a cocaine habit."

Jenny appeared visibly shaken by the news.

"How long?"

"A year. No, more than a year."

"But why?"

"I'm sorry, Jenny."

Kate faltered, tears rushed to fill her eyes. Once they began, Kate became voiceless. She flopped back into the chair and buried her face in her hands as if too ashamed to face her friend.

Jenny could say nothing. She was torn between reaching out to Kate and screaming at her to leave. Could Kate have been responsible for her accident? Would Kate try to kill her to save face for what she had done?

"The police think I tried to kill you because of it. Jenny, you've got to believe me, I would never want to see you hurt. I was going to pay the money back. I was just trying to cover up my addiction. I'm sorry. Please, Jenny, you've got to believe me that I would never try to hurt you."

When Kate finished, Jenny let the thick silence linger for a long time. They seemed to work well together. They trusted each other for four years. Now this. But nowhere in her mind could Jenny find reason for Kate to want her dead...except for the insurance money. Kate would never. Would she?

"I believe you, Kate."

"Jenny, what happened that night? What happened on that road?"

"I don't know."

Jenny began to cry, carrying now the full weight of her friend's betrayal along with the terror that now controlled her life. How could anyone have wanted her dead?

Jenny attempted to focus on the events of that night. Was there something locked in her memory that might help bring out the truth? Jenny searched deep inside, scraped out every corner of her memory, but still found nothing but a blank slate.

"How can I ever trust you again?"

"Jenny, I'm going to get help. I'm checking myself into a drug rehab upstate. I'll find a way to pay back the money I stole. I'll find a way to put everything right. Please just give me a chance to make things right."

"How could you have done this to me?"

"I'm sorry. I got caught up in the power. I liked being on top. I liked what drugs and money gave me."

"What about the agency? How can we survive? I can't run the business right now."

"When can you come back? When can you take over the responsibility for the business?"

"I don't know. Kate, I'm not ready for this. I can't handle this right now."

"You don't have to. I've brought in a consultant to manage the day-to-day until you can go back in. We can stay afloat for at least two quarters. Jenny, I'm going to fix my problem. I'm going to get back in line. Please don't hate me for what I've done."

Kate rose, sought the courage to go to Jenny, but turned away and charged out of the living room. A moment later, the front door closed. Jenny remained paralyzed on the sofa. She was consumed by the thought that someone wanted her dead.

29

Rick sat in the interrogation room with his eyes squared off against Kevin Murphy's. Kevin's unshaven face hung as if his skin had been draped over his skull. His eyes, reddened by exhaustion, alcohol and who knows what else, maintained a level stare. When he had been brought in, his clothes were a crumpled mess and his body emitted the odor of a garbage dump.

"You've got to believe me. I had nothing to do with Kate beyond manipulating the books."

"You lying piece of dog shit," Rick spat, enjoying every word and every squirm. "You probably masterminded this whole conspiracy."

"Please, just call Umberto at the Concord. He'll confirm that both Kate and I were there on September fifteenth. We ordered room service between nine and ten. There's no way we could have been at Diamante's that night."

Rick rose and slid in beside Kevin, as much as it dismayed him, and breathed heavily down his neck, avoiding the odors as much a possible by breathing in through his mouth and exhaling through his nose.

"You know, we're going check every little detail of everything you've told us here."

Just then, Jenkins slipped into the room. He whispered into Rick's ear. Then he smiled with diabolic pleasure at Murphy, who had turned around to observe the exchange.

"You are absolutely sure you don't want to change anything you've told me so far?"

Both Rick and Jenkins glared at Kevin.

"I'm telling you the truth. I wouldn't have anything to do with attempted murder. I'm not a killer, I'm just an accountant—a stupid fucking accountant."

"You can say that again, shitbag," Jenkins said.

"You think about it a while. I'll be checking out your story," Rick said before leaving Murphy alone.

The interrogation room door closed with the kind of thud that intimated incarceration, leaving Kevin Murphy to stare at his trembling hands.

****

Rick doled out Murphy's information to Jenkins and Wilson, asking them to make preliminary telephone inquiries to check out Murphy's story. He hadn't had this much fun in months. In the meantime, Rick had someone waiting for him in his office. Someone important enough to warrant pulling Walker out of his interrogation when it had just begun getting interesting. Rick was hoping he might get that little Murphy weasel to wet his pants before too long.

"Good morning, Mrs. Garrett," Rick said with obvious surprise on his face.

"Detective Walker," Jenny said, acknowledging him without the slightest trace of a smile.

"Have you remembered anything regarding the accident?" Rick hoped she would answer positively.

His case still resembled a sieve and Rick knew in his heart he'd never be able to fill enough holes to get the case before a grand jury.

"Kate Matheson, my business partner, came by to see me earlier."

Rick sat down. He expected this.

"Why was she questioned about attempted murder? Namely mine?"

"Jenny, we know now someone tried to kill you. Our evidence is strong enough to stand up in court. We just don't know who yet."

"I've heard this tune before. Can you just give it to me straight for a change?"

"You want it straight? All right. We know for a fact that your car was tampered with on the night of September fifteenth. Someone wanted you dead, Jenny. Someone very close to you."

"And you thought Kate would try to kill me?"

"We uncovered Kate's embezzlement and cocaine habit. Do you think she had a change of heart and wanted to confess to you? Killing you would have greatly uncomplicated her life."

"How could anyone have tampered with my car?"

"Jenny, I'm not at liberty to divulge anymore. But I desperately need your help."

Jenny said nothing. The words rose into her throat, but she couldn't spit them into the room.

"Jenny, now it's my turn."

Rick stopped himself. If he said what he was thinking at that moment, it might compromise his investigation.

"There is only one other person close enough to try to kill me," Jenny said.

"I know."

"So you suspect Warren?"

"Did Warren have access to your car that Friday? Before you went to the restaurant?"

"I don't know. I can't remember."

"Please, think very hard. Someone had to have access to your car in order to tamper with the bolt and cause your accident. Did Warren use your car?"

Jenny narrowed her eyes, concentrating on that one solitary question with all her power. Why couldn't she force her memory to work again? What was wrong with her?

"Yes! Warren used my car. He had a meeting and his car was in the shop."

Jenny experienced soaring elation one moment for remembering it, terror the next for what it implied. It was a small piece. But a piece. Something from that black void had surfaced. Now she needed more.

"When?"

"I'm not sure. I needed the car that day also."

"Why Jenny? Why did you need it?"

"Having lunch with someone...dog food?"

Rick reached into his desk, pulling out Jenny's calendar from her office.

"That's my calendar?" Jenny asked, staring at it while Rick flipped through the pages.

"Wednesday, September thirteenth. You penciled in a lunch with an Alvin Welmont."

"Yes. I was supposed to meet him for lunch to discuss an ad campaign for his company's new gourmet dog food. I had to cab it because Warren used my car."

Jenny stopped, closing her eyes.

"Jenny, talk to me. Help me."

"Warren used my car two days before the accident."

30

Jenny sat sullen and silent on the sofa. Dying sunlight streamed in through the living room windows to warm her face and cast long narrow blocks of light across the Persian rug which consumed most of the open floor. So much had happened in the past week that thinking clearly began to feel like something out of her reach. How could she go on? More importantly, how could she deal with her problem? Suicide was a concept that had never even entered her head before a few days ago. Now it seemed like she must consider it. The torment of something beyond comprehension and the realization that nothing short of death could free her of it cast her into a dark depression. How could she possibly broach the subject with Warren? How could he understand what she was feeling?

Warren finished his newspaper, folded it neatly in half, then set it beside his chair and left the room. He seemed so restive these last few days. Something was wrong, but he refused to confide in Jenny. Something had been occupying his mind.

The house seemed lifeless and vacant without Chips. Jenny felt his absence in every room she entered. He used to lie at her feet and chuff, forcing his eyes closed in a light sleep, and stretching his back legs rearward in what certainly appeared to be an uncomfortable position for a canine. Whenever Jenny moved from one room to another, Chips dutifully followed right behind. Now there was nobody and she felt no craving to replace her companion of six years.

A few minutes later, Warren returned from the kitchen and withdrew a cigarette from his pocket. He studied the flame as he lit the cigarette, returning to his chair and browsing through an Investor's Business Daily. Watching him, it seemed he intentionally avoided Jenny's eyes. He mumbled on occasion, flipping back and forth between the pages. She knew by the way he focused on anything but her that something had grown between them. Something Jenny felt responsible for.

It had been twenty-four hours since Dwight's last call, and Jenny began to feel like Dwight was also suddenly avoiding them. He had said little regarding his investigation and had brought no other colleagues into the house to investigate the evidence he had gleaned. Perhaps even his colleagues scoffed at his evidence? Perhaps he, himself, now refuted what had happened in her bedroom. Could he be too afraid to come back?

"You up to going out?" Warren asked, finally lowering the wall of newsprint he had raised between them.

"No, I think I just want to sit here."

"How are you feeling?"

"I'm okay."

It was a lie. Jenny wanted to cry, scream, yell and tear apart anything within reach. Her once neat and orderly life had become an unmanageable chaos. Warren barely spoke to her; he never touched her. She was scarred and ugly. But those were insignificant matters compared to...

She feared going to sleep at night, for in the darkness, the voices came. She awoke each morning terrified—terrified that this day the ghost would succeed in killing her.

Was death the only way to escape this torment? Thoughts of suicide again crept into her mind. No person on earth could end the pain in her life. Yet she had to find the strength to go on—to hope.

Jenny held it all in—knew if she let even a sliver of it out, if she tried to voice what she felt, she would end up strapped to a bed in a New York hospital psychiatric ward. From where she sat on the sofa, Jenny noticed a black sedan roll to a stop before the house. She said nothing when she saw who stepped out of the car. Somehow she had expected this.

"How about pizza for dinner?" Warren asked behind the lazy drifting smoke from another cigarette. He had chain-smoked three in the last fifteen minutes.

"I don't know, maybe..." she said, preoccupied now with the scene unfolding out her window.

Jenny glanced across the room at the clock upon the mantle. It was nearly dusk outside and dinner had to be dealt with. Or did it?

"Whatever..." Warren's voice trailed off.

The doorbell brought Jenny around. Her heart beat frantically. She sensed what was about to happen. Yet, there was no way she could alter or stop it. It was out of her hands now.

Jenny rose unsteadily, but Warren waved her off as he pressed his cigarette out and sauntered to the door.

"Detective Walker," Warren said with obvious surprise.

Jenny had said nothing as she watched him come up the drive. Somehow she knew why he had come. Maybe it was the stone face Rick brought with him or the determination in his eyes.

Rick asked to come in. Two uniforms followed in his wake.

Warren waited until the three entered the foyer, then he closed the door against a brisk north wind that tousled his hair. Though he tried to hide it, his face had turned ashen. He forced a weak smile.

When Rick and the two officers entered the living room Jenny was steadying herself at the sofa.

"Mrs. Garrett, you're looking well this evening. It is really great to see you getting around more."

"To what do we owe this honor, Detective?" Warren asked once they were all gathered in the living room. Instead of moving to be at Jenny's side, Warren just stood there and fumbled with another cigarette.

"More questions, I presume?"

The officers took up retral positions, standing like uniform-store mannequins just at the edge of the foyer.

"Mr. Warren Lawrence Garrett," Rick said in a suddenly official tone.

"Yes?"

"I have a warrant for your arrest. You have the right to remain silent."

While Rick continued reciting Warren's rights, a uniform stepped forward with handcuffs.

Warren's eyes turned white in disbelief. His stammer bore his surprise to what was happening.

"Why? What's the charge?" Warren demanded.

"The attempted murder of your wife, Jennifer R. Garrett."

Jenny fell back, grabbing for the sofa arm. The second uniform reached her in time to help her down onto the cushions.

"Warren?" she pleaded with both voice and eyes. He had to say something. He had to say this was all a mistake.

Instead, Warren shook his head.

"This is crazy. You are fucking out of your mind, Walker. I'd never try to kill Jenny."

"What is...Detective?" Jenny stammered.

"Mrs. Garrett, we have firm reason to believe your husband tampered with your car, thereby causing you to lose control after you exited Diamante's restaurant on the night of September the fifteenth."

"I don't believe..." Jenny muttered.

"We're booking your husband. He'll be arraigned in district court within forty-eight hours. The judge will decide if he'll remain in custody or be released on bail."

"Jenny, I'd never do something like that. I love you, Jenny. I could never want to kill you."

Rick moved Warren to the front door. He wanted Warren to struggle, to fight his authority, to give him a reason to bash his face in. Rick knew better than to let a case 'become personal, but he didn't care. Warren resisted at first, then succumbed when the uniform delivered a commanding tug on the handcuffs.

"Call Whitmauer. Wait, damnit, we can't leave Jenny alone in the house."

At the door, Warren suddenly fought free of the uniform's grip. He turned back to face his wife; his words had turned Jenny's face to parchment.

Instinctively, Jenny glanced up the stairs into the darkness.

"Detective, I'm frightened of being alone. I...I"

"It's all right, Mrs. Garrett. Nothing's going to happen to you now. We're taking care of it."

"You don't understand..."

"Jenny, call Mackenzie," Warren said, jerking his arm free of the uniform so he could remain turned toward her for a second longer. He wanted to kiss her—to assure her this was all a mistake—but he was too far away and Jenny made no move to come toward him.

"Jenny, don't stay here alone."

"Mrs. Garrett, is there someone you can call, if you're afraid to be alone?"

"Call Mackenzie!" Warren shouted again as the two uniforms moved him out the door and down the stairs.

Jenny's heart leapt into her throat at the thought of being alone in the house. She snatched up the telephone the moment the door closed. What if the ghost appeared? What if it tried to kill her?

Trembling, she dialed. No answer after three rings. Had she misdialed? After the fourth ring, she listened to an unfamiliar answering machine announcement.

"Please Dwight..."

She left a frantic message. She was alone in the house and frightened. Could he come over right away?

Then Jenny started to dial Kate's number. By the third digit, she remembered that Kate had checked herself into a drug rehab program in an upstate New York hospital.

Her fingers misdialed the next number twice; each time Jenny had to cut off the line before the first ring.

"Come on, Jenny, hold on," she commanded herself with a faltering voice.

Bridget's voice chimed in wonderful beyond words. Sure she could come right over. She would be there in less than thirty minutes. From Jenny's trembling voice, Bridget must have deduced the grave importance of Jenny's need.

Jenny checked the clock. Thirty minutes. She had to hold on for thirty minutes alone in the house. Before leaving the phone, she dialed their attorney's number, reached his service and left a brief message asking him to call.

She could make it. She told herself again and again—she could make it.

Not a sound could be heard, save for her own terrified breathing and her frantically pounding heart. Jenny moved through the first floor rooms quickly and efficiently, switching on every light. She refused to attempt the stairs to the second floor, terrified of what she might find if she did.

Leave, her inner voice commanded. Get out of this house now. But Dwight had said the ghost was part of her. There was no place to run from it; no safe place where the ghost could never reach her.

Jenny curled herself into a ball on the sofa, forced her back into the corner, wrapped her arms tightly around her doubled-up legs and found comfort from the sofa's hard stiff frame.

She must remain calm.

As she subdued her fears one by one, she focused every ounce of her energy inward. It was then that her head began to fill. It filled with images as if someone had opened her up and was now pouring in her memory. At first, they came all jumbled, flashing across her mind chaotically. Then she began to see them in the chronology in which they had occurred in her life.

Warren *was* late that Friday night for dinner. Where was he? Could he have been tampering with her car in the parking lot?

Wait, there was something else. It took everything Jenny had to hold in her excitement. *She was pregnant!* They were going to have a baby. It was to be a surprise for Warren during dinner.

That's why *she* had made the reservations for Diamante's. They were celebrating. But Warren seemed worried, almost frightened at the prospect when she broke the news to him. He complained his business was slipping. He was plunging deeper and deeper into the red. They needed Jenny's income from the agency to handle the month-to-month living expenses. How could they afford to have a baby now?

Why had Warren kept her pregnancy from her after the accident? Why wouldn't he tell her she had lost the one thing she wanted most in her life?

The champagne that night was to be Jenny's only alcoholic drink until after the baby was born. She had only had that one glass of champagne. She couldn't have been drunk. She nursed the one glass throughout their dinner.

She relived the toast Warren made to their marriage, their love, and their baby. He had accepted it, welcomed the joy it would have brought them. Both pledged to love each other forever. Hearing those words again inside her head sent shivers up her spine. My God, could Warren have told her he loved her when he knew she was about to die?

Jenny checked the clock.

Sixteen minutes had elapsed. Bridget would be crossing the halfway point by now.

Jenny thought she heard noises emanating from Warren's den. Fourteen more minutes, she told herself, just hold on fourteen minutes more.

Was there something upstairs? Was her spirit beckoning her into the darkness?

Jenny had to get up, had to move. She went to the staircase, flicking the light on over the stairs. It still left deep chasms of darkness on the second floor.

"Please, Bridget, please hurry," Jenny cried for the fifth time in the last ten minutes. "Dwight, where are you!"

Twenty minutes had passed. Ten more minutes.

Jenny paced, reassembling those lost hours and days in her life. But all the while, her eyes kept watch over the stairs, and her ears remained perked for any sound that might drift down from up there.

A jolt of fiery pain shot up her side. Walking started to hurt. She curled into a fetal ball on the floor in the corner of the living room, tucking her arms before her chest for protection.

It was up there. It was creating noise to torment her. It was waiting for her—waiting for the right moment to appear and kill her.

Jenny remembered now. They were about to leave the restaurant. She was so excited she would have made love to Warren in the back seat of the car if they could have fit. She desperately wanted to hold Warren and feel him inside her. The excitement was on the verge of exploding within her. It was a glorious time for her. Everything seemed perfect that night.

Jenny recalled now that she had actually left the restaurant alone. For some reason, Warren had paused at the door. He said he had to make a call.

Five more minutes. Please Bridget don't be late.

Jenny saw herself pull out of the parking lot, accelerate around a turn and start down the winding road that led to the bottom of the hill. But there were car lights behind her; insistent lights that filled her rearview mirror and shone into her eyes. Lights that roared into her wake like an angry beast.

The car in her wake bumped her hard on the left rear just as she began a sharp right turn. Jenny remembered hearing a loud metal-against-metal thump. The noise came not from the rear, but rather from under her hood. Something had snapped, she had thought at the time.

The car in her wake receded, but then roared up again.

At the next bend, she started to turn the wheel, but the car lurched in the direction opposite the direction of her turn. She slammed her foot on the brake. The back end came around on her. As her car spun wildly, Jenny saw the headlights coming straight at her.

Jenny's heart hammered as headlights blinded her. She again felt the ton of steel careening out of control just like it did that night. As hard as she tried, she could do nothing to avoid the oncoming car.

Headlights splashed in through the living room windows. Jenny screamed. She saw nothing, felt nothing.

Gasping, her face dripping in sweat, Jenny raced to the window, but the car continued past her house, turning at the corner.

"Bridget, where are you?"

The house was coming alive around her. A low rumbling arose out of the kitchen, as if someone were beating fists on a table. Jenny curled further into her corner and slumped lower onto the floor. It was here, making those incessant sounds, taunting her.

"Damn you! Leave me in peace!" she issued with a voice empty of strength and courage.

If only she could cry, scream, do something to vent the pressure building inside.

Her ghost, the torment of her very existence, waited at the top of the stairs, beckoning her to come up.

Jenny began to mewl.

Another set of headlight beams brought Jenny up from the floor. The car stopped in her drive.

Bridget!

Jenny ran to the door and threw it open wide as Bridget bounded up the stairs.

"Jenny, what's the matter?"

Their embrace sent waves of relief through Jenny. She was no longer alone. No longer vulnerable to that thing waiting at the top of the stairs in the darkness. Jenny hurried Bridget into the living room, never once glancing up the stairs into the murky darkness.

Bridget tossed her coat over Warren's chair and helped Jenny to the sofa, rubbing the palms of her hands vigorously across Jenny's arms and shoulders to warm her.

"Jenny, you're freezing."

"The police arrested Warren."

"What for?"

"Attempted murder. They said Warren tampered with my car. That's why I had the accident. They said he tried to kill me."

"That's unbelievable. Warren would never do that."

"I can't believe it, either."

There was something in the way Jenny spoke that caused Bridget to wonder whether Jenny was telling the truth.

"Why did they..." Jenny started.

"Let me make us some tea," Bridget countered.

While Bridget went to the kitchen, Jenny sat on the sofa, replaying in her mind all those bits and pieces that had surfaced concerning the two lost weeks. Bridget's presence fueled her courage, and for now, Jenny tucked away her fear of what lurked unseen up the stairs.

Jenny realized there was more to that night. Had she unwittingly played into Warren's deception? Did he know the car was set to go out of control? Is that why he stayed behind to purchase cigarettes? Did he need to put distance between himself and her so he wouldn't witness the accident and see his own wife die in a tragic crash? Was it the Saab behind her that night bumping her as she made the turn?

"Here's some hot tea. This should help."

Jenny accepted the cup in both hands, sipped a little, then set it on the side table.

"Did you call your attorney?"

"Right after I called you. His service said they would get a message to him. I don't know how long it will take before he can get to Warren and sort this thing out."

Bridget sipped her tea in silence while she browsed the books on the shelves across the room.

Jenny remained on the sofa, staring into her cup. There she saw something rising up out of the black liquid. Something that could shed further light on that fateful night.

"Could you stay with me until Warren can return home?"

"No problem. I'd be happy to, Jenny. So, the police are saying your accident wasn't really an accident after all?"

"They believe Warren did something to my car that caused it to go out of control."

"That's ridiculous," Bridget said, returning to the sofa beside Jenny. They were eye to eye now.

"What could he have done?" Bridget asked.

"I don't know."

"Why would they think Warren would be crazy enough to do something like that?" Bridget persisted.

"Warren was having an affair," Jenny stated. That's what she saw in the liquid. She had learned that Warren was involved with another woman. The words just popped into Jenny's head. Another lost memory regained.

"What? He was? With who?"

"I don't know...I remember...I thought I was losing him to another woman. This was before the accident. Before I knew I was pregnant."

"Jenny, you were pregnant?" Bridget asked with surprise.

"Yes."

Another lost memory played across the front of her mind.

"But you knew that, right? I remember now. I got the call from my doctor at the office. You were there with me at the time."

"Jenny, I couldn't have been there. I would have remembered that."

"It was about two weeks before the accident. You came by and we were going to lunch, except I got tied up on the telephone with a client. That new panty hose account, remember?"

"No, Jenny, I don't," Bridget said.

There was an odd insistence in Bridget's voice.

"My doctor called before we could get out the door. I took the call, and she told me I was pregnant. Remember, you promised not to say anything. I was going to surprise Warren at a special dinner...the dinner at Diamante's."

Jenny stopped. *The dinner at Diamante's.*

"I don't remember that, Jenny. It must have been someone else."

"No, Bridget, I'm sure it was you."

Bridget left the sofa. She returned to the book case, placing her back to Jenny.

For a moment neither spoke. Jenny stared at her back in disbelief. Everything had returned so clearly now. She saw it as if it had just happened yesterday. Why was Bridget saying these...

"You're right, Jenny. It was me. I was there and you *were* pregnant."

Bridget's voice turned cold and distant.

"God, I thought my mind was playing tricks on me. I remember it so vividly now."

"I know. You and Warren were going to have a baby. Your life was *so* perfect."

As she spoke, Bridget's voice completed its diabolic transformation. A voice now more of conscience than of person. She turned to face her friend with eyes white hot in anger. She dropped her tea cup, the liquid spilling into an inky stain across the Persian rug.

"I was pregnant, too, Jenny. You didn't know that, though. You didn't know I was pregnant."

"Pregnant? Bridget, what are you saying?"

"I was pregnant, Jenny. But you never knew. You know why you never knew? Because I aborted it in the first trimester. I killed the one thing I wanted most in my life."

"I'm sorry. I didn't know. I didn't even know you were involved with anyone."

"I was. I was in love, really in love, for the first time in my life. I was in love with someone who just wanted me."

"Bridget, I'm sorry. Why didn't you tell me?"

"I couldn't. I couldn't tell anyone."

"You could have told me. I would have helped you through it."

"Would you? Would you have helped me through it when I told you it was Warren's baby? Would you have helped me through it when I told you Warren loved me and wanted to divorce you? Would you have helped me through it, Jenny?" Bridget was screaming now.

"Oh God," Jenny moaned, clutching her chest.

"Yes Jenny, I'm the one Warren was fucking on the side. I'm the one who made him feel like a king. Not you!"

"What?"

"That's right, Jenny. But don't worry about your precious little hubby now. You know what the sentence is for attempted murder? He'll do ten to twenty in a federal prison. You know how I know that, Jenny?"

Jenny abandoned the sofa and started backing slowly toward the front door. Get out, her mind screamed to her body. But her body had difficulty comprehending.

Bridget sprang like a leopard, slipping quickly past her to block the way out of the house.

"You know how I know that, Jenny?" Bridget persisted, growing more venomous.

"No."

"Because Warren didn't try to kill you. He doesn't have the balls for something like that. But I do, Jenny. Why should you have Warren's baby when he made me kill mine? Tell me why, Jenny?"

Jenny bolted for the stairs, pounding up as fast as she could. Her stomach felt like it was being ripped in two. Up there was the darkness and the...

Bridget lunged from behind her, but missed Jenny's foot by a scant inch. Her face smacked the stair causing blood to trickle from her nose as she climbed, using hands and feet to regain her footing.

Jenny reached the second floor a stride ahead of Bridget. She dashed into the bedroom and slammed the door just before Bridget could reach her. Against Bridget's pounding and pushing, Jenny held the door in place long enough to turn the lock.

Bridget pounded the wood with both fists. Then silence, horrifying silence.

"Actually, I didn't want to kill you, Jenny," Bridget whispered sinisterly through the door. "I just wanted to kill Warren's baby. I wanted to make sure your baby died the same way mine did."

Granite silence returned for a long moment.

Jenny feared stepping away from the door even though she had locked it. Could Bridget break it down? Then Jenny saw the telephone by her bed.

She snatched up the receiver. A dead line.

"It's off the hook in the den," Bridget said into the phone, "No one can help you now."

"Bridget, please don't do this. Please let me go."

There was no answer.

****

Dwight jumped into his van, cranking it and pumping the accelerator until it droned like a dying lion. He had to get to the Garrett house. Damn that mechanic. He said the van was fixed.

The worst possible situation for Jenny now was to be left alone in that house with her spirit. Dwight held no doubts that the ghost intended to kill her—needed to kill her—in order to free itself from the torment of being caught between worlds. He had no inkling of what he might be able to do to prevent that death from happening; he only knew he had to get to her and do everything in his power to save her life.

Dwight realized it would take at least thirty minutes to get to Jenny's after he got his van to start. The busy telephone line he got when he tried to call only heightened his fear. Maybe Jenny was on the tele-

phone. Or maybe something else had happened causing the phone to come off the cradle.

Finally, the engine caught and Dwight roared out
of his friend's driveway, fish-tailing down the street
in the dark.

****

Jenny flinched when something heavy bashed her
door. Bridget had gone for one of Warren's hammers
from the basement. The interior surface of the six-
paneled door began to splinter with each successive
blow.

"Please, Bridget, please don't do this."

"You could have lived if you would have let Warren divorce you. I wouldn't have tried to kill you if
you hadn't gotten pregnant. Now I have to finish the
job. Then they'll let Warren go. You see, Jenny, I'm
going to have him after all."

"No you won't. The police will figure out you're
the one who tried to kill me."

Bridget's hideous laugh seeped through the
wood.

"Don't worry, I took care of everything. You
remember Reggie Dickerson? Poor Reggie, the *gopher*
you fired a year ago for screwing up at the agency.
Dumb Reggie got himself so strung out on heroin
that he'd do anything for a fix. He's the one who
rigged your car. But don't be fooled, it was my idea.
Something I learned from a racetrack mechanic. Reggie helped make sure my plan would work."

"Then he'll..."

"Don't worry about Reggie. I paid him in heroin.
Paid him so well, the shit died four days after your
accident. You're the only one who knows the truth,
and you're not going to be able to tell anyone."
Bridget was screaming through the door, pounding
incessantly with maddening blows.

Jenny opened her window. If only she had
engaged the alarm. She gazed down the twenty feet

to the shrubbery below. No way to get down from here. In her mind's eye, she saw Mr. Chips lying dead in the grass.

31

The interrogation room was deathly quiet; Warren sat completely alone. He knew they were watching him through a mirror on the wall. Still, he lit another cigarette as soon as he finished the one between his lips. His hands had to be occupied, doing something, anything. The cigarette helped. The nicotine had yellowed his index finger.

He checked his watch for the fourth time in ten minutes. His hands had to be occupied, doing something, anything. Twenty minutes had elapsed since they had placed him in the interrogation room. Part of the game, Warren figured. He just had no idea how long this part of their game lasted. He hoped Jenny had gotten someone to stay with her; someone to safeguard her until he could get back. As much as he hated Mackenzie, he hoped he had arrived to watch over his wife.

Warren fought down the urge to stand up, walk over to the mirror, and stick his middle finger right in their faces. But he knew better. Instead, he sat complacently tapping the cigarette on the edge of the ashtray, waiting.

These shits, I'll play their game and beat them at it, he thought as he waited. He started to hum a tune, an eighties ballad he dug up from deep in his memory. Inspiration was what he needed most right now. It was the song Jenny and he shared on their honeymoon. It offered him strength.

Finally, Rick Walker entered the room. He entered alone.

Warren fell silent.

"What? I don't deserve two of you shits? Don't you need a partner to play your good cop, bad cop game on me? You must think I'm a fucking moron."

Rick said nothing. He took up the chair beside Warren and opened the folder he carried in with him.

"You know you're going to get ten years for attempted murder, don't you?"

"Thank you, Sgt. Friday. This is so fucking ridiculous. You know I didn't try to kill Jenny. This is the most insane bullshit charge I've ever heard of."

"Let's start with the basics. We know your commodities trading business is in serious trouble. Man, you're drowning out there, and you're all alone. You're facing bankruptcy."

"I'm down for the year. I've lost more in a day than you make in a year. I've lost ten times your fucking salary and came back. You think I'd kill Jenny for money?"

"You stood to gain a cool million if she had died in that accident." Rick emphasized the last word.

Warren's eyes fixed themselves on Rick's. They were squaring off, one against the other.

"That's ridiculous. Jenny was a partner in an ad agency and we needed to keep her adequately insured. Who knows what problems I'd have to face if she died. Christ, I've got a million dollar policy on myself."

"But no one tried to kill you. And Jenny had Partners' Insurance with the agency. That would have taken care of any business-related financial difficulties resulting from her death."

"Yeah, and Kate would have collected on that if Jenny died. You pull her in for questioning, too? Maybe she tried to kill Jenny for the money."

"We've cleared Kate. She didn't have opportunity."

Rick's immediate response surprised Warren, so much so, that he stumbled for his next words. They had suspected Kate of attempted murder.

"Opportunity. Opportunity to do what? What the hell are you talking about?"

"You figured the crash would destroy any evidence, didn't you? You figured no one would ever connect Jenny's accident to premeditated murder?"

Rick edged closer, making certain Warren could feel his breath against his face. Then Rick slowly reached into his pocket and removed two bolts in a sealed plastic bag. Very carefully, Rick set the bolts on the table in front of Warren.

"You know what's different between these two bolts?" Rick asked, his eyes never looking up at Warren's.

"No. They're both broken."

"Very good. But if you look real close at this one here," Rick pointed, "you'll see cut marks on the end where the locking nut used to be. Cut marks that come from a hack saw blade."

"Good work, Sherlock!"

"The other bolt head busted by sheer force. You notice how smooth the surface is where the break occurred?"

Warren fumbled for another cigarette, never looking at the bolts now in Rick's hand.

"Yeah, scumbag. You figured the crash would destroy the evidence. You figured you could kill Jenny, collect the money and keep right on screwing your girlfriend."

"You're out of your fucking mind."

"This bolt here came off the right front stabilizer strut support of your wife's car. When the locking nut was snapped off, the strut was free to come loose from the mounting, and Jenny lost control of the car. But you knew that. You planned that to happen. You just needed to get Jenny on a winding road, so you could make sure she'd lose control."

Sweat worked its way down Warren's neck. He crushed out the cigarette he had just lit and reached for another.

"How did you do it? Tell me exactly the steps you took. Start at the beginning..."

"I didn't do a fucking thing!"

"Yeah right. You made the reservation at Diamante's knowing you needed to get Jenny on a winding road. And you were late. While Jenny was inside waiting, you were out in the parking lot. It was dark, and even if someone questioned you, you'd just have said it was your car."

Rick paused long enough for his words to sink into Warren's brain.

"You went up to the car, popped the hood and whacked the bolt with a hammer. That made the nut snap off. But you stupid shit, you forgot to take the locking nut with you. We found it in the parking lot of the restaurant and matched the cut marks to the bolt from Jenny's car. You left just enough evidence behind to allow us to throw your stinking ass in prison for twenty years."

If this kept up, he'd have the sentence for attempted murder trumped up to fifty years by the time Warren confessed. Rick reached into his pocket, pulled out a hexagonal nut with threads intact and encased in plastic.

"The saw marks here match those on the bolt. They're an exact fit. You see, we know the strut was rigged. I found it where you left it."

Warren refused to even acknowledge the nut sitting before him on the table.

"What did it feel like?" Rick asked with a perverse tone to his voice.

"What did what feel like?"

"Sitting across from Jenny during dinner, laughing, talking, even holding hands—all the while knowing you were going to send her to her death? What did you think about during those two hours in the restaurant?"

"This is ludicrous. I did *not* try to kill my wife! I love Jenny."

"You sat across from her and ate your dinner. What did you have, prime rib? You entertained her with your sick witticisms, knowing that in less than an hour she was going to be killed. But you love her."

"You are out of your mind!" Warren screamed.

Rick grabbed a fistful of Warren's hair, jerked his head back and seethed into his face.

"I hate fucking scum like you. Tell me how it felt, you sick fuck! Tell me, I want to know how it felt to raise a champagne glass in a toast. Were you toasting your freedom?"

Rick released him.

Warren rose out of his chair.

Rick stopped him with an iron hand to his chest.

"Sit the fuck down."

Warren complied.

Rick's eyes turned to steel. This was no longer a game. Rick was no longer toying with him.

"How did you know you could make it work? We've been digging real deep into your background."

"I didn't try to murder Jenny."

Warren pushed the ashtray away, refusing to even look at the two bolts still sitting on the table before him.

"At any time, you can stop me, and we'll wait for your lawyer. I don't want scum like you finding a way to slip out of here. You're going down for this, you shitbag."

Rick forced himself back into his chair, silently combing his fingers through his hair in what had to seem like an eternity to Warren. It was time for Rick to stop talking and Warren to start. If a confession were to be forthcoming, it would begin to flow now.

"I love my wife. I'd cut off my arms and legs before I'd do anything that might hurt her."

"I get it, scumwad, you love your wife, but you fuck her best friend."

Warren wanted to lash out against Rick, scream into his face, but the sudden rush of guilt stole his strength. Only through surveillance could Walker have known Warren was seeing her.

"Tell me where you went that Wednesday, September thirteenth? Two days before Jenny's accident."

"What do you mean? I was at my office, working."

"All day?"

"All day."

"Maybe you need a little refresher, Warren. Maybe you don't understand my question. Where did you go on September thirteenth?"

"You're right, Detective, I don't understand your fucking question. I was working at my office in the financial district."

"We're getting closer now. Where did you go in your wife's car on September thirteenth of this year?"

Warren swallowed involuntarily. He had forgotten about that. He had borrowed Jenny's car because his was acting up. He didn't want to risk the Saab stalling out in traffic, so he instead went to Jenny's office and borrowed her car.

"What are you trying to say?" Warren asked, staring directly into Rick's cold eyes.

Rick knew he needed the words. He needed Warren to say the words. Confess that he did it. Rick knew he had no case unless this scumbag confessed. All the circumstantial evidence in the world couldn't convict this asshole. And Rick knew it. He hoped Warren didn't know that. Rick needed a confession.

"I'm saying that you used your wife's car, the car destroyed the night of September fifteenth, two days prior to Jenny's accident. I'm asking you nicely where you went that day?"

"I met with a client. Edward...Jawecki...we had a meeting about an investment program I was putting together."

"How long did the meeting last?"

"A couple of hours."

"Where did you go afterward? Where did you go to rig the car? How did you know to cut that bolt?"

"I didn't rig the car. I never did anything to the car."

"Okay, Warren, I'll let you think on that for awhile. Why don't we talk about Bridget Sterling?" Rick asked in a sardonically casual way. The words almost knocked Warren out of the chair.

"What about Bridget?" he stammered.

Rick tightened his proverbial grip around Warren's neck. Now it was time for the kill. Warren was hanging at the very edge of the precipice. Rick just needed to topple him over.

"Bridget is Jenny's best friend. What about Bridget?" Warren persisted, feigning innocence.

"We know about your affair with her. How long has it been going on?"

"I don't know what you're talking about. Bridget Sterling is Jenny's friend. I see her when she comes to visit Jenny."

Rick opened his file, flipping to the interior sheets.

"And you also see her when you want to get your rocks off, don't you?"

Warren shifted uncomfortably on the chair.

"November eleventh, ten twenty-two, you entered the Glen Oaks Apartments."

"Bridget had asked if I could take a look at her bathroom plumbing. Her shower was leaking."

"You remained there the entire night. Jenny was in the hospital. How long did it take you to fix the shower?"

"How long...."

"Why was your hair wet when you left in the morning? Did you have to test the shower to make sure the leak was fixed?"

"I was upset. I needed someone to talk to. Bridget offered a sympathetic ear."

"Yeah, she offered you a *helluvalot* more than just an ear, didn't she? You spent the night with her."

"I did...."

"You didn't go home. You went for an all-nighter with Bridget. She's one hot lay, isn't she?"

"You've had *me* under surveillance since that first time you came to talk to Jenny, didn't you? I'm the one you've been focused on the whole time."

"We know all about you, Warren. We know exactly what you're doing. Is that why you wanted Jenny dead? Is that why you set up the accident? You wanted the money *and* Bridget?"

"No. All right. I've been seeing Bridget for a little more than a year. It was casual. We were lovers—but I still loved Jenny. I wouldn't leave Jenny for Bridget."

"Did Bridget know that?"

"Yes. She didn't care."

Rick felt a burning in his gut. The words were ripping him apart. In a flash, he saw Bridget's outstretched body on the bed, beckoning him. She was so beautiful. Now Rick was glad he never told Bridget how he really felt.

"Why don't you tell me about you and Bridget."

"What do you mean?"

"What happened on March third of this year?"

"Are we playing Jeopardy or something?"

"We're not fucking playing anymore. What happened with you and Bridget on March third of this year?"

"I want my fucking lawyer," Warren said, then he picked through his pocket for another cigarette.

"Yeah, I figured you were going to say that."

****

"You can't call for help, Jenny," Bridget's cold voice rasped. She was no longer the sweet woman Jenny thought of as her friend. Bridget had become some kind of demon out of a nightmare.

Jenny screamed into the night.

Minutes later, exactly how many Jenny couldn't be sure of, all the lights in the house went dead. The only light entering her bedroom sifted in from the moon overhead.

Jenny shuddered, suddenly afraid.

"God, no please..."

She felt a presence in the darkness. The thing that had haunted her had returned. She listened to more than one heart beating in that bedroom. And the other wasn't Bridget's; she knew that for certain because the bedroom door remained intact.

Her spirit had entered the room with her.

But beyond the bedroom door, Jenny heard Bridget's pounding feet moving frantically up the stairs.

****

Rick sat behind the mirrored glass panel, browsing through the notes in the Garrett file. He was dead tired. He wanted to go home to sleep and forget about this damn Garrett case. But Warren refused to crack, so Rick needed to stay, hoping for a break. He had played his hand as skillfully as he could. Now he had to wait and hope it was good enough to trip Warren up.

Rick's only worry was that Warren's attorney might materialize and ruin everything. He would end up having to release Warren and be forced to close the investigation for good.

Inside the interrogation room, Warren rose from his chair to pace. He moved in a tight circle around the table with his head down, his eyes tracking his feet. In doing so, he defied the guilty suspect's behavior profile. Guilty suspects, once confronted with the evidence against them, and then left alone, invariably put their heads to the table and sleep, unfazed by having been confronted with their crime. Either Warren was innocent, or he was breaking the unwritten criminal code.

Warren stopped pacing, walked directly to the mirror and tapped lightly on the glass.

"All right. I want to talk."

Rick slammed the file closed and rubbed the exhaustion out of his eyes. He was too tired to even become excited about this turn of events.

Warren stood at the table when Rick returned, sat in his chair as Rick settled into the chair beside from him.

"Bridget and I had been lovers for about six months when she told me she was pregnant. I didn't believe her at the time. I figured it was just some lame trick to pry me away from Jenny. You know the scam. The girl tells the guy she's pregnant so he will split from his wife. Then she says: *Surprise! I just missed my period. That never happened before.* Initially, I didn't bite."

"When was this?"

"February."

"Why didn't you believe her?"

"Because she had hinted she was looking for more than just a sleeping arrangement. She whined regularly about how she wanted a real life. You know, a husband and someday, children. I figured she was just trying to manipulate me. I..."

"You planned on leaving Jenny?"

"No. Bridget knew I would never leave Jenny. I made no promises, nor did she ever come out and say she expected me to."

"So then what?"

"So then...we met with her doctor, and I confirmed that she really was pregnant."

"Then she asked you to leave your wife?"

"No. I told her...I demanded...she abort it. There was no way I'd leave Jenny under those circumstances. It's not that I didn't want children. I just wouldn't have them under those circumstances."

"So, on March third you accompanied Bridget to the abortion clinic and paid for her abortion."

"That's right."

"How did Bridget handle it?"

"Good, I guess. She understood."

"Did you lead her to believe there was a future for the two of you?"

"No...well maybe. I don't know."

"What happened after that?"

"When I learned that Jenny was pregnant, I broke it off with Bridget. I knew I couldn't keep it..."

"What do you mean, when you learned Jenny was pregnant?"

"Jenny and I were going to have a baby. I learned by mistake just before Labor Day."

"How did you learn?"

"Bridget told me."

"Bridget told you?"

The words triggered something in Rick's mind. His gut began rumbling and bile backed up into his throat.

"Yeah, she said Jenny got it confirmed a few days before and was planning a big surprise to tell me about it. Why Jenny confided in Bridget before me is beyond my comprehension."

"Wait a minute. Jenny told Bridget she was pregnant?"

"I guess so. I figured Bridget told me out of spite. Figured she'd ruin the surprise as a way of getting back at me."

"Jenny told Bridget she was going to have a baby. And Bridget told you."

"Yeah, I had to play dumb, so I wouldn't spoil the surprise."

"Yeah right, scumbag. You had to play dumb or Jenny would know about you and Bridget."

Rick suddenly sat back in his chair. Something Warren had just said had knocked his whole thought process helter-skelter. He forgot about everything and turned in a new, uncharted direction.

"Why would Jenny tell Bridget that she was pregnant?"

"I don't know? But Bridget knew. She flew into a rage when I told her it was over."

"You told her this when?"

"I guess around the fifth of September."

"What did Bridget do?"

"Nothing. I mean she calmed down and said she understood."

Rick left his chair. It became his turn to pace. Something Bridget had said to him earlier was now toying with his brain like a spiteful child. Something elusive sidetracked his thinking, steering him away from Warren and into a new...

"Warren, could Bridget have had access to Jenny's car?"

"I guess. Jenny often let her borrow it if she needed to go out of town on a shoot. The agency's insurance covered a list of people on the car. I think Jenny put Bridget's name on the list a year or so ago."

Rick swallowed the coppery fluid accumulating in his throat. Bridget knew Jenny was pregnant; she might have wanted to harm Jenny in an attempt to force a miscarriage. Or could Bridget have decided to kill Jenny and keep Warren all for herself?

Rick left the interrogation room and dialed Jenny's number. The busy signal sent a shudder through his insides. He dialed for an operator.

"Operator, this is Detective Rick Walker. I have an emergency situation. Could you break into 555-6980?"

Rick waited a long moment.

"I'm sorry, sir, I get an off-hook indication for that line. There is no call in progress."

Rick slammed the receiver down. He tried Bridget's number. No answer.

****

Bridget hammered at the bedroom door until the wood jamb finally splintered. The door moved inward.

Jenny screamed when the door creaked and gave way.

Despite gut-wrenching pain, Jenny managed to slide the corner of the bureau in front of the door. But even that did not long deter the determined Bridget.

When Bridget heaved against the door the first time, it moved the bureau a few inches. She forced her fingers in through the slit to gain a better leverage point.

"You fucking bitch!" Bridget scowled from the hall, seething and puffing. Saliva drooled from the sides of her mouth as if she had become some kind of crazed animal. She squeezed more of her hand through the opening, running it down until she came to the bureau.

"You stupid bitch, do you think you can stop me? Do you think I'd ever let you keep Warren's baby?"

"Please Bridget, please, don't do this."

"You're going to die for this, bitch."

Grunting, Bridget pushed at the door. Her effort backed the bureau another inch further into the room. She had almost enough space to stick her head through.

"Let me in, you bitch!" Bridget screeched.

In the pale moonlight that washed over the door, Bridget's eyes were wide white bulges against a pallid face. Dripping blood lined her chin. With another heave, she gained another inch of opening and stretched her neck full length to get her head completely inside the bedroom.

Jenny screamed, backing into the corner. Then she saw her ghost emerge through the wall at the far side of the room. The black orbs stared at Jenny, indifferent to Bridget's scowling face at the door. Somehow the apparition knew. She had arrived to witness the final moment; the moment when she would be set free from her prison.

"God, no," Jenny whimpered.

Then Jenny heard her name being called. It rose from down below her window. Someone was outside.

Dwight screamed her name from the yard.

"I'm up here!" Jenny screamed, pulling herself to her feet.

"Damn you, Jenny. I'm going to kill you for killing my baby!"

Jenny clutched her side, ignored the spectral image standing across the room staring at her, and started moving toward the door.

Bridget's eyes flashed with terror when she realized Jenny's intent. In a panic, Bridget knew what she must do. She squirmed to pull her head free of the opening before Jenny could get there to ram the door closed.

And she almost made it. Almost. Bridget's fingers failed to clear the door before Jenny crashed into it and forced it closed.

A scream of pure agony wailed through the entire house.

Dwight attacked the front door a second time with his full body weight. It held solid and locked.

"Jenny!" he screamed with all the force his lungs could muster.

A faint cry came back from deep within the bowels of the darkened house. The cry of a desperate woman trapped by both a mortal killer and a spectral one.

Bridget pushed with all her might and forced the bedroom door back into the room. She would let nothing stop her. The harder she pushed, the more the crease widened. She rammed first her leg in, then her arm.

Jenny tried to push against the bureau, but her strength was frail compared to Bridget's. For Bridget, adrenaline had taken over, pumping her veins with the strength of three men.

The bureau slid further—Bridget now filled the doorway with her entire body.

"This time I'll make sure you're dead!"

With a weight-lifter's grunt, Bridget pushed her way completely into the bedroom, forcing Jenny to retreat to the bed.

But Jenny was not ready to succumb.

As Bridget lunged toward her, Jenny grabbed the lamp and crashed it into the side of Bridget's face. Bridget silenced Jenny's scream with a hand to her mouth, partially deflecting the lamp with her other arm. A ceramic shard cut into the side of Bridget's face, sending a steady stream of inky blood running down her cheek.

As Jenny fell back against the mattress, she could see her ghost rising above Bridget and drifting further into the room.

Bridget's hands circled Jenny's neck, clamped over her throat and squeezed with a force driven by hatred and loathing.

Jenny gurgled a scream.

Her ghost closed in, but made no attempt to interfere.

Downstairs, glass shattered. Jenny knew she just had to hold on—help was here. Dwight was in the house. She forced two fingers under Bridget's hands to break the death grip.

Bridget scowled as she pulled her hands away and grabbed the pillow to cover Jenny's entire head.

"Die, bitch!"

Jenny kicked, but Bridget's weight and driving arms proved too much on top of her. She sucked hard for a breath of air, feeling her lungs burn as if they were being pulled up through her throat when no air could be brought in.

Then Jenny felt no more.

Dwight flew into the bedroom, saw the blood-stained creature kneeling over Jenny and dove. In one fluid motion, he grabbed Bridget's hair, yanked her off the listless body, and as she came around to face him, his fist toppled her to the floor.

Bridget groaned, tumbled feet over head and landed with a thud.

Dwight held his stance, but only for a second to make certain Bridget would not rise against him. Then he stripped the pillow from Jenny's head and felt for signs of life.

"No!" he screamed.

There was no movement, no breathing, no life coming from Jenny's body.

"Jenny!" Dwight barked, shaking her wildly.

Still Jenny's body moved with a horrible looseness.

Dwight checked, found no pulse.

Jenny was dead.

In anger, he slammed a fist into her chest and did the only thing he could remember from his CPR training. With head tilted back, he worked a finger in her mouth to remove her tongue from within her throat and began puffing air into her lungs.

"Breath, Jenny," he commanded desperately.

Nothing.

"Breath damnit!"

He refused give up. From behind, he heard a moan. He glanced over to see Bridget still lying on the floor, her left leg twitching wildly.

Dwight pounded sharply again on Jenny's breastbone, and still getting no pulse, resumed his CPR.

"Come on, Jenny, come on back to us and breath," he whispered between breaths. He could only hope he was doing it right; he only knew he had to keep trying. He couldn't give up now.

Sweat rolled off his chin as he alternated between pumping her chest and blowing rapidly into her mouth. A minute seemed like an hour and Dwight's arms were losing sensation.

Downstairs, the door banged open, feet rushed in.

"Up here, hurry!" he screamed.

A uniform flooded the room with light, leveling his gun on Dwight's back.

"Freeze!"

"I can't. I've got to save her."

The uniform lowered his weapon.

"Help me, goddamnit," Dwight urged as a second uniform added his light to the scene.

The first officer dropped to his knees and began breathing frantically into Jenny's throat. The second uniform raked his light over Bridget's body, then instructed Dwight to move away from Jenny. He, in turn, replaced Dwight and fingered Jenny's chest until he found the exact spot for the compressions.

"Blow, blow, bl..."

He struck Jenny's chest with such force that the body flinched. He checked the carotid for a pulse.

Nothing. But then...

"I got it! I got it!" he chimed while his partner still blew into Jenny's mouth.

"It's getting stronger. I'm getting a pulse at the carotid."

The first uniform backed away. Jenny began breathing on her own.

As the officers moved away, Dwight moved in to cradle Jenny's head in his arms, smoothing his hand along her hair.

"You the husband?"

"No."

"Then who are you?"

"It's a long story."

Feeling Dwight's hands on her face, Jenny opened her eyes.

"Jenny?"

"Warren."

"No, it's Dwight...Mackenzie."

"Oh God," Jenny cried out, pulling away in terror.

"It's okay, Jenny. The police are here."

A uniform pulled a groggy Bridget into a sitting position.

"She was suffocating Jenny when I broke in. She's..."

"She's the one who tried to kill me..." Jenny said.

"Jenny, you're safe now," Dwight said, and on impulse, bent down to kiss Jenny's lips.

A wild rush of emotion swarmed over Jenny when she felt Dwight's lips kiss hers. Something inside came alive, blossoming into a brilliant star burst of desire.

Jenny reached up, bringing Dwight's lips back to hers.

"I'm back. I can feel it. I feel it inside!"

In those moments of death, Jenny's spirit had been given the opportunity to cross over from the dark side and return—she knew it the moment Dwight's lips touched hers. She felt what had been missing since her accident, she felt her spirit dwelling inside her body.

Jenny Garrett was whole again.

The End.